MURDER
PLAYS SECOND
FIDDLE

A PEARLY GIRLS MYSTERY

ALSO BY HEATHER WEIDNER

THE PEARLY GIRLS MYSTERIES
Murder Strikes a Chord

THE JULES KEENE GLAMPING MYSTERIES
Vintage Trailers and Blackmailers
Film Crews and Rendezvous
Christmas Lights and Cat Fights
Deadlines and Valentines
Teddy Bears and Ghostly Lairs

THE MERMAID BAY CHRISTMAS SHOPPE MYSTERIES
Sticks and Stones and a Bag of Bones
Twinkle, Twinkle Au Revoir
A Tisket a Tasket, Not Another Casket

THE DELANIE FITZGERALD MYSTERIES
Secret Lives and Private Eyes
The Tulip Shirt Murders
Glitter, Glam, and Contraband
Male Revues and Subterfuge

MURDER PLAYS SECOND FIDDLE

A PEARLY GIRLS MYSTERY

HEATHER WEIDNER

KEYLIGHT
BOOKS
AN IMPRINT
OF TURNER
PUBLISHING

Keylight Books
an imprint of Turner Publishing Company
Nashville, Tennessee
www.turnerpublishing.com

Murder Plays Second Fiddle

Cover design by J. Kent Holloway
Book design by William Ruoto

Library of Congress Cataloging-in-Publication Data

Names: Weidner, Heather, author.
Title: Murder plays second fiddle / by Heather Weidner.
Description: Nashville, Tennessee: Keylight Books, 2026.
Identifiers: LCCN 2025005727 (print) | LCCN 2025005728 (ebook) |
ISBN 9798887981154 (paperback) | ISBN 9798887981161 (hardcover) |
ISBN 9798887981178 (epub)
Subjects: LCGFT: Detective and mystery fiction. | Novels.
Classification: LCC PS3623.E4257 M85 2026 (print) | LCC PS3623.E4257
(ebook) | DDC 813/.6—dc23/eng/20250210
LC record available at https://lccn.loc.gov/2025005727
LC ebook record available at https://lccn.loc.gov/2025005728

Printed in the United States of America

MURDER
PLAYS SECOND
FIDDLE

A PEARLY GIRLS MYSTERY

1

The bells on the front door to Celebrations at Ivy Springs clanged like they were in a windstorm, sending Elvis, the black-and-brown chihuahua, into full-on yip mode as he greeted everyone. Cassidy Jamison, the event planner and owner of the property, scooped him up, tucking him under her arm like a football before he bestowed a lickfest on any guests.

Two bottle-blonde thirty-somethings followed a taller blonde in red stilettos through the door, glancing around at the front room of the converted farmhouse like they were casing the joint. Cassidy had an instant flashback to high school, when these three former cheerleaders had ruled the school and sent the nerds and bandies running for cover. Shaking off the bad memories, she pasted on her best smile.

"Well, hey there, Cassidy," Britt Rogers Mahoney cooed, waving both of her bejeweled hands around. "It is so good to see you again. You remember Kelly Mason Todd and Anastasia Young from our days as Springers? Gals, Cassidy was a freshy the year we graduated. I don't think she hung out with our crowd. But you might remember her."

Before anyone else could speak, Britt wandered through the seating area, where she paused to pick up a vase full of teal sea glass, inspecting it like she was a judge on *Antiques Roadshow.* Setting the vase down, she continued, "We're so excited that you're hosting our mega-reunion here. Your property is so cute—in a shabby chic, rustic sort of way. That stupid pandemic messed up all of our plans for our big milestone bash, but we've regrouped and planned a sensational party." She fanned her face with her hand and continued. "We want this one to be a two-weekend epic event that everyone will be talking about for years. And your amphitheater, barn, and garden will be perfect for what we have planned. I've got the signed contract and the check for you. We want to go over the schedule and make sure everything is perfect. We don't want to miss any details. This party is going to be one for the ages."

She waved her hand again and then paused to stare at the sparkly diamonds on her ring finger. The other two blondes nodded furiously behind Britt like they were her backup singers.

"Definitely an event to remember," Kelly said, continuing to bob her head behind Britt.

Cassidy hoped her big smile didn't look fake. *Wow. They've got a lot planned.*

"Of course," Cassidy said. "We want every facet of the celebration to be special. Come into the conference room, and we can make sure my team knows what you all want. Can I get you some coffee, tea, or water?"

"No, we're fine," Britt said. "I brought my own mineral water with me. Bottled water and tap don't always agree with me." The other two continued to nod, and Anastasia, the brassier blonde, made an exaggerated sympathy face. The three women took seats across the table from Cassidy.

Cassidy opened a manila folder and a legal pad. "We didn't get a chance to chat last time," she said. "What have you all been doing since high school? I just moved back to the area recently, so I've been out of touch with a lot of folks from back in the day."

Britt smiled coyly and replied, "College. Marriage to the quarterback. Divorce. Totally rejuvenated. New supportive husband. Full-time beauty blogger and influencer. It feels amazing. Like the complete package."

As Anastasia opened her mouth to speak, Britt interrupted. "Gals, we have a tight schedule today with lots to do. Let's cut the chitchat and get right to the chase. Here's the schedule. We need to set up on Wednesday. The dance and mingle is Thursday night in your fabulous barn. On Friday and Saturday, we're using your garden for afternoon goat yoga. It'll be adorable. The wine tour's not on your property, so you don't have to worry about that. Anastasia is taking care of that."

Anastasia opened her mouth, but closed it again when Britt continued to rattle off the schedule. "Friday night is the big bash in the barn, with fireworks afterward. Saturday is meditation in your garden, hiking and fishing daytrips, a tour of our illustrious high school, and dinner and a repeat of our Homecoming to round out the evening. Sunday wraps up the first weekend with meditation at sunrise and brunch in the barn. A fabulous experience."

Britt took a breath and then chugged on with the schedule for the second weekend. "Whew. That's a lot. Our guests will get their money's worth. We have something for everyone," she said with a smile that showed all her perfect pearly-white teeth. Then she quickly added, "Did you get all that? Details are important. I would hate to have to repeat myself."

Cassidy nodded. "Yes. I have the schedule here, and my team is ready to meet your caterers and bartenders and have the facilities set for all your events. It sounds like two fun weekends. And I have security scheduled to help with parking and traffic control, if it's needed."

"All righty, then. That's about it. Now, for a walk around the property. I want to show the gals where things are," Britt said, picking up her red Coach bag.

"Let me get the keys," Cassidy said, rising.

"I know you're busy. We'll wander around by ourselves. It'll give us some precious time together, and we can just multitask while we're making our rounds. Our jam-packed schedules have us all going a hundred miles an hour every day. Plus, I have so much to tell them about our newest committee member, Darcy Branch. You remember her. I think she did things you were interested in, like the newspaper stuff. Anyway, she's a famous journalist, and she promised to do a story on our big shindig. I am over the moon that she agreed to join the team." Britt's eyes sparkled and her cheeks turned a slight pink. Anastasia and Kelly didn't echo her excitement.

After a pause, when no one commented about Darcy, Britt stared down her long, pointed nose at Cassidy. The other two women giggled like schoolgirls, and Britt gave them a wilting look. "These gals already saw the barn online. We're going to pop over to the outdoor sites and then head out for our luncheon. We want to see the garden and the view of the valley for our fireworks extravaganza. What'd you call it? A serenity garden? But wasn't that where that rock star was killed? Not so peaceful for him. We'll have better luck." Britt waved her hand dismissively as she rose. "Ta-ta, Cassidy. We'll see you on Wednesday." The other two followed her out the front door.

When the door shut firmly behind the trio, Cassidy picked up her folder and returned to the office. "Well, Elvis. It may be an interesting couple of weekends, but at least it's all paid up and ready to go." Before she could settle in at her desk, her phone alerted her with a series of rapid-fire texts.

"Oh, look, it's things Britt forgot to tell me when she rattled off all her other key points five minutes ago." She replied with **All**

taken care of. See you on Wednesday for setup, and then jotted down Britt's list of demands on her legal pad for her team, made up of groundskeeper Levi Jenkins and the Pearly Girls, all friends of her late grandmother. They would be thrilled with more demanding guests. *We've seen our share of bridezillas and mothers of bridezillas. Hopefully, I can keep the peace. It's only for two weekends.*

The front door popped open and the bells jangled. This time, Elvis, in full-on security mode, zoomed into the front room, skidding around the two teal couches in the seating area. Aileen Roberts, a retired schoolteacher, bustled in with her lilac-and-plum tunic blouse flowing behind her. Her purple-tinted hair matched her outfit right down to her tennis shoes. She paused, and Ruthanne Carmichael, Cassidy's bookkeeper, almost slammed into the back of her.

"Don't stop in the doorway," Roxie Matthews groused from behind her two friends. "Kate and I haven't even made it through the door, and already there's a pileup. And it's kinda warm out here for a fall day. Shoo." She switched her oversized magenta Michael Kors purse to the other hand and stepped around Ruthanne.

"Aileen, what is going on?" Kate Carlson asked. The retired nurse picked up Elvis for a cuddle.

"I got this email about Linkydinking." Aileen stared at her screen. "It's from my housekeeper's daughter. She wants to become a teacher, and I said I would help her if I could. But I'm not sure about this. It might be one of those scam things. And I certainly don't want to get mixed up in a group chat with a bunch of people I don't know."

"What are you talking about?" Roxie asked, leaning closer to see Aileen's phone. "Cassidy. Come over here. She needs some of your tech support."

"Oh, my stars, I don't need to get mixed up in some pyramid

or crypto scam," Aileen muttered. "What if it's a sex ring or something?"

Cassidy leaned over to look at Aileen's phone. A slight smile crossed her face. "That's LinkedIn. It's a social media site for professional networking."

Aileen let out a long stream of air. "What a relief. I thought it was some kind of swingers' thing or dating site. I am not up for any canoodling or Linkydinking right now."

"You don't know what you're missing," Roxie mused as she headed for the conference room. She continued: "It's an email invitation to join the site and to network with other members. Your friend's daughter is probably looking for anyone with a background in education to help her find a job. If you want to set up a page, I can help you."

"Nope. Don't have time for that. I'm too busy with all the in-person social stuff. I deleted it. End of problem." Aileen dropped her phone in her straw purse, which sported three large daisies.

Kate slid her tall frame into one of the chairs in the conference room, and Elvis settled himself in her lap. "Cassidy, we wanted to check in and make sure we had the schedules for the reunion events. It's the talk of the town. That Britt always seems to stir stuff up."

"And not always in a good way. I heard from several people over at the beauty salon that she is going way overboard, as usual," Aileen said.

"You just missed her," Cassidy said. "She and her team are headed to the garden."

"Is that Britt's humongous Cadillac out front? I was wondering whose car that was," Kate said.

"Speaking of cars, hey, Cassidy, I saw your new Wrangler in the parking lot," Ruthanne remarked, rummaging through her colorful purse. "I like it. It suits you. Very sporty. I want to go for a ride in it."

"I figured it was time to stop doing my personal stuff in the Celebrations van. Elvis and I are enjoying the winding roads and the Jeep life."

"Be prepared for Duck, Duck, Jeep," Kate said. When everyone stared at her, she continued. "My grandson has a fancy Jeep, and he said other owners leave a rubber duck on your car to tell you that you're it. They save them on their dashboards and such. It's a thing in the Jeep world. It sounded fun."

"Cassidy, pick a day when you're going to town. Elvis and I want to do a top-down tour of Main Street," Ruthanne added. Glancing around the room, she rose and headed to the office. "And I love that it's red," she yelled from the back.

"And we all know red cars go faster than regular ones," Roxie winked. "So, what's going on with the reunion plans? I saw Britt and her gang toddling toward the garden."

"Those girls always traveled in packs and never wore sensible shoes or clothes," Kate muttered. "I'm surprised they haven't taken a tumble in those heels."

"They have lots of ideas for their event, and Britt wants to make sure we understand that details are important," Cassidy said, trying to hide a smirk.

"Of course we do," Roxie said, rolling her eyes. "Does she think we were born yesterday?"

"That girl. I had her in my middle-school English class and on Student Council. She was a handful back then. Always the center of attention. Always chasing the boys," Aileen said, settling in across from Roxie and Kate.

"Don't start without me," Ruthanne yelled from the back. "Does anyone want anything while I'm near the kitchen?"

"Water," Roxie yelled.

"Make that two," echoed Kate.

Before Cassidy got her folder open, Ruthanne bustled in and plopped down, pushing a silver curl off her forehead. She dealt out the water bottles like she was playing a high-stakes poker game. "Okay. All settled. Thanks for waiting. So, what's on the docket?"

Cassidy spent the next twenty minutes outlining the events for the upcoming weekends, and she wrapped up with the long string of requests from Britt.

"Yep. That sounds like that girl," Aileen interjected. "She had to be the queen of everything."

"More like the queen of mean," Kate interjected. "She and her brother used to come to Dr. Kellam's office regularly when they were kids. She's a piece of work. Can you say 'spoiled'?"

"She married her high school sweetheart, Mac Gibson, right after graduation. The parents put on quite a show wedding. Too bad it didn't last," Roxie said.

"She didn't want him to go away on a football scholarship and date college girls, so she insisted on a wedding right after graduation. Too bad he blew out his knee in practice the summer before his freshman year, and the rest of the college thing didn't work out for him," Aileen added. "He's been working at his father's tow company ever since."

"Britt married Vince Mahoney a couple of years ago, and she's doing quite well for herself. Haven't you seen her zip around town in that flashy red Cadillac? And I heard Vince left his wife Margaret for the younger Britt. It was quite the scandal," Ruthanne whispered.

"That's Britt's style. She caused quite a kerfuffle at the high school when she stole Mac from her friend. What's her name? Kip Young's daughter," Aileen said.

"The pushy girl—Anastasia," Kate added.

Cassidy's eyebrows shot up under her red bangs. "They must have made up. Anastasia was with her today."

Kate's eyes widened. "Who says there's not a lot going on in small towns? Speaking of that, I heard at the last council meeting that they're budgeting for a third stoplight to slow people down at the end of Main Street, where it merges into the residential district."

"Where all the bed-and-breakfasts are popping up?" Aileen asked.

Kate nodded. "Can you believe it? Three stoplights in Ivy Springs. And I heard a new couple from Roanoke is restoring one of the Victorian homes near the Baptist church. That'll make three B and Bs when they're all done and spruced up," Ruthanne said.

"More places for our guests to stay. That's always good," Cassidy said.

"Besides Sid Pro Quo's no-tell motels out by the highway," Roxie added, rolling her eyes.

"You would know," Kate said with a grin.

Roxie gave her a friendly poke in the ribs. "Oh, y'all don't act all innocent. We've been around each other for so long, we know everybody's secrets. So don't try to pretend you weren't part of the action back in the day." Turning to Cassidy, she added, "It doesn't look like we have much to do until setup tomorrow. Anything you need, Cassidy, before I hightail it home and get ready for my date tonight?"

"Who's the lucky guy this time?" Ruthanne asked.

"Karl. He's from out near Natural Bridge, and he and his son own a racing team."

"Varoom. That sounds exciting," Ruthanne said. "I'm going to skedaddle too. Aileen, Kate, and I have our knitting group tonight at Spin a Yarn. Are we meeting for dinner first?"

"Yes on dinner, before Operation Knit Stuff," Aileen giggled, looking at Kate and Ruthanne.

The three gal-pals exchanged glances and followed Roxie to the lobby. Aileen stopped short again. This time, Ruthanne—not as quick to catch herself as she had been earlier—ran into the back of her, making a loud "umph" sound.

"What now?" Roxie asked, reaching for the doorknob.

"I forgot to ask Cassidy if she ever called that cute deputy and asked him out to dinner. He was hanging around here quite a bit last summer." All eight eyes turned to focus on Cassidy.

"You know, the one who arrested the rock 'n' roll murderer," Roxie said.

"And don't forget the kidnapping. We helped him solve that too," Kate added.

Cassidy's face flushed, and she nodded in agreement with Roxie and Kate. "He's all business. I haven't seen much of him since he got promoted. We're both super-busy, and I'm not interested in dating anyone right now."

"He's a detective now, not a deputy," Kate said, wiggling her eyebrows. "And he wasn't just here for his investigations. It wasn't all murdery business last summer. He liked you. We could tell."

"I'm sorry he had to be here because of the awful murder," Aileen said.

Ruthanne let out a heavy sigh. "We finally got to meet the Weathermen. I'm still brokenhearted about Johnny Storm's murder." Her voice trailed off as she wiped a stray tear from the corner of her eye.

"I've been busy with my volunteer business council work and this place. You gals know how much goes into keeping our event calendar fully booked." Cassidy paused and added, "And I appreciate all the help from you. I couldn't run this place without such a great team." *The Pearly Girls do help me, even if I have to bail them out of trouble from time to time—and be their tech support.*

The four surrounded her and Elvis for a group hug. The mutual admiration fest broke up when Cassidy's phone alerted her with a string of texts.

"You on some group chat?" Kate asked.

Cassidy shook her head and glanced at her screen. "Nope. It's Anastasia with some new demands from Britt for the Rockin' Reunion festivities."

"That's our cue to go," Roxie said. "Come on, gals, and try not to get in any trouble with the wild knitting crowd."

"You never know what we'll do next," Ruthanne giggled, and the fab four disappeared out the front door, leaving Elvis at his people-watching spot by the front window.

"Six texts in under a minute with—count them—twenty-one new things for me to check on. Come on, Elvis. It's going to be a long couple of weekends. But if we do all the planning, the party should go smoothly. Right?"

2

EARLY WEDNESDAY MORNING

Elvis tugged on the leash and dashed across the dewy grass. Shivering in the early morning breeze, Cassidy followed the tiny dog to the edge of the serenity garden, where he had raced to check out his fish friends in the koi pond. Shaking off the memories of the dead rock star she had found floating amongst the lily pads last summer, she tried to focus on the remaining items she needed to take care of this morning before Britt and her bunch arrived.

After the chihuahua had sniffed every blade of grass and Levi's fall flowers, the pair headed to the office to get a jump on the day's tasks. As they rounded the corner, Elvis's ears perked up, and he let out a low growl.

Anastasia Young was heading toward them, tugging on a rolling cart and fumbling with two large bags on her shoulders.

"It's okay, Elvis. She's a client. And she's here awful early for their afternoon setup," Cassidy whispered. Then, louder, "Hey, let me help you with that." She headed toward the other woman, who was dressed in a navy suit with red heels.

"I'm good. I wanted to start dropping stuff off and getting everything prepped before Britt gets here. She likes everything to be just so."

"You've got your hands full. Let me take your bags, and Elvis and I will let you in the barn."

"Thanks," Anastasia said quietly. She dragged the black canvas cart behind her as they walked down the path to the converted red dairy barn. "It's a nice place you have here. I've been here a couple of times over the years with my parents for events. It was somebody's wedding." She paused in the grass and glanced around. "Your grandma did a nice job with the amphitheater and converting the old barn. It's a cool place. If I ever get married, I'd like a spot like this." Her voice trailed off as she stared at the weathered barn.

"What have you been up to lately?" Cassidy asked. "Since the move back, I haven't done much reconnecting. I've been so busy with the events here. I know I need to get out more."

"It's not all it's cracked up to be," Anastasia replied. "Most people have moved away. A few of us stayed here. I moved back in with my mom after my dad died. She needed someone to take care of the house, so we're still in the place on Clover Lane."

"I love all those old Victorian houses in town that look like something out of a picture book. When I was little, I thought they were dollhouses," Cassidy said.

"Yep. Ours is the pale pink one. It's a lot to maintain, though. I'm trying to talk my mom into selling it, but she won't hear of it." Anastasia paused and looked out at the mountains. "Sometimes I wish I'd left for a life in the big city. There's not very much excitement around here."

They approached the large sliding doors. Cassidy unlocked the barn and typed in the security code on the keypad. "Here we go," she said, flipping the switch. The overhead lights and the twinkles in the rafters and the loft area popped on.

"Wow. It looks magical in here. It'll be perfect for tomorrow's dance. Britt ordered a bubble machine and a laser light show. It should be something," Anastasia said, gazing around at the large room with a bar and the loft overlooking the dance floor.

Cassidy nodded. "The bubbles and the lights should be fine. There are plenty of outlets for your DJ and all the equipment. Just no smoking or any pyrotechnics inside."

"Don't give Britt any ideas." Anastasia wrinkled her nose. "The caterers will be here this afternoon, and they'll take care of serving. I'll work on the registration tables and figure out where the photo booth should go." She walked over to the area below the loft and stared into the dark area on the first level. Anastasia took several tentative steps in, and then backed up like she had seen a ghost.

"We use that for extra space. I had seating under there, but Britt didn't like it," Cassidy said, pointing to the dark, empty area.

"Yep. She has a vision of how things should be." Anastasia looked lost in thought as she continued to peer into the empty open area under the loft.

Cassidy set the two bags down on the nearest table. "We arranged the tables and chairs around the stage to match Britt's drawing. Let me know if you need help with moving any of them."

Anastasia twirled and waved her arms as she looked around the room. Her frizzy blonde hair rivaled something from an '80s rock band and stood out in all directions. "I think we'll be okay. Let's move those two tables over here for registration. And I think the photo station will go over in that corner. They may need a table or two for their props."

"I'll get you two more and a couple of chairs," Cassidy said.

"Cool. I'm going to snap some quick pics and send them to Britt, so she can see it before she gets here this afternoon. I know she'll have feedback on everything. She wants this event to set the tone for the weekend."

After locking the long tables' legs in place, Cassidy said, "There you go. Call or text me if you need anything else. Elvis and I will be in the office."

"We'll be fine as soon as Britt takes her happy pills. She's in a tizzy because she's not sure the caterer's tablecloths will be the right shades of fuchsia and teal. She wants the ambiance to be perfect."

Cassidy nodded and picked up Elvis's leash. "Call us if you need anything. My team will be here this afternoon if you need more helpers."

Anastasia held her phone up and started narrating her walk around the venue as Elvis and Cassidy slipped out the door.

Back in the office, after filling a mug with the strongest coffee she could find, Cassidy settled down at her desk to send emails to local businesses about possible events for next spring. Elvis circled his puffy bed several times and settled in for a morning snooze, uninterested in the business calendar.

Around ten o'clock, a roar in the parking lot sent Elvis and Cassidy scurrying for the front window.

Britt's giant Cadillac zoomed in and took two parking spaces in the first row. She slammed the door and stomped across the grass in her stilettos, heading toward the barn. Before Cassidy could say anything, a Volvo pulled into the spaces beside Britt's car, and Kelly climbed out, adjusting her sunglasses.

"Stay here, Elvis. I may need to do some firefighting. If the Pearly Girls show up, let them know where I am."

Bored with the drama, Elvis strolled to his bed, rolled over, and kicked all four legs in the air.

Cassidy dashed off a group chat to her team and hurried after the former cheerleaders.

Britt's shrill voice drifted out of the barn as she barked orders at Kelly and Anastasia. Cassidy stepped out of the way as Levi helped the gals move the round tables and chairs closer to the stage. Before Cassidy could comment, Kelly said, "Britt, dear, they were set up according to how we drew up the plans."

"I know," she snapped. "But it will be better this way, and if the tablecloths don't match, the caterer will have to replace them with black and white. The balloon arches will be here by three. Everything needs to match. They will be our focal point for the entrance and the stage. This is going to be the best reunion ever and the talk of the town for years to come. I need to be out of here soon to get home to get dressed for the gala." She clapped her hands like it would make the work go faster.

"What can I do to help?" Cassidy asked.

"Nothing. They've got it. They're moving the first three rows of tables for a big entranceway." Britt threw her arms wide open. "Kelly and Anastasia will ensure that the caterers and balloon people are ready to go. And they'll be back here to make sure the volunteers are in place for registration and the other stuff before the guests arrive."

"I laid out the badges and the welcome packets at the front two tables," Anastasia said, pausing to wipe the perspiration off her brow.

"I see," Britt said. "When you're done over there, come here, and I'll show you how the registration table should be arranged."

Kelly snickered under her breath as she moved two wooden chairs.

Anastasia pursed her lips and swallowed whatever remark she was about to make. She headed to the table where all the badges were laid out in neat rows.

Cassidy nodded to Levi, who dusted his hands on his jeans. His face twitched with a wry smile.

"Levi, do you need any help?" Cassidy asked.

"Nope. I'm headed outside to knock down the tall grass before our guests arrive. Y'all let me know if any more furniture needs to be rearranged again." He headed out the back door before Britt could comment.

"I hope he doesn't stir up dust and pollen before the dance. I have allergies, and we don't need a mess," Britt said, moving all the badges to the side and starting an arc pattern on the table. "Like this and in alpha order," she snapped at Anastasia.

"I thought it would be easier for the volunteers if the tags were in rows."

"Nope. I like this better. Thanks for fixing it for me." Britt snapped her fingers and pointed to the table. "Okay, this seems to be under control. Kelly, make sure the caterers know what to do. Annie and Austin will be here at three. Maurice, the balloon guy, will be here about two. Balloon arches at the entrance and at the back of the stage. They should fit the doorways precisely. I want the color to pop in here. And tell Annie I'm going to be really disappointed if I come back and find white and black tablecloths. She was supposed to have checked the dye lots with the samples I gave her. I want color everywhere." Britt splayed her fingers and waved her arms around. "Oh, I almost forgot. I need photos of the before-and-after. I promised my followers they'd get a sneak peek." Britt whipped out her phone and took several shots. Then she made everyone stop what they were doing for a happy group picture.

"There. That was fun. I'll post these later with the ones of the decorations," Britt said. "See you this evening. Byeeeee, everyone." She blew air kisses as she sashayed out the door.

Wow. She's over the top.

Cassidy slipped out of the barn to get Elvis while Britt's team scurried around to attend to the last-minute changes. Cassidy and Elvis enjoyed a long, quiet walk around the amphitheater.

After exhausting every possible stall tactic, Elvis finally gave up on his quest to find the ever-elusive squirrel and followed Cassidy across the grassy area. With no burning tasks that had to be done for her business, she trotted upstairs, with Elvis hot on her heels.

She replenished his water bowl and slipped him a couple of snacks. "You're in charge. I'll be back as soon as I can."

Changing her mind about returning to the office, Cassidy hustled back to the barn to check on things. Inside, a large balloon arch greeted visitors at the entrance. Its twin took up most of the room on the elevated stage in the back. Annie and her helper, dressed in all black, zipped around the kitchen and serving tables. The tablecloths were white. *I'm sure Britt will have something to say when she arrives. Hopefully, she'll have other things to keep her occupied, and the linens won't cause any drama.*

Before Cassidy could check out any more of the decorations, Britt breezed in the front doors. "Love the balloons. Maurice outdid himself. Not happy about the tablecloths, but I'll deal with that later. Oh, Cassidy, just the person I wanted to talk to. Would it be a problem if I trucked in a couple loads of sand for next week's events? I want to switch it up to a beach theme for next Saturday. We all have great memories of beach week. I don't know why I didn't think of it earlier. It'll be a blast."

"Inside?" Cassidy asked, hoping that her smile looked sincere. "We will have to adjust the cost for the change and the cleanup."

"Well, I guess we could put the sand outside if it's a problem," Britt said. "Let me think about it, and I'll text you. I want to create our own little beach party. Fabulous, huh?"

Cassidy nodded, wondering what she'd do with the makeshift beach after the party and how she would break the news to Levi.

Interrupting Cassidy's thoughts, Britt said, "Oh, I forgot to tell you. We're going to open the doors at five for a meet-and-greet for the VIPs and the volunteers. I told the caterer, and she said she could make it work. I know we didn't plan to start that early, but it's okay with you, right? The guests should be arriving for cocktails between five and six."

"I'll let the security team know." Cassidy hoped her voice didn't reveal the annoyance of the last-minute changes. "Enjoy the evening and let me know if we can help with anything." She pulled out her phone and sent texts to Mateo Domingo, her security guy, and the Pearly Girls.

A slew of texts arrived within seconds.

Aileen: That girl. She's always soooo demanding. I'll be there soon to help.

Ruthanne: Wow, nothing like last-minute. I'm in the office. I'll be over as soon as I finish with these files.

Roxie: I'll be there when I can. Tied up with something.

Kate: Aileen, I'll pick you up. See you gals in a bit.

"Any problems?" Britt asked, staring down her ski-sloped nose.

"No. No problems. Just letting my team know to be here for our early arrivals," Cassidy said with a smile she hoped didn't look fake.

Cassidy's phone trilled. She smiled at Britt. "I need to take this... Hey, Ruthanne. What's up?"

"Remember, I told you that reporter was coming tomorrow to talk to you about the history of the property and the old honky-tonk?"

"Uh-huh. It'll be some free publicity for us."

"Well, she's here in the lobby. A day early," Ruthanne whispered in the phone.

"I'll be right there." Cassidy disconnected and fluffed her hair as she power-walked to the office. *Nothing like chaos right before an event.*

3

STILL WEDNESDAY

Cassidy took a couple of deep breaths and tried to look composed as she entered the farmhouse from the back patio. *Nothing like an impromptu interview.* "Thanks, Ruthanne," she said, patting her friend on the shoulder as she headed through the office to the lobby.

"Trish Campbell is out there. She said she'd schedule photos with you later," Ruthanne whispered.

"Yay." Cassidy winked and grabbed a bottle of water from the fridge. Stepping out into the public space, she said, "Good afternoon, Ms. Campbell. It's so nice to meet you."

"I hope you don't mind me stopping by early. We're headed to Staunton for an interview at the Woodrow Wilson Presidential Library, and I was hoping to squeeze you in today. Thanks for seeing me on short notice. I'll bring Noah by in a couple of days to get some pictures of you and the property."

"Not a problem. Just let me know, and I'll make sure to put it on my schedule. May I get you something to drink?" Cassidy asked, settling on the teal loveseat across from the reporter.

Trish shook her head. "Your place is lovely. The garden and the magnificent view of the Blue Ridge Mountains are amazing. Okay. I want to know all about the history of the place and the cave. I'm going to record this so I don't miss anything." She clicked a button on her phone and set it on the coffee table. Then she pulled out a small notebook and flipped to an empty page.

Cassidy smiled. "My grandfather owned a honky-tonk here. It had been in his family for decades. The road out front used to be the main road to Nashville, and many bands would stop in on their travels back and forth. It was before my time, but he had lots of memorabilia from famous acts who sang on his stage. It was quite the place to be, back in the day."

"The fire was so tragic. Was anyone hurt?" Trish asked.

"No. I don't think so. It was in the eighties. My grandmother said it was a lightning strike, and most of the old wooden building burned before the volunteer firefighters could get here. Unfortunately, the bar, stage, kitchen, and memorabilia were destroyed in the fire. The Pearly Girls, my grandmother's four friends, work here, and they have lots of tales about sneaking into the bar when they were younger to hear the musical acts."

"Pearly Girls?" Trish wrinkled her nose and turned her head slightly.

Cassidy picked up a glossy Celebrations brochure from the coffee table. "Roxie, Ruthanne, Kate, and Aileen were best friends with my grandma since 4-H and the church youth group." She tapped the brochure with her index finger. "They grew up in the days of Camelot, and of course they were known for their signature pearls. Someone nicknamed them that, and it stuck. I'm so fortunate to have them help me with events here." She pointed to the group picture of the five of them, all sporting strands of pearls.

Trish smiled. "We certainly want to get them in our photo session, and I'd love to come back and talk to them if they're willing. I can't wait to hear some of their stories. They look like a fun bunch."

"They definitely have stories." *The question is do you have the time?*

"I'll text Ruthanne and set up some time. She was so helpful. Okay, so how did the event-planning business come into being?"

"After the bar burned down, my grandfather was never the same. My grandma said it broke his heart. He died when I was young, but I do have a few memories of him. The Pearly Girls have all kinds of tales about the music scene here in Ivy Springs. When my grandfather passed away, my grandma decided to make some changes to the property. She converted the old dairy barn to a place for indoor events and added the garden and amphitheater for plays and concerts. She always loved a fun party."

"Ruthanne said you've also used it for weddings and memorial services."

Cassidy nodded. "It's hosted a bunch of different events. We have a big high school reunion planned this weekend."

"Okay, what about the cave? That sounded so cool. Noah and I want to see that on our next visit. It's wild that you have your own cave," the reporter cooed.

"It is cool. I played there as a kid. I was always searching for hidden treasure or dinosaur bones. We found some cans and discarded tools from the past, but that was it. Rumor has it some of my ancestors used it as a place to store their bootleg liquor during Prohibition."

Trish's eyebrows shot up under her chestnut bangs. "Oh, the adventures you could have had as a kid. It's safe to go in, right?"

Cassidy nodded, and Trish continued, "And I would be remiss if I didn't ask you about what happened in your garden last summer. I'll weave it into the story, but I don't want it to be the focus of the article."

"It was tragic. We thought we were hosting a Groovin' through the Decades concert series, and sadly all the fun and nostalgia were marred by the murder of Johnny Storm."

"The band was before my time," Trish mused. "But I know some of their songs. My mom loved the Weathermen. I heard you found the body in your garden." Trish leaned forward like she was waiting for a secret to be revealed.

Cassidy closed her eyes for a beat, trying to blot out the memories of Johnny Storm floating in her koi pond. "Yes, Elvis, my chihuahua, and I found him one morning."

"And you helped the police apprehend the killer. I'm still stunned at who it was," Trish interrupted. "You're quite the sleuth. I saw some stories online about it."

"It was a sad story, but I was glad that I was able to help out."

"Wow. You are quite modest. I'm sure you were more integral to the capture than that. Anything else you want to say about it?"

Cassidy shook her head.

"And you have a dog named Elvis. Tell me about him," she said.

"He's a brown-and-black chihuahua mix." And as if on cue, Elvis trotted in and sniffed the reporter's shoes.

"This is Elvis," Cassidy said, reaching down to pick him up before he jumped on Trish. "His black sideburns reminded me of the King. And growing up here with my grandma and the Pearly Girls, there was no question I'd be a fan of the King of Rock 'n' Roll."

Trish smiled and jotted something in her notes. "For a small little town in the mountains, your place seems to be ground zero for a great deal of action, past and present. I think that gives me enough for now. I may have some more questions when we come back. I'll text you some dates for the photos, and hopefully I can score some time with the Pearly Girls." She turned off the recording and rose. "Thanks for seeing me today. What a great story!"

"Thanks for covering us. We love to share our little corner of the Blue Ridge."

"My pleasure. I'll see you soon." Trish waved and headed for the door.

Ruthanne popped her head in as soon as the front door closed. "Oh, we'll have stories for her. I hope she adds us to the article. We'll be famous."

"Careful. No embarrassing stories about my teen years." Cassidy winked.

"Never. We'll keep it to our adventures and the fun we had at your granddaddy's bar that our parents didn't know about," Ruthanne said. "Among the four of us, we have plenty to tell."

"Oh, I lost track of time," Cassidy said, looking at her smartwatch. "It's almost time for Britt's early, unplanned event. I need to give Elvis a walk and then head over there."

"I'll close up here and meet you there in a few. I need to wrap up a couple of things." Ruthanne breezed back to her desk.

Elvis was in no hurry to end his walk. He dawdled and pursued every scent he encountered. Cassidy finally coaxed him back to the apartment with the promise of a treat, and then she hurried to the barn to make sure there were no issues.

Hearing loud voices, she wended her way around the tables with the fuchsia-and-teal flower arrangements. *So much for a quiet evening.* The volume increased as she headed toward the kitchen and serving area. Rounding the corner, she bumped into a muscular guy in all black who appeared out of nowhere.

"Oh, excuse me," the guy who looked like a cross between an athlete and a member of a boy band said, setting two crates full of glasses next to the counter.

"My apologies. I wasn't watching where I was going." Cassidy stared at his ice-blue eyes and sandy blond hair. His bangs draped casually across his forehead.

Wiping a hand on his black jeans, he offered it to her. "Hi, I'm Austin. Bartender and resident gofer for my sister's catering company, at your service."

"Annie's brother. It's so nice to meet you," she said, staring up at him.

"Yep. She tortures me at home and at work," he said with a snicker. "After my tour in the Army was up, I moved back here with her, and she put me to work."

Annie walked by and punched him lightly in the shoulder. "He needed something to keep him off the streets. Plus, he has to earn his keep. He was eating me out of house and home." She smiled and set down two platters of hors d'oeuvres. "Just kidding. Austin has been a huge help with his amazing bartending skills, and I'm lucky to have him until he figures out what he wants to do in civilian life," Annie said. "I'll put the platters in the prep-area fridge, and then we'll move in the wine and the rest of the booze."

"There are two smaller fridges and the ice machine back here behind the bar if you need them," Cassidy said, pointing to the large machine humming by the back counter.

"I'm on it," Austin said to his sister. Turning to Cassidy, he continued, "It was nice meeting you. I've got to go unload the van before my boss gets testy and fires me." He shook her hand again and held it longer than a friendly shake. The warmth sent tingles through Cassidy.

"It was nice to meet you too," she said as he dropped her hand.

A megawatt smile lit up his face. Before she could say anything else to him, he hustled out the back door. "Hey, Annie, let me know if I can help with anything," Cassidy yelled into the main part of the barn.

"We're good to go here. The scramble was earlier when I had to prep for the new meet-and-greet, but it's all good. Hopefully, everyone will have fun."

"Whoooo hooooooo," echoed through the barn, and Cassidy poked her head out in the main area. Britt breezed in, wearing a sequined royal blue pantsuit with silver stilettos and a tiny tiara in her big up-do. Anastasia, Kelly, and another woman with long brown hair and glasses stood behind her in casual outfits.

"This place is looking faaaaa-buuu-lous," Britt said. "You all made my vision come to life. Awesome. Just how I wanted it. I need to touch up my makeup. Be right back. Anastasia and Darcy, find your places. Kelly, you're the mix-and-mingle queen. Big smiles, everyone. What a way to kick off our extravaganza, and all the future reunion committees will have to really hustle to top us. So excited. We still rock Ivy Springs, ladies. Teamwork makes the dream work."

When she had disappeared in the back, Anastasia and the other woman, a brunette in a flowing top with batwing sleeves, headed for the tables flanking the balloon arches.

"Hi, I'm Cassidy Jamison. Let me know if you all need anything. The caterers are in the back, and the bartender is setting up now."

"I'm Darcy Branch," the brunette said, shaking Cassidy's hand.

"She's the big-time reporter," Anastasia whispered, not so softly.

Darcy smiled. "Thanks. But this weekend, I'm one of Britt's army of volunteers to make this a Springer event to remember." She fist-pumped the air and made a face.

Kelly drifted by the table and added, "And Britt is dying for you to do an article on the event and mention her. She'll do whatever you ask her to do if you keep teasing the idea of a big story. I'm just sayin' you have the power. Use it wisely."

Anastasia's eyes widened. The other two women paused, waiting with bated breath for Darcy's reply; but she simply continued straightening the name tags on the table.

Before anyone said anything, Britt breezed back in and shoved two large bags under the first table closest to the stage. "There. All ready. Everyone knows what they're supposed to do tonight? Wait, who moved the name tags?" She glared at Anastasia.

"I did," Darcy said. "I thought they'd be easier to locate if they were in columns. There. See how nice that looks." She stepped back to survey her work.

Anastasia froze and watched in anticipation of Britt's impending explosion.

"Oh, great idea," Britt said, glancing at the balloon arch on the stage.

Anastasia's eyes widened, and she chewed on her bottom lip.

Britt did a half-twirl and waved her arms around. "The photographer and the photo-booth guy will be here soon. Oh, whooooo is that?" She followed Austin to the bar.

Kelly and Darcy tagged along behind her. "Well, hello," Britt said to Austin. "We're so glad you're here tonight to celebrate with us."

"Thank you. Annie and I are glad to be here." Austin set three tins full of cut fruit on the counter.

"What's your specialty?" Kelly asked with a cougary leer.

"I do all kinds of mixed drinks. I have what I call a pink poodle. It's sweet and creamy, with a little kick to it. It'll go with your decorations if you want to give it a try. Gimme a second to finish here, and I'll whip up three for you."

"And me," Anastasia yelled, dodging chairs and tables as she scurried to the bar. She tripped over her own foot and caught herself on one of the chairs. *Looks like a bad case of FOMO, or as Kate would call it, fear of missing out.*

"Cassidy, would you like anything?" Austin asked, turning on his Hollywood smile.

"Water's fine." Cassidy stepped closer to watch him. He washed his hands and pulled out glasses and ingredients. His routine almost looked choreographed: it reminded Cassidy of the old Tom Cruise movie *Cocktail*. *Austin sure knows how to entertain his audience.*

After presenting the foamy pink drinks with dainty paper umbrellas, he took a slight bow and headed to the back. Cassidy picked up her water and wandered around to look at the bubble machine and the photo-booth setup, making a mental note to get the vendors' cards for her collection. *You never know when an event might call for their services.*

A shriek echoed through the empty barn, and Cassidy's head jerked toward the bar as Annie and Austin rushed in from the back.

Kelly had both hands planted on her hips. "You did that on purpose."

"I'm so sorry," Anastasia said. "It was an accident. My hand slipped on the damp glass."

"Now I have to go home and change." A thunderstorm brewed behind Kelly's hazel eyes. "Britt, I'll be back as soon as I can," she bellowed as she stomped out, the large pink stain spreading across her white slacks. "Anastasia, you're going to pay for this."

Cassidy hurried to get several damp paper towels to wipe up the wet floor as Austin mopped down the bar and cleared the glasses.

Britt rolled her eyes and said to Anastasia, "You better watch your back. You've made an enemy of the wicked witch. And we all know about Kelly's mean streak."

Anastasia shrugged. "It was an accident. She'll be fine," she said, walking toward the registration table. "I'll pay for her dry cleaning."

Cassidy tossed the damp paper towels and sidled over behind Darcy and Anastasia as the guests started to arrive.

"Britt, dear," a tall man in a tailored gray suit with a tie that matched her jumpsuit called out. All eyes were on him as he strode across the room.

"You made it! I thought you'd be tied up for hours with work. I'm so glad you're here," Britt said, rushing toward him and air-kissing both of his cheeks. "Everyone, this is Vince, my rock and best friend."

He nodded at the small group and picked up his name tag. "Nice to meet you all. Lovely place." Anastasia stared at the older man, who had a slight resemblance to Harrison Ford. Cassidy's glance flitted to Darcy, who stood nearby. The brunette pushed a strand of hair behind one ear and exchanged a slight smile with Britt's husband. Then she quickly focused on the table and made a show of straightening the name tags.

"Oh, Cassidy, why don't you join us for the meet-and-greet? It'll be good for you to connect with people from school. Some of the folks still live around here." Britt looped her arm through her husband's and led him to the table near the stage.

"Thanks," Cassidy said. "My team and I will be around throughout the evening if you all need anything." By the time she finished her sentence, Britt and her crew had dispersed to the tables and the bar. Cassidy found an unobtrusive spot near the bubble machine and away from the DJ's large speakers. She had a perfect view of Austin, who put on a show with every drink he made. He knew how to garner tips, especially from the female patrons.

Around ten o'clock, the guests started to drift toward the door. Britt held court at her table with Kelly, Darcy, and others. But there was no Anastasia in sight. *I wonder if the gals are still feuding over the spilled drink. Any grievance seems to generate big drama with this crowd. Not much has changed since high school.*

||||||||||||||||||||||||||||||||||||||||||||

Cassidy did a walk-through of the downstairs area as the DJ carried off the last of his bags and boxes. She locked the back door and flipped the kitchen lights off. Annie and Austin had already left with all their gear. She checked the loft and the hallways that led to the bathrooms.

"All clear in the bathrooms," Ruthanne called out as she turned off the lights in the back. "I think we get to call it a night." She met Cassidy midway in the back hall.

"Thanks for all your help. I think we're done here until tomorrow." Cassidy set the alarm and pulled the main doors closed behind them.

The pair stepped out into the cool night air and quickly moved out of the puddle of light from the overhead floodlights. Cassidy had to blink several times to allow her eyes to adjust to the darkness. In Ivy Springs, the ambient light that cities generated didn't exist, so the stars were brighter, and the darkness was inky.

Cassidy pulled out her phone and clicked on the flashlight app. Ruthanne froze and grabbed Cassidy's forearm. "Did you hear that? It didn't sound like the normal night woodsy noises. I think I heard footsteps," she whispered.

"I saw something move over there," Cassidy replied, taking a few steps toward the tree line. Before she could continue, a woman in a flowing blouse or a cape of some sort and a tall man in a suit rounded the corner of the barn. The pair, backlit by the lights, hugged and kissed for what seemed like forever, and then they walked off in separate directions.

In several seconds, the man closed the distance between the barn and where Cassidy and Ruthanne stood. When he crossed their path, the man, who turned out to be Vince, said, "Good evening, ladies. Nice place you have here," so casually that the little rendezvous by the barn seemed not to have happened.

"Enjoy your evening," Cassidy managed to say as he headed toward the parking lot.

Ruthanne poked her in the side when the man climbed into his large Mercedes and roared out of the main entrance. "That was Britt's husband. And I'm pretty sure that wasn't his wife with him out by the barn."

The alarm buzzed, and Cassidy rolled over after she turned the noise off. Hours later, she woke up to Elvis licking her nose. "What, puppy? You need to go out?"

She glanced at her phone and gasped. "I must have fallen back asleep. We need to get a move on!"

After a quick shower, she threw on jeans and a long-sleeved polo branded with her company's logo. She fluffed her curls and added a couple of swipes of lipstick and mascara. "There. That'll have to do in a rush. I should never have turned off the alarm."

She picked up her messenger bag and slid a yogurt and banana in the side pocket. "Let's go for a quick walk and then see what the Pearly Girls are up to."

At the mention of the "W" word, the chihuahua bounded down the steps and waited impatiently at the back door for Cassidy to catch up.

The walk around the patio and the serenity garden did nothing to calm Elvis. He was high-energy when she opened the door to the office, and he bolted over to greet Ruthanne, who was knitting at the table. Kate sat nearby, scrolling through something on her phone. Ruthanne's pile of yarn and what looked like an unfinished scarf sat nearby.

"Good morning, all." Cassidy dumped her things on her desk and headed for the coffeemaker.

"Hello, Sleeping Beauty," Roxie said as she breezed in from the front. "I even beat you in here this morning. That's not normal. Please tell us you had a hot date. Did he sneak out the back?"

Thoughts of the cute bartender flashed across her mind, but she decided not to make up a story about having a date. "Nope. I was super-tired after the exciting first night of the reunion. What's going on around here? Ruthanne, is that a scarf?" Cassidy pointed to the long brown creation that spilled from the accountant's lap and looked like a small pile of laundry on the floor.

"She got a little carried away," Kate said.

"This project was so much fun. It started out as a place mat. Then it became a scarf," Ruthanne added. "Now, I've got other plans for it."

"It's a twelve-foot monstrosity," Roxie said, rolling her eyes.

"I'll find a use for it," Ruthanne said with a mischievous grin. Aileen and Kate giggled like schoolgirls as Ruthanne stood and folded the python-sized scarf and stuffed it into her satchel.

Cassidy booted her laptop up and settled in at her desk to check her business's social media sites.

"Oh, Cassidy," Kate said. "We ran into Ahni Rao at our last knit-in. She wants you to contact her about a bookfest she'd like to bring to the area."

"Sounds like fun. A Novel Idea is such a cute store. We've needed a bookstore here for so long." Cassidy whipped out her phone and fired off an email before she forgot about the lead.

"Soooo, Roxie, tell us about your latest fling. We all saw you chatting him up in the barn last night. And he didn't look like a race-car driver," Aileen said in a sing-song voice.

"I haven't seen Martin in years. It was good to run into him again. You all remember Martin Ellis. He used to teach History and Poli Sci at the high school. He retired and moved to Florida," Roxie said, pulling a mug from the cabinet.

"It was nice of some of the teachers to come back for the reunion. And it worked out for you." Ruthanne wiggled her eyebrows.

"We were chatting. Catching up. We're going to have drinks tonight before the big shindig," Roxie replied.

"Oooh, so you have a plus-one for the dance," Aileen said.

"No. Just a friendly meetup. Not sure how long I'll stay at the dance unless Cassidy needs me. I'm not too keen on music after the '90s," Roxie said.

"Tonight's supposed to be the hits of 2009 from the class's senior year," Cassidy added.

Roxie wrinkled her nose. "Not my cup of tea. I'll stay as long as I can stand it."

‖‖‖‖‖‖‖‖‖‖‖‖‖‖‖‖‖‖‖‖‖‖‖‖‖‖‖‖‖

At around four o'clock, when all the Pearly Girls had headed off for other activities, Cassidy packed up and took Elvis for a walk around the property. *I wonder if we'll have more drama tonight. Roxie and the retired teacher. Vince and the mystery woman. And the general cattiness of the planning committee. Mixed together, it could make for a lively night.*

Cassidy's thoughts bounced to Austin, and a little charge jolted through her. It would be nice to see him again. She chided herself for looking forward to running into him. He was just being attentive, good for his business.

Elvis and Cassidy strolled through the serenity garden, enjoying the quiet place next to the rocky grotto wall near the cave with the view of the valley on the other side. Her glance settled on the flower bed near the koi pond. The plaque honoring the memory of Johnny Storm looked good in the middle of Levi's irises and lilies. She shook off the dark thoughts of the tragic murder and looked out at the view that reminded her of why she loved this place. Life after college in the big city was fun, but the mountains would always be home.

Cassidy's eyes flicked toward the cave, by far the most interesting and unusual feature on the property. *What other twenty-something has her own cave? I really need to do something with it.* All kinds of ideas for the space bounced around her head. What if she turned it into an underground music venue or a spot for parties? "Elvis, maybe I should pursue this. If the construction to make it doable is reasonable, then I should think about it. It's not doing anything for us in its current state. I could create something that celebrates the history of the property and brings in its own revenue stream. A win-win."

Not interested in the ways to use the cave, Elvis decided he was ready for dinner. Cassidy hustled home, fed him, found some leftover pizza to heat up for herself, and changed outfits a couple of times. She finally settled on a rust-colored cardigan with a cream camisole and black leggings that paired with her low-heeled Peter Pan boots. Tonight was all about comfort.

"Okay, pup. I'm headed out in a few." She slipped the little dog two miniature treats and patted his head. "You're in charge of security here."

Pocketing her phone and keys, she headed toward the barn, where DJ Magic Mike's white SUV, covered in an advertising wrap, and the two vans from Annie's Eats sat in the grass near the back door. She eased in through the open door and paused for her eyes to adjust to the dim interior.

"Hey, there," boomed a male voice from the other side of the kitchen, and Cassidy let out a squeak.

Austin laughed. "Sorry. I didn't mean to startle you. I thought you saw me over here. You ready for another night of fun?"

"Always," Cassidy said, trying to will her heart rate to slow down. "Do you need anything?"

"Nope, we're good. It's a rinse and repeat from last night with a different menu. Let me know if you want to sample anything or you need a drink."

Cassidy smiled. "Thanks. I'm going to check on the reunion committee. Hopefully, tonight will go off without a hitch." She glanced over her shoulder. The DJ station looked lonely in the corner without all the pulsating lights from last night. No Magic Mike in sight.

Movement near the main doors caught Cassidy's eye, and she threaded her way through the tables and chairs to the registration area. "Hi, Anastasia. How are things?"

The woman turned her head and zipped toward the restrooms. *That was odd. I'm sure she heard me.*

Cassidy looked around. No Britt, Kelly, or Darcy. Glancing at the time on her phone, she wondered where everyone was.

A shrill "Excuse me. Can I have a gin and tonic, light on the ice?" broke the silence and interrupted Cassidy's thoughts. *Anastasia. She's too close this time to pretend she didn't hear me.* She sidled up to the bar next to the brassy blonde, who was scrolling through something on her phone.

"Hi, there. Are you the only one here from the planning team?" Cassidy asked.

"Here you go," Austin said, setting the glass in front of the woman who hadn't looked up from her phone. "What can I get you?"

"Ginger ale, please," Cassidy said.

"Neither of these drinks is a challenge, but okay. I brought some of my fancy gear with me and everything. Y'all are going to have to come up with something else later to test my mixology skills." Austin winked.

Cassidy smiled as he put the glass in front of her with a plastic sword full of cherries and pineapple chunks and returned to his bar prep. She glanced at her own phone to make sure she hadn't gotten any last-minute emergency messages from her clients. *The reunion gals are cutting it kinda close this evening.*

"I always get stuck doing the crap work," Anastasia said. "When will I learn? I guess they'll be here any minute, especially now that all the heavy lifting is done." She reached for her drink and took a long swig.

"Heyyyyyyy there," echoed through the seating area. "Anybodyeeeee here?"

"We're over here," Anastasia said without turning around.

"Where's Britt and Darcy?" a breathless Kelly asked. "I need Britt to try this on. She wanted my red sequined outfit for tonight. She must want to make an entrance as usual." She draped a dry-cleaning bag over the nearest chair. "Hey, barkeep. Could you make me a hurricane?"

"Coming right up, ma'am," Austin said, wiping his hands on a dish towel.

"I'm not old enough for 'ma'am,'" Kelly said with a coy smile and wink. "Hey, Anastasia. What happened to your face? It's puffier than usual."

The other blonde bit back her reply and stared at Kelly for a couple of heartbeats that created an awkward pause.

Austin tried to break the glarefest with "Can I get any of you ladies a refill?"

"No, we're good," Anastasia said. "We need to be on our game.

You know Britt will be here any minute to bark out orders for things we need to change at the last minute. And for your information, everything is fine. My face is a little swollen on this side. It's allergies. I think it's all the hay in this place."

"There's no hay in the barn," Austin said before Cassidy could offer a retort.

"I meant all the tall grass around the property. It makes me sneeze and wheeze." She slugged the last few drops of her drink down and then set the glass down on the counter with more force than needed. "I'll be back before Britt gets here."

Cassidy looked up to see Britt pushing her way through the guests streaming in through the door, blowing in like a thunderstorm coming over the mountain ridge. "Kelly, where are you? I finally found the matching shoes. Where's the outfit? Help." She skidded to a stop in her tennis shoes and snapped her fingers for Kelly to follow her.

"Let me know if I can help," said Anastasia, who looked torn between making her escape and cozying up to her fearless leader.

"Thanks. I think I've got it with Kelly's help," Britt called from the back. "She's always a lifesaver."

As more guests poured in, Cassidy found herself a quiet corner near the bar to people-watch. Singles and couples arrived and filled most of the seats near the dance floor.

When the DJ played "Party in the USA," Britt and Kelly made their entrance like royalty. They had matching sparkly outfits. Britt's was red, and Kelly's was a shimmery white. *They should have had Anastasia in blue for the full patriotic effect.*

After greeting all her friends, Britt took the microphone from Magic Mike and tapped on it with her giant ring. The thunks echoed through the room, and the audience groaned. "Sorry about that," Britt said quickly. "I was trying to get your attention for a big announcement. Kelly Mason Todd and me, Britt Rogers Mahoney, have news you're going to want to celebrate. Where is the famous Darcy? If you're in the building, please come up here." She paused and shaded her eyes with several oversized index cards as she scanned the crowd. "Oh, well. We'll catch her up later."

"We want to thank our generous donors from the amazing class of 2009, Mac Gibson, Darcy Branch, Keith Emerson, and Britt and Vince Mahoney," she said with a giggle. "With all the contributions and the golf tournament, we raised fifteen thousand dollars for the Ivy Springs Athletic Fund. We'll do the official presentation at the school, but I wanted you all to hear it here first. We rock!"

The audience clapped and drowned out Britt. When it started to die down, she whispered, "Thank you. Thank you all so much. The class of 2009 is and always will be amazing. Go, Springers!" She dabbed her eyes and followed Kelly to the bar.

About an hour later, Cassidy cruised by Austin's station for a Coke, and a flash of red caught her eye. Britt waved her spangled arms around. "I am fine," she said to Vince, pulling away from him. "I'm stressed out. Darcy and Anastasia have skipped out, leaving Kelly and moi to do all the work as usual. Sometimes I have to do everything *and* be the one in charge," she whined.

Vince leaned over and whispered something to Kelly, who then said to Britt, "Come on. I have some CBD goodies in my purse. Maybe that will make you feel better. Let's take a little break, and we'll look for the gals later." She took Britt's elbow and led her through the crowd to the restrooms.

"What can I get you?" Austin asked after pouring shots for a group of guys at the bar.

"Coke, please. It's a lively evening." Cassidy glanced toward the dance floor.

Austin nodded and set a drink with a pink flamingo stir stick in front of her. "Great tips. I'll take it over the alternative any day. Enjoy." He winked as he turned his attention to a group of women vying for his attention. A tingle of excitement surged through her. *He definitely knows how to cater to his audience.*

Trying to stay awake and hoping the caffeine from her drink would kick in, Cassidy walked the perimeter of the room and then stepped outside for some fresh air. A small crowd had gathered near the path to the parking lot. Cassidy trotted over to see if she needed to put out any embers before they flared up into bigger problems. Kelly and Mac, Britt's first husband, were trying to ease Britt into the back seat of a gray Honda. "Come on, Britt. You've had too much to drink. Let the Uber guy take you home."

"I need to talk to Vince," Britt whined. "First Darcy, and now Anastasia. Ha. Anastasia. You remember her, she's the one I stole you from. And it wasn't that hard." She waggled her finger at Mac, who looked down at his shoes. "Mac, you remember the good old days. We were hot. We had it all. What happened to us?" she sniffed.

Britt wiped her heavily mascaraed eyes on her sparkly sleeve. "Ow. Okay. Just take me home. Kelly-poo, promise me you'll take care of everything here. And don't tell folks I couldn't find Darcy and Vince. You know how people talk. They'll spread rumors," she slurred. "He can't do that to me again. Just like you, Mac," she hissed through her clenched teeth.

Mac didn't reply and used the pause in the conversation to shut the car door and tap on the roof for the driver. He and Kelly returned to the barn, and the onlookers dispersed and headed to their own vehicles.

That was interesting, Cassidy thought. *There is definitely something brewing behind the scenes with these folks. We've got only one more weekend of this. We've endured worse. We'll make it.* She let out a sigh and headed back to the barn.

5

Cassidy willed the office coffeemaker to finish sputtering and fill her mug. Maybe the caffeine from a second cup would ward off the headache that was building behind her eyes. Last night, Britt had sent her a string of texts that went on until two in the morning. At first, they were requests for today's activities and ideas for next week. Then the tone turned whiney when Vince hadn't returned home. Cassidy finally muted her phone and tried to get some sleep. *Let's see what Britt comes up with today. Hopefully, she and Vince have worked things out.*

Elvis yipped and pawed at her jeans. "Okay, let's take a break. Maybe the fresh air and a nice walk-about will be better than the coffee." She clicked his leash in place, and he danced out the door.

The warm breeze, probably the last nice temperatures before fall arrived in full force, tousled her hair and brought with it scents of grass and pine trees. Elvis took full advantage of the outside time and pranced to the garden. They walked the perimeter of the flower beds and around the wrought iron furniture, and paused at the pergola that served as the wedding chapel near the pink and white rose bushes that still had a few remaining blooms. The variegated camellias along the back had a handful of lingering flowers too. The chihuahua sniffed the mulch and then started to paw around.

"Come on, buddy. Levi will not like you digging in his flower beds. He had a conniption when the squirrels did it."

The sun glinted on something metallic. "What is that?" Nudging it with the toe of her shoe, she bent down and picked up a gold metal lipstick. "Audacious Flame, a bold color. Hmmm. What's that over there? This is like an Easter-egg hunt." Several feet away, a green key chain with Sid "Pro Quo" Proctor's motel logo poked out of a tuft of grass. "Come on, Elvis. This is stuff to add to our lost-and-found collection. Somebody will be back for these. Let's get a move on. We need to get some work done before the reunion folks get here for goat yoga in the garden."

Not all that interested in goats or yoga, the little dog barked and trotted off toward the farmhouse.

"Uh-oh," Cassidy said. She'd almost stepped on something black. "Somebody dropped a bunch of stuff here. And they'll be looking for this car key fob. What was going on around here last night? Know anyone with a Toyota?" Cassidy's voice trailed off as she fingered the key and tried to remember if she had seen any of the reunion crew in a Toyota.

Still not interested in the conversation topic, Elvis led the way around to the parking lot. Away from her Wrangler and company van, Ruthanne's Mini Cooper and Kate's silver Volvo sat at the other end of the lot. A black Toyota with the racing package sat alone in the last row. Cassidy clicked the fob, the car beeped, and the headlights flashed. She locked it again. "We'll keep an eye out for the owner."

Inside, Cassidy put the items in a plastic bin on the counter and sent a text to the Pearly Girls in case they heard from anyone about the missing items. Before she could check her email, Kate and Aileen buzzed in and instantly covered most of the back office with large shopping bags and oversized purses.

"Morning, Cassidy," Kate said. "We stopped by to check on things and to see if you need us this afternoon. Ruthanne roped us into a new project, and we've been spending all our free time on that."

"But we're having fun," Aileen said, rummaging through her pink canvas bag. "We're trying to get the new project finished. If you need us tonight, we'll gladly come back. Ruthanne's on her way in. She's out there wrestling with her fifty-foot scarf. If it gets any bigger, it's not going to fit in her car anymore."

Cassidy laughed. *What does one do with a scarf that size?* "The reunion stuff is under control. You all might want to swing by the barn sometime today. They've gone all-out decorating for tonight's events. I think you all will get a kick out of some of their creations. Maybe it will provide some ideas for our other events. They're creating vignettes all around the barn of musical tributes from their high school days. It should be entertaining."

Kate's eyebrows shot up, and Aileen paused and leaned forward. "Like what?"

"Frenemy fights, love triangles, and cougars trying to get the attention of the new bartender," Cassidy said, settling in her office chair.

"Ah, Austin. I bet Annie's still having to protect her little brother from all his adoring fans. He was the Brad Pitt of the elementary school scene," Aileen said.

"He has caused quite a stir on the dating front in Ivy Springs since he returned to town," Kate added. "He doesn't know how cute he really is. And it doesn't hurt that he's so nice and has that amazing smile."

"Who has an amazing smile?" Roxie asked, showing off her pearly whites with an exaggerated grin.

"Austin Taylor, Sylvie's grandson," Aileen said.

"Oh, yes. All the gals know he's back in town and single. Word spread like wildfire." Roxie reached for a mug and a coffee pod. "Cassidy, you should ask him out."

Ignoring the comment, Cassidy pretended to be engrossed in her social media feeds. The gals chattered on about town gossip; and Ruthanne wandered in, dragging a trash bag full of her latest knitting project. The other three paused and snickered at some private joke.

‖‖‖‖‖‖‖‖‖‖‖‖‖‖‖‖‖‖‖‖‖‖‖‖‖‖‖‖‖‖‖‖

Around four o'clock, all the Pearly Girls drifted out the door with promises to check in this evening in case Cassidy needed a break from the reunion gals.

"We'll be at Kate's house knitting, if you need us," Aileen said, closing the door behind her.

"Come on, Elvis. Let's go see what we can throw together for dinner. I got so engrossed in event ideas this afternoon, I didn't get to the other stuff on my list. But I did send an email to that concert promoter to see if he was interested in doing another event in the summer. Fingers crossed."

After kibble for Elvis and leftover lasagna for Cassidy, she got him settled on the couch and did a quick check on her hair and makeup. She had time to change outfits before heading over to the reunion.

The barn looked empty through the balloon arches. *Wow. They went crazy with all the musical decorations.* Vignettes from CD covers and music videos filled every empty space around the dance floor and loft. Huge 2009 balloons hung over the main doors and the DJ's booth. The balloon arches swayed when the AC blew through the nearby vents. Cassidy recognized tributes to Hannah Montana, the Kanye and Taylor Swift dust-up, Katy Perry, and a tribute to the cast from *Jersey Shore*. She walked to each set of decorations and snapped pictures for her collection.

A scratching sound in the kitchen caught Cassidy's attention. She tiptoed around the corner, and Annie popped up with a metal tin and a large tray. "Ooooh."

"So sorry to startle you," Cassidy said.

"I thought the reunion people would be here by now. The fireworks guys have been setting up all afternoon. They roped off the area over there behind the barn, and I had to drive on your grass to get to the back door. I hope I didn't damage anything."

"I'm sure it's fine," Cassidy said. "The fireworks should be fun. Hopefully, it won't spook any of the wildlife or my neighbors."

Noises in the main area drew them both to the bar. Kelly and Anastasia, along with the DJ and his helper, moved around like bees in a hive.

"I haven't seen Britt or Darcy," Anastasia said.

"Britt's probably working on her social media stuff. She said she had a couple of new contracts to promote some products," Kelly said. "She always has a busy calendar. She'll show up soon."

"After all the work is done," Anastasia said under her breath. "I haven't seen Darcy in a while. I hope she didn't get bored and leave town. I'm sure there can't be much around here to hold her attention for very long."

Kelly shrugged. "Who knows. She's a big-time reporter and writer. I'm sure she's used to a much faster pace. And she may have even been called out for another story. Britt will be ticked. She was expecting her to do an article on her and all the fabulous reunion events and the money we've raised. She was looking for a big spread with photos. She said she needed it to boost her reach as an influencer."

"At least Britt isn't doing those candle or essential oils parties anymore. She kept insisting that my mother and I host her parties. I mean, how many candles can you buy in a year?" Anastasia plunked one hand on her hip. "I have allergies. Candles and scented oils aren't my jam."

"Vince has funded many of her business opportunities. She's trying to find her niche," Kelly said in a low voice, straightening the tablecloth on a nearby table.

"I have a feeling Darcy has flown the coop. Britt will be so bummed. I wonder if she told Britt she was leaving." Anastasia made a frowny face. "You know what, I haven't seen Vince around much either. If I didn't know better, I might think he and Darcy had a thing going. They always seem to disappear around the same time. Has anyone else noticed? He lights up when she's nearby. Poor Britt. She'll be brokenhearted. It's like what Mac did all over again."

"I saw Vince and Darcy out back the first night together, and it didn't look casual. That's all Britt needs right now, another two-timing husband. For all her outgoingness, she's really fragile. A second cheater would shatter her," Kelly said.

Cassidy stepped closer to the two women, but their conversation faded when they zeroed in on Austin, who hustled in, hauling two crates full of bottles. His muscles bulged as he hoisted both crates on top of the bar. The reunion women forgot all about their busyness as they staked out spots at the bar to ogle Austin.

The line at the bar grew and encroached on Kelly and Anastasia's space as guests began to trickle in. The noise level increased until Magic Mike drowned it out with the top hits from the class's senior year. Not seeing anything interesting, Cassidy mingled with the guests. She thought she recognized some of the faces. It hadn't been that long, but some people had changed drastically since their teen years.

The pounding bass from the speakers and the loud conversations gave Cassidy a headache. Not noticing anyone on the reunion committee, she walked the perimeter of the room to try to ward off the pain building behind her eyes. As she rounded the corner near the stage, a shrill noise pierced through the chatter and caused all heads to turn to see what was happening. At first, Cassidy thought it was from the music; but when she heard it again, her brain registered it as a cry for help.

Rushing over to the area under the loft, she skidded to a stop behind a group of women. One doubled over like she was going to be ill, and the other continued to scream and point at the decorations. Cassidy stared at the vignette as the woman continued with a mix of shrieks and sobs.

The scene was supposed to be a recreation of Lady Gaga's bloody performance of "Paparazzi" from the MTV Video Music Awards, but that wasn't a mannequin in the center of it all. Someone had altered the vignette, and it now looked like something from a low-budget horror flick. Britt, in a white dress covered in red splotches, sat slumped over next to one of the railings. A long curly blonde wig hung askew over her face, and smeared red lipstick stained her mouth and cheek. Someone had pulled the white dress over Britt's street clothes. Had Britt been here the whole evening like this? How had no one noticed?

Cassidy's stomach felt like it was full of cement. She took a deep breath to fight off the wave of nausea and stared at the very dead Britt, surrounded by cardboard boxes that had colorful cameras painted on them.

Cassidy took a few more deep breaths. *Girl, you've got to get control of this now.* She cleared her throat and steeled herself to face the fallout of another dead body on her property. "Get back, but stay in the building," Cassidy commanded. She pulled out her phone and dialed the emergency dispatcher. "This is Cassidy Jamison at Celebrations at Ivy Springs. We're hosting a high school reunion in the barn this evening, and some of the guests found the body of Britt Mahoney, and she's unresponsive. I need police and an ambulance."

"Both are on their way. They should be there in a minute or two," the dispatcher responded. "Is she breathing?"

"No, I don't think so. I'm afraid to touch her. It looks like there's blood on her," Cassidy whispered in the phone. She took several deep breaths and glanced around to see if there was anyone who could help with the growing crowd. "We have an event going on right now. I'm going to ask someone to wait at the door to show you where the, uh, victim is. We need to move the guests to the back of the building, so you all will have some space when your folks get here."

"Don't let people leave," the dispatcher said. "The police will want to talk to them."

"Okay. Time for some crowd control." Cassidy disconnected. Spotting Kate and Aileen in the back, she waved them over.

"What's going on... Oh, my. Not again," Aileen said, stopping to stare at the scene. "What in the world happened here?"

"Did anyone check her?" Kate asked, shifting into caregiver mode.

Cassidy shook her head, and Kate the former nurse nimbly climbed over the props in the vignette and leaned over Britt. "No pulse. And she's not breathing." She paused and wiped her stained fingers together and took a sniff.

Kate then carefully retraced her steps out of the decorations. When she was closer to Cassidy, she leaned toward her ear and said, "I don't think that's blood, but I couldn't tell what happened to her. The red stuff smelled like paint."

"Police and EMTs are on their way. Can one of you watch the front door? We don't want witnesses leaving until the police have a chance to talk to them. And can one of you hang out at the back door?" Cassidy asked, relieved that all the blood spatter wasn't real. But what had happened to Britt? Cassidy's thoughts flitted to all the drama in the woman's life.

"We're on it," Aileen said, heading to the kitchen area. "Nobody will sneak past us."

Kate said, "There's nothing we can do for her. What an awful way to go. And why was she dressed up like that? Are they having some sort of costume event?" She didn't wait for an answer, taking a couple of steps toward the entrance. "I'll flag down the ambulance."

Cassidy inched closer to the stage and the DJ. When she couldn't get his attention, she tapped him on the shoulder. "I have an emergency announcement," she yelled over the throbbing music.

"What?" he asked, staring at her.

"I said there's been an emergency. I need the microphone."

He reached over to his soundboard, turned off the song, and handed her the mic.

"Good evening. Excuse me. Everyone, I'm sorry to disrupt the party. We have a medical emergency, and the EMTs will be here shortly. For the next few minutes, please stay in the area with the seating, and we'll have an update for you as soon as they take care of the situation."

A murmur rumbled through the crowd as guests strained to see what was going on. The chatter got louder as the EMTs, several deputies, and Detective Zac Turner hustled in and crowded around the loft area. It was hard to see around the perimeter of law enforcement and emergency personnel, but that didn't stop the crowd from trying to get a glimpse of what was happening as they edged closer and closer to the gruesome scene. Then every few minutes one of the deputies would guide the crowd back to the seating area.

Cassidy scrolled through Britt's Instagram and Facebook pages. There were no recent posts except for a couple of product endorsements from around lunchtime. None of the comments looked threatening or questionable. Not finding anything, Cassidy moved on and searched for Darcy. Her sites hadn't had a new post since last Sunday, and they were all work-related.

Striking out, Cassidy looked through the photos she had taken earlier in the barn. *Why don't I have one of the Lady Gaga exhibit?* Disappointed that she didn't have an earlier shot of the scene, she flipped through the others to see if anything looked out of place. Nothing seemed amiss. Was this staged earlier, or did someone put Britt here right before the event? *You would think one of us would have noticed.* Cassidy shivered at the thought. *This is kind of an out-of-the-way spot.* Maybe that gave the killer some time to create the horrific scene.

Cassidy stared at her phone for what seemed like an eternity.

Detective Turner, in black jeans and a teal Ivy Springs Sheriff's

Department polo, strode over and tapped her on the shoulder. "You okay?" he asked. "What happened?" He motioned for her to follow him to the kitchen.

"I was walking around, checking out the festivities, and I found her like that." Cassidy tried to blink back tears. It was going to be hard to get that final image of Britt out of her mind. "I have no idea how long she had been there. I took some photos earlier, but none of them were of this area."

"Send me them just in case," he said, patting her shoulder. "Did you know her? And what is she dressed up as?" He pulled out a spiral notebook from his back pocket and flipped to a blank page. He stared intently at her with those intense hazel eyes that she remembered so well from before.

She nodded slowly. "It's Britt Rogers Mahoney. She's married to insurance salesman Vince Mahoney. Britt's the head of the reunion committee. Tonight's theme is music from 2009, their senior year. That's supposed to be Lady Gaga at the Video Music Awards," she said in a low tone.

"When was the last time you saw Britt? Tonight?" he asked, scanning the room.

Cassidy shook her head. "Yesterday. She wasn't here for the setup this afternoon."

"Did you notice anyone hanging around back here? It's kinda dark, and not really that close to the bar or the stage. Was this like this when you got here?" he asked, glancing past her at the crowd the other deputies were trying to corral on the other side of the room.

She closed her eyes for a beat. *I can't remember anyone back here. We weren't using the loft for this event.* Most of the crowd was near the bar, where Austin held court with his mixology tricks. Cassidy retraced her earlier steps in her head, trying to remember her last encounter with Britt. She opened her eyes and shook her head. "We didn't use this area, so there wasn't much traffic back here. Maybe someone on the committee has pictures of it from their setup."

A forensic team cordoned off the area with police tape as noise from the crowd increased. Detective Turner looked over his shoulder at the three deputies. "Get those people's statements and then start letting them go. We don't need onlookers hanging out while our guys work. I want to talk to anyone on the committee, her friends, and any staff working the event, but the guests can leave after you get their info. And see if you can tent off the area," he said to the three deputies, who fanned out around the seating area.

"The members of the committee are Kelly Mason Todd, Anastasia Young, and Darcy Branch. Vince Mahoney, the current husband, and Mac Gibson, the ex-husband, are also supposed to be here tonight, but I haven't seen any of them in a while," Cassidy added.

"Uh-huh." Turner jotted notes. "Does she have any enemies that you know of?"

Cassidy paused, and the detective stared at her until she answered. "She's very direct, and she steps on toes from time to time. Her inner circle seems to be her biggest fans. She is very demanding and expects to get her way. Let's say not everyone agrees with her."

An ear-splitting shriek, followed by wails, caused everyone to freeze.

Kelly Mason Todd had slipped through the crowd and stepped behind the two forensic technicians who were snapping pictures. Stumbling backward, she shrieked again. Kelly sank to her knees, crying and pointing at the lifeless Britt. "What happened? Who could have been evil enough to do this? I hadn't seen her all evening, and now I'll never get to talk to her again." She seemed to melt onto the floor. A tall man with a goatee gently lifted her to her feet and led her to a nearly empty table near the bar. She buried her head in his shoulder and sobbed loud enough to be heard over the crowd noise.

Anastasia pushed her way through the small groups of people clustered nearby. "What is going on? Holy sh—. Who would do this to our decorations? This is not the epic reunion that we had all hoped for." She grimaced. "It'll be memorable, but not the way Britt wanted." Her voice trailed off as she stared at the scene. "This scene was Darcy's idea. She loved the gothic look. Britt hated it. But she let Darcy do it. Britt was trying to ingratiate herself for a primo spot in an article that Darcy might write. Geez Louise. Now everybody will remember our reunion because it's where Britt died. I can't believe this is happening." Anastasia ran both her hands through her straw-like hair, causing it to stick out at all angles like she'd been caught in a windstorm.

Cassidy paused for a couple of seconds, struck by Anastasia's callous comments about her friend and wild look about her. Before Cassidy could speak, Anastasia said, "What are they doing over there? Nobody told the DJ he could pack up." She scrunched up her face and stomped toward the stage.

As the minutes and hours ticked by, the crowd thinned as the deputies finished gathering statements. By eleven-thirty, only a handful of people remained. The occasional whispers in the eerily silent barn created a surreal feeling as the forensics team worked under their bright portable lights. Cassidy scrolled through her social media feeds, trying to pass the time until the police provided an update.

Word had already leaked out on Facebook about Britt's murder. Nothing compared to the speed of a small town's gossip grapevine. The comments were a mix of condolences and rumors about who could have done it. The latter listed names that included serial killers and zombies.

"Well, that was not what I expected to see tonight. Gruesome," Aileen said, shuddering as she plopped down in the seat next to Cassidy.

"As tragic as tonight was, I was surprised people were grousing about cutting the evening short and canceling the fireworks. They seemed more concerned about that than they were for the dearly departed," Kate said, sitting in the chair opposite Aileen. "I can't believe there wasn't more sympathy about what occurred here tonight and the life that was cut short."

"I'm wondering if we'll need to cancel the rest of the events. I can't see folks wanting to celebrate after tonight," Cassidy said in a low tone.

"If their earlier comments and morbid fascination with the gory details are any indication, they'll all want to come back to the scene," Kate muttered, rummaging through her purse. "They like to gossip about the infamous Britt. I heard tales of her romances, bad marriages, and a couple of pyramid schemes where she lost a boatload of money. Nobody was singing her praises, except Kelly." She gave a little one-shoulder shrug.

Before anyone replied, Austin strode over, carrying three water bottles. "In case you need a drink," he said.

"Many thanks. I'm parched," Aileen said.

"Sure, Mrs. Roberts. It's good to see you. It's been a while," he said with a grin.

"You've grown a bit since you were in my class," Aileen sized up Austin and winked. "I hope life is treating you well."

He nodded. Before he could comment further, Kate blurted, "Hey, did you hear any chatter over at the bar while the deputies were questioning people? What were people saying about what happened to Britt?"

He paused and scanned the room before he said anything.

"There was some talk. A lot of people seemed shocked. Others were tired and just wanted to leave. And a bunch were annoyed about no fireworks. They gossiped about Britt and her husband and their troubles, but no one seemed too broken up about it except the blonde woman who's always with her. A couple of people wondered about where her ex-husband was."

"What about Darcy, the one with the darker hair?" Cassidy asked. "She was on the committee too. Did you happen to see her?"

"I haven't seen her in a while. She's the one they fall all over themselves when she's around. Can I get you all anything else? I'm packing up. As soon as the detective says we can leave, Annie and I are headed out."

"Thanks," the three women said at the same time.

"It's been a long evening," Kate added. "I'm ready to go home too."

"We have to finish that thing," Aileen gave her a sideways look. "No rest for the weary."

Kate rolled her eyes. "I need a break from our project." She wiggled her fingers in the air. "I think I've lost feeling in these babies. After this, I won't be doing any crafting for a while."

Before Cassidy could ask about what the thing was, Detective Turner sat down in the seat across from the women. "I know it's been a difficult night. Is there anything else you all can remember?"

"You want something to drink?" Cassidy asked.

The detective shook his head. "Did you happen to hear anything from the other guests?"

The three shook their heads. "What happened?" Cassidy whispered. "Should we be worried about a crazed killer on the loose? And do you think we'll need to cancel the rest of the events?"

"You always need to be aware of your surroundings. I don't think there's any imminent danger, but it's always good to be vigilant."

He stopped and glanced at the forensic technicians. "We'll be out of here tonight or maybe early tomorrow. That shouldn't interfere with your events."

"How did she, well, you know...die?" Aileen whispered. "I heard there was blood everywhere. Was it a stabbing or something? I was in the restroom and some gals were talking about it and the fact that Mac, her ex, was an avid hunter with a huge gun and knife collection."

Detective Turner nodded and wrote something in his notebook. "Keep this to yourselves, but it may ease some worries. It'll hit the paper tomorrow, I'm sure. But let's not spread it until we have to. The scene here was all staged. It wasn't real blood. We have to wait for the medical examiner's report on the official cause of death, but there was no evidence that she was stabbed or shot."

Kate let out a stream of air that sounded like a leaky balloon. "I knew she was covered in paint. It didn't have the consistency of blood. But it was foul play, right? I've seen enough episodes of *Dateline*. But why would someone put her there in the decorations unless they were trying to make a statement?"

Detective Turner's lips formed a straight line, and something in the distance caught his eye. "Y'all are free to go and close up here. Forensics is packing up. If you hear anything related to the murder, let me know."

I can't figure him out. Sometimes he acts like he's willing to share information or ask for my help, and then other times he clams up and tells us not to get involved. He's cute and smart, but he puts out too many mixed signals. He's impossible to get a read on.

"We definitely will," Aileen said with an impish grin. "We'll have Cassidy call you right away. Right, girls?"

"And you may want to stop by for a chat or coffee or something sometime later in the week too," Kate added with a wink.

Great. The Pearly Girls are looking for every opportunity for a fixup. Cassidy could feel the heat rising in her cheeks. She and the detective had a flirty relationship that never led to anything. She felt like he would have asked her out if he were truly interested, but the Pearly Girls still wanted to take every opportunity to stir the pot and push them toward a date. *He's vexing, and right now, that's not working for me.*

"Thanks for all of your help. Let us know if we can answer any other questions." When she realized no one had said anything, Cassidy added, "I'm going to check the kitchen and lock the back doors. If you two feel like it, could you make sure the loft and restroom areas are clear?" She and Aileen rose and made their way around the empty tables as the detective walked in the other direction.

"Not a problem," Kate said, rising. "It looks like the only ones left are the police."

Cassidy stopped, and Aileen almost crashed into the back of her. "I'll have to see if the reunion folks want to cancel the rest of the events. I wouldn't blame them under the circumstances." Cassidy blew out a long puff of air.

"Don't fret until you know something definite." Aileen patted Cassidy's arm. "I'm gonna check the bar area and then help Kate."

After locking the doors behind the forensic team, Cassidy made her way home on autopilot.

She cast a bleary eye at her phone one last time before she crawled in bed. One o'clock. She yawned and turned the light out, but her thoughts about who could have killed Britt drowned out any of her attempts to fall asleep.

7

SATURDAY MORNING

"Come on, Elvis. Sleep didn't come easily after last night's horrible discovery. And now I can't seem to wake up. Let's get a move on and see what's going on downstairs." His pointy ears shot skyward as he darted for the door.

Downstairs, she dropped her things on her desk and took Elvis for a walk in the cool morning breeze. That car was still sitting in the parking lot. She made a mental note to let the detective know about the lost keys, in case they might have something to do with his case. In all the hubbub last night, she had forgotten to mention what she had found in the garden.

Elvis chased a bug to the edge of the pond, looking befuddled when he could no longer find it.

"Come on. We need to get back. I hope you didn't accidentally swallow that bug." Cassidy wrinkled her nose, and Elvis reluctantly followed her to the office.

Hearing a car door, the pair hurried closer to the parking lot for a better view as a deputy closed the passenger door. Detective Turner slammed the driver's side and strode toward Cassidy and her dog.

"Good morning. We'd like to take one more look at the barn," Turner said. Today, he had on jeans and a long-sleeved shirt that hugged his biceps and chest.

Cassidy shook off thoughts of his physique and said, "Sure. Can I get you some coffee?"

Both men shook their heads and followed her to the office. She handed the keys to the detective and jotted the security code on a sticky note. "If the alarm is flashing, this is the code."

The tall detective folded the paper and put it in the front pocket of his jeans, palming the keys. "I'll bring these back when we're done." *He's all business today. Not even a smile.*

The younger deputy remained silent, shifting his weight from foot to foot and adjusting his utility belt packed with his holstered gun, a taser, a baton, a flashlight, and what looked like twenty pounds of other gear.

"Uh, Cassidy Jamison," Detective Turner said, "this is Diego Sanchez. He joined the force about three weeks ago. We were fortunate to pick him and another deputy up for our team."

"Hello," Deputy Sanchez said with a nod.

"It's nice to meet you. If you all change your mind about coffee or water, just let me know."

As the pair turned to leave, Cassidy remembered the lost-and-found items. "Oh, the other day, we found a lipstick, a motel key, and a car key in the garden. Nobody has asked about them, but the car key is to the black Toyota Avalon TRD in the parking lot."

Detective Turner nodded at Diego, who pulled a small evidence bag and a pair of gloves out of his Batman utility belt. He snapped on the gloves.

"They're in a bag in the office. Let me get them," she said.

She headed to the office and realized Detective Turner was right behind her. She punched in the code for the door and retrieved the found items from her desk. "Here you go. Nobody claimed them."

"Thanks. We'll check on it. If anyone asks about the car, send them to the sheriff's office. I'll run the plates on it." Detective Turner stepped outside and jogged toward the barn.

She felt her pulse race. *You're amped up because of another murder investigation. It has nothing to do with the tall detective and his spicy-scented aftershave.* Cassidy retrieved her phone and fired a text to the Pearly Girls that the police were back in the barn. As she hit send, her phone lit up with a flurry of texts from Anastasia.

Met with the team. The rest of the events are still on. It's what Britt would have wanted.

Plus, everything's planned and paid for. The yoga people should be there soon. We'll be there after lunch to set up the barn.

I'm surprised they decided to hold the rest of the events. Cassidy settled in her office chair and tapped a quick reply.

Staring at her computer screen for what seemed like forever, she finally opened a blank spreadsheet and started typing names. The list of people who had had issues with Britt was long. And whatever had happened to Darcy? *That has to be her car, right?* She opened her browser and did a search. *Nothing recent on her work page or her socials.* She added the gals on the planning committee to her list of suspects, along with Britt's former and current husbands. *At least hosting some of the upcoming events will give me a chance to poke around and pick up some more ideas about who really had it in for Britt.*

"Hey, Cassssssssidy," Roxie yelled, stepping through the front door. "I'm surprised they're continuing with the reunion. The Britt thing should have been the nail in the proverbial coffin. Though everyone in town seems to have an idea about who could have killed her. For a popular girl, she had quite a list of detractors. It's all that anyone is talking about today."

Footfalls on the porch turned Elvis into the morning greeter. Kate and Aileen hustled in with several bags stuffed with yarn spilling out the top.

"I'm sure Britt would have loved being the talk of the town, but she probably wouldn't have liked what they're saying," Kate said, dropping her bags near the couch in the lobby. Squeals rang out and the Pearly Girls, Cassidy, and Elvis rushed outside onto the porch. Elvis let out a low, guttural growl after another squeal and a "Noooooooooo!" came from the front lawn.

Ruthanne scurried closer, waving both arms and yelling as a small goat chased her across the grass. "Nooooo. Go back with your friends. Stop chasing me."

"Who's your friend?" Aileen asked as Ruthanne scooted up the porch steps and used a white wooden rocker to block the charging goat.

"Oh, my stars," Ruthanne said breathlessly. "I went over to see what the goat yoga was about, and this little guy followed me to work. Now he doesn't want to go back and join the others. He's a tad aggressive. So much for peace and Zen in the serenity garden. He's cute, but I'm afraid he's going to hurt me with those little horns. He nipped at me already. Naughty goat." Ruthanne waggled her finger at the goat, who bleated three times and put his front hooves on the base of the rocking chair.

"Maybe he doesn't understand goat yoga or peace and harmony," Aileen said, reaching out to pat the brown and white kid. "He's kinda cute. Did you wave a red cape or something at him to get him all riled up? He seems friendly enough to me."

Cassidy scooped up the wiggly Elvis before he could get in on the action. He wasn't quite sure what the new critter was.

"No. I just patted his head. Then he turned into an attack goat when I tried to leave," Ruthanne said.

"Maybe he bonded with you. You said goat yoga?" Kate's eyebrows shot up under her straight silver bangs.

"The goats frolic and hop on the participants. It looks like fun, but I wasn't dressed to give it a whirl this morning." Ruthanne tried to shoo the kid back toward the garden, but he climbed on the porch and wound around her legs like a cat. Elvis let out a low growl to let the intruder know this was *his* territory.

"They hop on the people doing yoga?" Kate asked with a look like someone was trying to pull a prank on her.

"Yes. It's supposed to be relaxing, and it allows the participants to be one with nature. They have kitten and puppy yoga too," Ruthanne said.

"And they hop on the people on the mats?" Kate repeated.

"Yes, it's a real thing," Ruthanne said, still trying to shoo the little goat away. "Oh, no. You need to go back to your yoga friends. You can't hang out here." Ruthanne inched toward the door.

"Here," Roxie said, stepping closer to the kid. "Goat, come on. You need to go find your little barnyard pals." She put her hand on his neck and guided him down the wooden steps and across the grass. She continued to talk to her new four-legged friend as they crossed the grassy area.

"Well, I'll be. Roxie, the goat wrangler," Aileen said.

"The goat whisperer," Kate said, snickering. "You never know about someone's hidden talents. Aileen, I thought *you* would have corralled it. You've been herding kiddos for years." She tapped her friend lightly on the arm and retreated to the back office as a black Camaro roared into the parking lot and kicked up gravel and dust when it skidded to a stop next to the black Toyota.

Anastasia hopped out, threw her purse over her shoulder, and slammed the door. She waved. "Is the barn open? It looks like I'm the only one here. That doesn't surprise me," she yelled, glancing around the parking lot. "You're still giving the cave tour at two, right?" Before Cassidy could answer, the brassy blonde lumbered toward the porch. "People will be interested in your cave. Today's other events are offsite. I have to spend the afternoon getting ready for the dinner. Britt wanted it to be a tribute to our homecoming where she and Mac were crowned king and queen. Not sure how many people will be in a festive mood. I'm guessing it'll be more somber, but we'll see how it goes. The caterers are on their way. I sent her a list of things for tonight. I can't believe Kelly and Darcy left me to do everything. Tonight's festivities are going to recognize anyone who ever served on a homecoming court. I have a ton of things to get ready, and those brats abandoned me."

Ruthanne turned her head but swallowed whatever she had planned to say.

"Let me get my phone and keys, and I'll be right there to help you," Cassidy said.

She followed behind Anastasia, who strode across the lawn with long steps. "We need to pull down all the decorations from yesterday but leave the balloons. Britt wanted crepe paper and more balloons, but I think we'll go with what's already there. It's going to be an endeavor to pack up all the musical vignette stuff and cart it out of here. Hey, what did the police want this time?" Anastasia stopped suddenly and tapped her foot.

"They came back to wrap up their investigation of the murder scene," Cassidy replied as Anastasia looked exasperated.

"Exactly what could they be looking for?" Anastasia gave her a glare that could have wilted a flower.

"They said they wanted to see the scene again. They didn't share any details," Cassidy said, wondering where the sudden interest in the police came from.

Then, without reply, Anastasia continued her march to the barn.

No police in sight. Only the occasional bird or cicada could be heard over the rustle of the breeze through the trees. Cassidy flipped on the overhead lights and wandered around the first level of the empty barn.

"I have ten signed up for the cave tour," Anastasia yelled from somewhere in the dark interior. "I told them to meet outside the doors here at two and to wear comfortable shoes. Let's see who shows up."

"Oh my gosh!" Anastasia fell silent, and Cassidy strained to listen for any clue to figure out where she was.

"Are you okay?"

"Just stressed. Look at all this stuff from those stupid musical scenes. I have no idea where to put this junk. I swear, the ones with the big ideas never put in the work." She stomped her foot on the wooden planked floor.

Cassidy made her way to the bar, where Anastasia stood with her arms wrapped tightly around her chest. Before Cassidy could reply, Anastasia pulled out her phone. "I mean, who wants all this junk? I'm telling Kelly we're ditching it. Do you have a dumpster we can put it in? It's a lot of crap. And who has time for this?"

Cassidy nodded and pulled out her phone and dashed off a text to Levi. After he responded, she continued, "My maintenance guy will bring the trailer around, so it will be easier to haul it away if you don't want any of the decorations. We can help you load it."

"This was Darcy and Britt's big idea," Anastasia said. "They thought it would be fabulous to relive high school." She wrinkled her nose and made a "pfffft" sound. "Darcy up and vanished," she said, "and, well, we know what happened to Britt. At this point, I don't care. I'm making an executive decision. I'm not hauling the mess home and storing it, just to throw it away later." She headed for the

Katy Perry display, and Cassidy zipped over to the Lady Gaga one to see what was left besides smudges from gray fingerprint powder.

In the dark corner, a square red carpet, surrounded by cardboard boxes decorated to look like colorful cameras, sat alone in the space. Many of the boxes had been knocked over or shoved against the wall. Cassidy closed her eyes for a second, trying to remember what she had seen here last evening, but her thoughts kept flashing to the gruesome scene with Britt.

Shaking off a creepy feeling, Cassidy dashed off a quick text to the detective to let him know they were dismantling the displays and throwing out the props. When he didn't respond, she flipped on her phone's flashlight and stepped under the loft area. Three or four chairs had been pushed back under here. When she swept the light around the perimeter of the space, she jumped and let out a squeal.

A bald mannequin lay on the floor up against the wall. Taking a deep breath to calm the butterflies inside her, Cassidy stepped closer and dragged it out near the carpet. The killer must have used the blonde wig and the bloody dress from this on Britt. *Okay, so someone had time to kill Britt, ditch the mannequin, and dress Britt in the costume. No easy feat, especially if it were one person. Someone on the committee? Someone who had sneaked in before the event?* Questions popped up in Cassidy's head like the fuzzy critters in a Whac-A-Mole arcade game. Lots of questions and no answers.

Dragging the three chairs and the small table to the storage closet, Cassidy cleared the area as Levi backed the ATV and a trailer into the barn.

Shutting off the loud engine, he said, "Here you go, Cassidy. I'll be back in an hour or so to haul it away. Do you need any help? I can stay and pitch in. I was headed over to the garden to clean up after all those goats. I had to chase a couple out of the flower beds before they got any ideas about eating the mums. It was a bit chaotic, if you ask me." He wiped his brow with the sleeve of his work shirt.

"I think we're good. Thanks, Levi. The Pearly Girls will be here soon, and we should be able to dismantle the decorations quickly," Cassidy said as she piled the colorful cardboard boxes in the back of the low trailer.

Levi saluted with two fingers and trotted out through the giant doors.

Thoughts of a killer on the loose wormed their way back into Cassidy's consciousness as she walked, and the normal sounds of bird-chirping and the hum of the ice machine in the kitchen suddenly sounded spooky. She took a couple of deep breaths to ward off the dark feelings. *Okay, girl. Another person has been killed on your property. This time, it's someone from town with an enemy list as long as my arm. Maybe I should leave this to Detective Zac and concentrate on making sure this doesn't scare away my business. But stuff that happens on my property IS my business.*

Cassidy surveyed what was left of the Lady Gaga display. She dragged the bald mannequin to the trailer and hoisted her over the low railing. All that remained of the display was the red carpet. Grabbing the corner of the remnant, she started to roll it up for transport. Somewhere in the middle, she tripped on something black. *What is that?* Cassidy froze when she spotted a large knife with a thick black handle, covered in red goo. She reached for it, and then recoiled when she thought it could be important to the investigation.

How did a knife, covered in red stuff, end up under the rug? Snapping a picture of it, she texted it to Detective Turner. Did his guys not move the carpet? Or had it been put there later? Too many thoughts swirled in her head.

Save it for me. We'll check it out. I'll send the deputy over, he responded. **She hadn't been stabbed, but it could have prints on it.**

Glad I didn't touch it. Cassidy hurried to the kitchen and rummaged through the cabinets and drawers until she found a plastic bag and a piece of cardboard. She grabbed several paper towels and turned and ran smack into Austin. "Ooof. I'm so sorry," she said. "I was thinking about something, and I didn't hear you come in."

Austin put his hands on her shoulders to steady her. "Are you okay? It looks like you're in the middle of putting out a fire. What's up?"

"We're cleaning up the decorations, and I needed a bag to save something. Sorry. I was lost in thought."

"I told Annie I'd start the setup for the taco and burrito buffets." He pulled his hands back and put one in the front pocket of his jeans. The other he ran nervously through his tousled blondish hair.

"I'm helping Anastasia in there, and we've got the cave tour at two." She smiled and took a quick step backward. "I get to play tour guide."

"You do it all around here. Cool. Sounds like fun. I'd love to see the cave if you've got space in your group. Annie won't fire me for sneaking off the job. And if she does, I'll tell Mom," he said with a wink.

"Sure. We'd love to have you. It's a neat place to visit. I can't figure out what to do with it. Right now, it's just your everyday ordinary cave."

"You should turn it into some kind of venue for cool events. People would love to rent it for concerts or parties. Is it big enough to turn it into a bar or club or something?"

"Maybe. I'm not sure how much work it would take to get it up to code. It's pretty big inside, and there are a couple of tunnels that open up into other exits," she said, looking up into his ice-blue eyes. "Meet us at the front at two, and we'll hike over." She did a finger wave over her shoulder and headed back to bag the knife before anyone else touched it.

"Hey, Cassidy. What are you up to?" Ruthanne yelled in her singsong voice that echoed across the main room.

"Just found something else for the lost-and-found," she said, sliding the knife on the cardboard and picking it up. She set it under the loft so it would be out of the way.

"What is all this stuff supposed to be?" Kate asked, pointing to the *Jersey Shore* display. She hefted a mannequin in both hands and tossed it over the trailer's railing. The dark wig fell off as the plastic body bounced around on top of the other junk. Ruthanne scooped up the wig and tossed it in with the rest of the items. "Maybe we should keep these. We could be Sonny and Cher or something," she mused. "You never know when you'll need a disguise," she giggled. "We could come up with some good costumes with all this stuff."

"It's from the *Jersey Shore*. You remember—Pauly D, Snooki, and JWoww? We used to watch it at my house years ago," Aileen said, dumping beach balls and other party props on top of the other stuff. "We should sort through this stuff before Levi dumps it. I think we could find homes for some of it. Hey, Rox, you need a couple of extra mannequins?"

She shrugged. "You never know. Maybe we could dress 'em up and leave them around town."

"Shhhhh," Ruthanne hissed like a leaky tire.

"I remember *Jersey Shore*," Aileen interrupted. "We played that drinking game when we watched it. Remember, it was Roxie's idea." She waved her arms around like she was swatting bees.

Anastasia strode in, tossing another mannequin and cardboard cutouts of firecrackers onto the heap. "I don't care what you do with it. I want it out of here for tonight's dance and dinner. I say good riddance. Help yourselves. It was all a stupid idea. I'll be back in a minute. I need to get something out of my car."

"That looks like the last of it. Time to head over to the office and get the big flashlights for the cave tour. Anyone else want to go with us?" Cassidy asked, wiping her hands on her jeans. Remembering the knife, she hustled to the loft and returned with it on its cardboard plate.

"What's that for?" Ruthanne asked.

"Zac wanted to take a look at it. I found it over there where we found Britt," Cassidy whispered.

"Oh," Ruthanne stared at the giant knife. Shaking off whatever she was thinking, she continued: "I had enough fun with the goat this morning. I don't need any other critter experiences, so I'll skip the cave tour today. Once we get this stuff out of here, we'll make sure the tables are ready to go. Austin said it was taco night. Yummy."

Cassidy spun around as Anastasia stormed over and dropped two large canvas bags on the floor. "The DJ and the photo-booth guy should be here soon. And Britt hired a florist to sell mums with ribbons. It was a thing back in the day at homecoming. Let's see how well that goes over now with adults. I'll need a table for the flowers near the door," Anastasia said, scrolling through her phone.

Cassidy pulled out a long table from the storage closet, and Ruthanne hurried to get two chairs.

"Here," Cassidy said. "The flower person can use this. Is it okay in this spot?"

Anastasia nodded. "It's fine. I need to check on the menu."

"We'll handle anything that pops up here," Ruthanne said. "You enjoy your cave tour."

On her way to the office, Cassidy spotted Deputy Sanchez trekking across the grass. "Good timing." She waved with her free hand. "The detective said you found something for us." He stopped near her, and she took a step back to look him in the eye. The new deputy had the build that looked like either a football or a rugby player.

She handed him the cardboard and the knife. "It was under the rug where we found Britt Mahoney."

"Interesting," he said as she stared at the hunting knife. "The forensic team searched the whole area. Not sure why they didn't spot it. Thanks. I'll take it to the car and bag it."

Cassidy swung by the apartment to give Elvis a walk around the farmhouse. It took a few moments to coax the chihuahua back up the stairs. On her way back out, she plunked a Nationals ballcap on her head, just in case there were any spiders or bats in the cave today.

Remembering her original task in the office, Cassidy hurried down the back steps and made a beeline for the storage closet for the flashlights. *Could the knife be important to Zac's investigation, or was it another prop?* A little spark zipped through her. She shook off the feeling and hustled back to the barn.

When she neared the giant doors, she found Austin leaning against the red wooden wall. His blond highlights shimmered in the sun, the longish hair giving him a casual, but hip, look, especially standing next to the weathered wood of the barn. He looked like he was ready for a photo shoot or to star in a Hallmark movie. *He could be a model.*

"Well, good afternoon, folks. I'm Cassidy Jamison, owner of Celebrations at Ivy Springs. And I'll be your cave tour guide this afternoon," she said, as he looked up and glanced around the empty area. "I guess we'll give the others a couple of minutes," she added.

He smiled and pocketed his phone. "I hope you have space on the tour to squeeze me in."

"I'll try. We may have an opening or three," she said, returning his smile.

About fifteen minutes later, Anastasia blew out the front door like something was chasing her. "What are you all still doing here? The tour was at two."

"No one else has shown up," Cassidy said.

"Oh, well, their loss. I hope they don't bail on the dinner. Or we'll have way too much food to take home." She waved her hand dismissively and retreated back inside the barn.

Cassidy handed Austin one of the large flashlights and said, "Well, you want to see it?"

He nodded and followed her through the garden and the grotto. "It's nice back here. It would make a good backdrop for pictures. That rocky area is cool. What's the plaque for?" He pointed toward the rose bushes.

Memories of Johnny Storm's murder flooded back. She glanced at the koi pond where she and Elvis had found the rock star. Shaking off the melancholic feeling, she replied, "We had a concert series here last summer, and Johnny Storm of the Weathermen was murdered and left back there."

"Annie said something about that. They're from before my time, but Mom and Dad used to listen to them. It's a nice memorial." Austin followed her over the rocky terrain and around the wooden barrier that sported a no trespassing sign.

"No bears or anything?" he asked with a half-smile.

"Nah. We have a few sightings every once in a while in the woods, but they don't usually come close to civilization unless they smell food. I've never seen anything in the cave but a bat, and the most dangerous thing in there last summer was the killer." She scrunched up her face like she had licked a persimmon.

Austin switched on his light. The temperature dropped several degrees once they cleared the mouth of the cave. Goose bumps covered Cassidy's arms.

"I used to play in here when I was a kid. This part goes back quite a ways, and it opens up into a nice-sized chamber. Then there are two tunnels that shoot off in different directions to exits on the other side," she said.

He shone his light around. "Kinda spooky. But really cool. It's bigger than I imagined. You could turn this into a club or something. There's a place in Tennessee that has concerts in a cave. They do light shows. Theirs is big enough to hold three or four hundred people. This doesn't look that big, but it could be a small venue for a club or parties. Hey, if you ever want to open something like that, I'd be interested in managing it for you. I can bartend and bounce too. Working for Annie is great, and I appreciate the job, but that's not what I want to do forever. It would be fun to be in on the beginning of a project, especially something as cool as this."

"I've been thinking about what to do with the cave a lot lately," she said. "I think it might be time to develop it. My relatives used to hide their bootlegging operations in here. All of this area has so much history. I think I need to capitalize on it. My grandfather and his father had a honky-tonk on the property that was part of the music scene years ago. It would be nice to add something that pays homage to the past."

"This room is bigger than it appears," he said. "You could put a bar up against the wall and a stage over there. I bet the acoustics are awesome down here." He yelled, "Hello," and it echoed through the empty space. "See? This would be cool. How big are the tunnels back there? I was wondering where you would put bathrooms and a kitchen prep area." He swept the area with the beam of his light. "It goes back pretty far. You could do something here. It'd be the only one like it around here and the perfect new spot for your events business."

"That tunnel is pretty wide. Both have exits. We could maybe do some kind of food prep in the tunnel. The ceilings are tall. You don't have to stoop. The floor kinda rises near the back exit, but there's plenty of room to move around." Butterflies bounced around in Cassidy's stomach. The more they talked, the more excited she got about repurposing the cave. "Maybe this would be a profitable addition to our offerings. I'm sure I could secure bookings for it."

"You could make this work," he said, flashing his light down the first tunnel.

"How would we secure it?" Cassidy asked, thinking aloud. "We'd have to build some kind of building in the front, so we could lock it. It's either that or make some kind of pull screen like the metal things that go across storefronts in the city. I want to make it usable, but I want to keep it as natural as possible." She flashed her light around. "I can always use another revenue stream. If I rent it out for private events, it may be hard to have regular hours. It wouldn't be like a nightly bartending gig."

"Maybe start out as rentals only and schedule monthly concerts or comedy tours. We could make it work, and you already have a following and reputation as a good events location. You could even do things like comicons or book events. I used to go to this club near the base that did Noir at the Bar every once in a while. It was interesting to hear authors read dark stories. And you've got the coolest place for bone-tingling tales." He flashed his light on and off like a strobe.

"It's something to think about. Let me talk to the Pearly Girls and Levi. If anyone can pull off the construction project, it's him. He did the barn conversion for my grandma. Hey, if you're interested, I'll keep you in mind. You're a great bartender. I've seen you in action." Cassidy felt her face blush, and she hoped he couldn't tell in the dim light.

"I managed supplies and logistics in the Army, so I do have some skills, and I managed the bar on base as a side gig. I'll get you my resume," he said. "It's a nice place, and I think it's unusual. People will want to see what you turn it into. And I can't wait to hear a concert down here. Thanks for showing it to me. I better be heading back. Annie's probably been blowing up my phone. I've got a low signal down here." The pair stepped into the sunshine, and Austin pulled out a pair of sunglasses and his phone.

Cassidy retrieved her phone too and glanced at a text from Trish Campbell. She and the photographer wanted to come back tomorrow for pictures for the article. Cassidy fired off a response and then a group text to the Pearly Girls. "Uh, thanks," she said, taking the large flashlight Austin held out to her. "See you around."

"I'll get you my resume," he called over his shoulder.

He'd definitely be an asset as a bartender. He knows how to work a crowd. Maybe I should pursue this. I'd be the only girl with cave parties in the valley.

8

Cassidy stretched in her office chair, and Elvis looked up from his puffy bed to see if anyone had any snacks. A noise in the front room distracted him, and he changed into six pounds of attack animal as he raced to the front. Stomping on the porch sent the black-and-tan dog into a full bark session.

Scooping him up in one arm, Cassidy looked out the front window and did a double take. The Celebrations mailbox and the nearby fence-post were draped with Ruthanne's giant scarf like it was some kind of banner. *What is that doing out there?*

The Pearly Girls, dressed from head to toe in black except for their signature pearls, tromped inside. *What are the ninja sexagenarians up to now?* She opened her mouth but didn't get a chance to ask.

Aileen let out a string of giggles and plopped down on one of the couches. Kate glared at her, and Aileen's face sobered. "Cassidy, I think attendance at this reunion thing has dropped off since the, you know..." She whispered, "*the murder.* Do you think anyone will show tonight?"

Before Cassidy could reply, Ruthanne said, "We decided to go to the spontaneous yoga session in the garden. It seemed to be pretty popular on Friday and Saturday, but today only Kelly from the committee, the instructor, and two other people showed up. By the way, Kelly invited us all over for brunch in the barn in a little bit," Ruthanne said.

"Well, that was before Roxie's ringtone disturbed the peace and the Zen," Kate mumbled. "I hope we're still welcome at brunch. We had to hightail it out of there."

"What happened?" Cassidy asked with a concerned look. *What kind of damage control am I going to have to do?*

"Nothing, really," Roxie said, waving a bejeweled hand at her friends. "We snuck in with our yoga mats and got settled, but we didn't have to sneak because nobody was there. And nobody cared that we crashed the party. The instructor started with her relaxation moves. It was kinda nice, and everything was fine."

"But someone forgot to silence her phone." Aileen pointed to Roxie.

"And it was a silent yoga class," Kate added with a slight scowl. "And your ringtone was 'Highway to Hell.'"

"I can't help it if they don't have a sense of humor." Roxie pulled out her phone and busied herself with whatever was on her screen.

"Hey, what's up with the matching Johnny Cash outfits and the scarf on the mailbox?" Cassidy asked, scanning the Pearly Girls' faces.

"Who's up for brunch?" Ruthanne asked, changing the subject. "Let's go before we miss the good stuff. I hate to be late."

"I doubt we'll have to stand in line. We might get doggie bags if no one shows," Aileen said.

"After today's adventures, I want a mimosa or two," Kate said, rising.

"Served by that hunky Austin. Now, *that's* what I call brunch," Roxie said, following the former nurse out the back door.

"Come on, Cassidy. Let's go check it out." Ruthanne gently

nudged her boss toward the back and away from the front window. "We all want to say hello to Austin."

Cassidy patted Elvis on the head. "Stay here and guard the place. I'll be back with a treat for you. The photographer will be here later."

"Oh, my lands. I forgot. Gals, we'll have to cut brunch short to go home and get ready," Ruthanne yelled out the back door. "We can't wear this for the photo shoot and the interview. We look like Cassidy's posse."

"We're like the Enforcers," Roxie said. "I vote we go with what we're wearing. Then we have time for two mimosas."

"We look good in black. Very slimming." Aileen smoothed out the hem of her long T-shirt.

Cassidy followed the women past the almost-empty parking lot.

"It's too bad the murder put a damper on the festivities," Ruthanne said.

Kate raised an eyebrow. "Cassidy, I'm glad you got paid up front. This would have been a disaster otherwise."

"Oooh, the place is empty," Aileen said, poking her head through the barn's main doors. "But the food smells so good."

"Come on. Let's get good seats for the Austin show." Roxie tapped Ruthanne on the shoulder and pointed to the bar.

Ruthanne shushed them as their tennis shoes squeaked on the hardwood floor. Their loud banter echoed to the rafters. Cassidy looked around. Kelly, Anastasia, Austin, and Annie outnumbered the guests who huddled at one of the tables near the stage. Cool jazz wafted through the speakers, and bacon, pepper, and onion smells drifted over from the steaming metal trays on the banquet tables.

"Hey, y'all," Kelly said. "Help yourself to brunch. I think our classmates have had enough reunion events. We'll have to pull up and decide what we want to do about the rest of the plans. And I have no idea what Vince is doing for Britt. I don't want to conflict with any memorial services he may have planned." She wiped the corners of her eyes as her voice cracked.

"We'll see. People may have wanted some quiet time after all that went on this weekend," Anastasia said, heaping a glob of steaming egg-and-cheese casserole on her plate. "I can't believe they'd bail on us like this. We'll have to make some phone calls, but I bet they'll be back for next week's party."

"I wish we'd heard from Darcy. She took off without a word to anyone," Kelly said. "Not very professional."

"We could have used her help. I bet Vince knows where she is," Anastasia said as a cat-that-ate-the-canary grin spread across her wide face.

Ignoring the snarky comment, Kelly turned to the Pearly Girls. "Please help yourselves to brunch. Our caterers outdid themselves on the spread. And if you have any other folks on your team, let them know too."

The gals smiled and made a beeline for the tantalizing smells. Cassidy stacked miniature waffles, bacon, hash-brown casserole, and fruit salad on the square plate and found a seat at a nearby table between Ruthanne and Kate.

As the gals tucked in to their food, the conversation drifted off. Cassidy reached for her phone, and Kate grabbed her wrist. "You don't need to check on anything. Let's just enjoy breakfast and the company. Why don't we be present in the moment?"

Cassidy acquiesced, as the Pearly Girls dissolved into a round of giggles. "What's going on? Y'all are acting strangely today," she said.

"No more than normal," Roxie said, from across the table.

"We've made a pact to cut back on social media and be more in tune with what's going on in the real world," Ruthanne added to a chorus of more snickers.

"Did you get that from today's mediation?" Kate asked. "Or was that a lesson from goat yoga?"

Ruthanne pursed her lips and made a face at her friend.

The gals fell silent again as Cassidy watched Anastasia and Kelly. Their reactions to Britt's death were on both ends of the spectrum. *And the reunion plans are falling apart. Maybe I can nose around and see if I can find Darcy. She probably got tired of all the infighting and decided to distance herself from the mean girls.*

Austin slipped behind Roxie and started to gather the unused plates, and the Pearly Girls immediately made him the center of attention. Trying to avoid any matchmaking embarrassment, Cassidy slipped two pieces of bacon in a paper napkin and rose. "Tell Annie y'all did a great job on the food. I enjoyed it."

Austin smiled, picking up unused place settings in front of the empty chairs. "She can cook. I knew if I came home for a while, I wouldn't starve until I found a job."

Cassidy's phone dinged, and she glanced down to see a message from Detective Turner. She waved at the Pearly Girls. "I've got to go meet the detective."

"We'll be back at the office in time to talk to that reporter, and don't you worry about things here. We'll take care of everything," Kate said.

"And she means 'everrrrrrythang,'" Roxie said with a wink.

Cassidy smiled her best customer-service smile. *They are up to something. Hopefully they won't gang up on Austin or do any more matchmaking.* She hustled to the office and just had time to slip Elvis his treat before Zac Turner stepped into the lobby.

"Good afternoon," he said. "I have a couple of questions about the hunting knife you found." Cassidy nodded, and he continued: "It was covered in the same paint as the dress. You found it under the rug?"

She nodded again. "I was taking down the Lady Gaga decorations. I tripped over it when I was rolling up the carpet." *How did it go unnoticed during the search? As soon as I moved the rug, it was in plain view.*

Like he could read her mind, he said, "I talked to everyone. The forensic guys moved the carpet and photographed the scene after the coroner left with the body. There was no knife when they searched the area."

Tingles erupted all through Cassidy's core. "So someone put it there after the fact?" she blurted. *Why? If it's not the weapon, was it to throw suspicion on someone?*

"It looks like it. We didn't get any clean prints off of it," he said quietly. "I need to go back through the interview notes. Someone mentioned a hunter in the group."

"I think the avid hunter was Britt's ex-husband. One of Britt's friends mentioned it." Cassidy closed her mouth to stop the babbling.

"Who?" he asked.

Cassidy shook her head. "Darcy or Anastasia, maybe. I don't really remember."

"The murder and the knife were staged."

Cassidy's eyes widened. *Who told me that? Kelly? Darcy? Now I don't want them to cancel next weekend's events. I need some time to poke around and ask more questions. It's very odd that someone would hide the knife after the investigation, especially if it wasn't the murder weapon. Who would want Mac to take the blame for Britt's murder? I haven't really seen much of him except when he helped Britt get a ride the other night.*

Interrupting her thoughts of how to accidentally run into Mac, the detective said, "Let me know if you find anything else. The car key belongs to Darcy Branch. And the motel key was for a room rented by Vince Mahoney." He turned and glanced out the window. "You never know when something will turn out to be important. By the way, do you or your employees know anything about any knitting bombers who have been prowling around town in the middle of the night?"

A puzzled look crossed Cassidy's face. "Huh?" Ruthanne's giant scarf flashed into her head. *The stealthy ninjas struck in Ivy Springs too?* Cassidy could feel her cheeks warming. *No wonder they were acting so weird.*

"Check out all the chatter around town on Facebook," the tall detective said. "Someone decorated lampposts, street signs, and fences with knitted things that look like giant sweaters and scarves like the one on your mailbox. It seems they hit your property too." He turned and left without sharing any more details.

"Elvis, can you believe it? Yarn vandals in town. Marauding intruders decorated large swaths of downtown in the middle of the night. Well, that solves the mystery of the suspicious sexagenarians all dressed like ninjas. Just wait until I see them. And Ruthanne can take down the scarf designed for a *T. rex* or a giraffe." Elvis yipped and stretched. Then he rolled over for a tummy scratch. Cassidy complied and then continued: "But for the real mystery...Darcy's car is in my parking lot, and the police have the key. Where did she go without her car? It looks like the rumors of her and Vince canoodling were true. I'm surprised Zac didn't ask me about the motel key. Let's go see what we can dig up."

Not interested in a love triangle or the knitting ninjas, and not finding any more bacon, Elvis settled in his bed as Cassidy turned on her laptop. "Oh, wow. This is what Zac was talking about," she said out loud. "Interesting handiwork. Where did they get all that yarn?" She scanned through thirty or forty pictures of their knitting designs. The gals had decorated downtown with a rainbow of colors. Lampposts, wrought iron fences, and even the town's statue of the pioneer had an oversized red sweater and a matching hat. "Knit bombing. Where did they get the idea?" She checked their social media accounts, and the only clue was a photo of Ruth's giant anaconda scarf stretched across the back of her couch on her Instagram site.

Cassidy spent the next hour searching for anything online about Darcy, Britt, Mac, Vince, Kelly, and Anastasia. Not having much luck with Google, she switched to the town's gossip blog, *Ivy Springs a Leak*. The website had grown in popularity over the last several years with its daily ration of announcements and gossipy posts. So far, no one had confessed to writing it, but the content was popular conversation at the coffee shop and church socials. Between that and Facebook, Cassidy struck gold. She pulled up her murder spreadsheet and started recording anything she found. *Like Detective Zac said, you never know what's going to be important later.* Thoughts of him sent a tingle of excitement through her, and she tried to focus on her spreadsheet. He was handsome and interesting. Sometimes he acted like he wanted her help, and then he changed into Dudley Do-Right who scolded her for asking questions or getting in the way. *Enough of him and Austin. Girl, you need to focus if you want to find anything that will help figure out who Britt's killer is. You're acting like a boy-crazy teen.*

The back door banged open, and Elvis made a run to check out the invaders.

"Cassidy," Ruthanne called. "The reporter and her photographer are here. Are you ready?"

"Give me just a couple of minutes." She saved her file and rushed to the restroom to touch up her makeup and fluff her hair.

"We'll stall. And don't think about changing clothes ten times,"

Roxie yelled. "You look fine in teal. It goes well with your eyes and red curls."

"You're one to talk. You always make us late," Kate said, as Cassidy disappeared into the bathroom.

After a quick minute to freshen up, Cassidy hurried to the porch to meet Trish Campbell and her photographer. They spent the next twenty minutes and what felt like hundreds of poses in front of the office, on the porch, and in the grotto. Cassidy's face felt like it was about to crack from all the smiling.

Trish stood and stretched. "Thanks, y'all. I think we got some really great shots. What do you think, Noah?"

"Yep. They look good. I'll have lots for the editors to work with. If you don't mind, I'm going to hang out while you do the interview to get some casual ones of the gals," the lanky photographer with curly dark hair said, adjusting something on the back of his camera.

"I'm thinking we can sit in those chairs over there and chat. Are you gals okay with that?" Trish asked, pointing to the grouping of white Adirondack chairs near the grotto.

"Perfect," Noah interrupted. "I can get those cool rocky out-croppings in the background." Staring at the back of his camera again, he waved the women toward the chairs.

"Okay, good. Ladies, I'm so glad you all could spend some time with me. Cassidy told me you were the best ones to ask about the honky-tonk and all the history of this place. I want to know all about the music scene, and she mentioned your interesting nick-name. I want to hear all about that too. She said you all have been friends for a long time," she said, waving her arms wide.

"A doofus in junior high school made fun of the fact that we all wore pearls. He called us the Pearly Girls, and it kinda stuck," Aileen said.

"It was during the days of Jackie Kennedy and Camelot. Everyone wanted to look glamorous like Marilyn Monroe or Audrey Hepburn," Ruthanne added, touching her necklace.

"By the way, we were all very young during the honky-tonk heyday," Kate added.

"Wee children," Roxie added. "We have hundreds of stories. You sure you've got the time?"

"Uh, we'll see how much we can cover," Trish interjected.

"Okay, let's see what she needs for her story. Cassidy's great-grandfather opened the bar, and then her grandfather ran it for years after he married her grandmother, Evelyn," Kate said.

"It was more like a neighborhood hangout," Ruthanne said.

"Quit whitewashing it," Kate sputtered. "It was a boozy, smoke-filled honky-tonk with soulful music, some cussin', and some fightin'. And we loved every minute of it."

"We had to sneak in with Cassidy's grandma. Luckily for us, her dad looked the other way," Aileen said.

"Our mothers would have tanned our hides if they'd known we were in there," Ruthanne said. "It was not a place for young ladies."

"The tonk was full of wood paneling, stale cigarette and beer smells, and a couple of pool tables. It's where we learned to smoke, dance, and swig moonshine. And we met so many famous musicians," Roxie said.

"In the early days, Cassidy's great-grandfather and grandfather hosted musical guests from all over. The road over there was the main road to and from Nashville in the days before the Interstate," Kate added. "The big acts would stop by on their way to and from Tennessee."

"So many of the famous country stars stopped by. Willie Nelson, Tammy Wynette, Loretta Lynn, Waylon Jennings, Hank Williams," Ruthanne said, counting them off on her fingers.

"It was Hank Williams *Junior*," Roxie said with a wink.

"She would know," Kate interrupted. "Let's say Roxie got a bunch of autographs in her book. Anyway, Cassidy's grandfather had pictures of them all over the walls. And anyone who sang at the watering hole had to sign the bar. He had it lacquered to preserve all the names. If walls or bar tops could talk."

"Lots of good memories," Roxie added.

"I'd love to see it," Trish said.

"Alas," Aileen sighed. "The bar got struck by lightning in the eighties and burned down. Everything was destroyed."

"How sad, and what a loss of so much history. I heard the bar was the place to be in the day. Tell me more," Trish said.

"Like we said, we shouldn't have been there in our younger years," Ruthanne said.

"But it was a wild ride," Roxie added. "And I'm glad we had the experience."

Kate smiled and waggled her finger at Roxie. "It wasn't proper, but it was loads of fun. I can still hear Evelyn's mother fussing at all of us now. That woman could be fierce. One night, she caught us sneaking back in, and she knew exactly where we'd been."

"Evelyn was Cassidy's grandmother. She was a Pearly Girl too. We miss her. She was always full of energy and fun," Ruthanne said.

"And she didn't care what other people thought," Roxie added. "Yep, we were right there in the middle of all the action. It was the only cool place in Ivy Springs, and we had front-row seats."

"The only other quote unquote nightclub was the lounge over at Sid Pro Quo's no-tell motel, and respectable people didn't go there in the day either. Plus, he only hired lounge lizards for his shows," Aileen said. "The honky-tonk was way more fun."

Thoughts of the motel key flashed in her head. It was near where she'd found Darcy's car key. Quietly excusing herself, she waved as the Pearly Girls continued their tales about all the famous people they had met during the honky-tonk's heyday.

As Cassidy walked back to the office, thoughts of Darcy zinged around in her head. The keys and the other stuff had been either lost or placed in the garden like Britt's staged body. *If Darcy took off like Anastasia said, why is her car in my lot? Something is not right about all this. And could she and Vince have something to do with Britt's murder?*

She paused and looked back over her shoulder. Roxie was waving her arms around as she recounted some tale of their antics. The honky-tonk really was a big part of this town's history. Cassidy smiled. *I should try to revive the musical past of this place.*

Cassidy opened the back door and picked Elvis up. She nuzzled her nose in the warm fur of his neck, and she felt the tension in her shoulders drift away. She kissed him on the head and plopped down in her seat. "What was that room number?" Cassidy opened her spreadsheet and scrolled until she found the bit of information. Dreading having to ask a favor of Sid Pro Quo, she debated with herself about whether she should call him. He was always a grumpy gus who seemed to want to argue with her at every business-council meeting. She made up her mind to call and ask about the room key before she lost her nerve. Swallowing her pride, she dialed the number to his office. *It's worth a try. The worst he can do is yell and hang up on me.*

After a couple of rings, a baritone voice greeted her. "Good afternoon. It's a fabulous day here in beautiful Ivy Springs. How can I make your day sing?" *His sing-songy rhyme sounds like he's trying too hard.*

"Sid?" she asked.

"Yes. This is Sid Proctor, the proprietor. How may I help you?"

"Hi, Sid. This is Cassidy Jamison from down the road at Cele-brations. How are you?"

"Just peachy. What can I do for you on this fine day?" His tone suddenly sounded more bored than friendly.

Ignoring his passive-aggressiveness, she continued: "I found a key in the garden the other night after one of my events. It was for room one sixteen at your place. Have any of your guests reported a missing key lately?" *And how could that tiny little roadside motel have a hundred and sixteen rooms? Even with his other motel, the room totals didn't go past sixty.*

"Let me see here." She heard pages turning in the background. "Nope. I don't think so. The guest in one-sixteen hasn't checked out yet. It's an extended stay. I'll make a note to let them know a key was found. That way, they won't lose their deposit. You can drop it off at the desk. Anything else I can help you with?" The constant drumming of his fingers provided a distracting background beat.

"Oh, who does it belong to? I can return it to them at one of the upcoming reunion events if that's why they're in town."

"Now, Cassidy. You know I can't violate the privacy of my guests. The relationship between the hotelier and his guests is sac-rosanct. Security and privacy, you know. I'll make sure to let them know. Is there anything else I can help you with?"

"No, you've been a great help. Thanks." Cassidy disconnected and made a pickle face. He didn't give any hints about the room owner. *Somehow, I can't see Darcy or Vince staying in a roadside mo-tel unless it was a hideaway. Why would Vince rent it for an extended stay?*

9

"Whoo-hoo, Cassidy. Are you busy?" Levi yelled, stomping his work boots on the mat outside the back door. He poked his lanky frame in the door and patted Elvis.

"Hey, Levi. It's good to see you. What's going on?" Cassidy looked up from her spreadsheet.

"I've been thinking about what you asked about the cave. You got a couple of minutes to go look at it? At first, I was deterred by the time and money it would take to convert it to something useful. But the idea kept popping into my head. The more I thought about it, the more ways I could think to make it happen. The idea kinda grabbed me and wouldn't let go."

Excitement jolted through her. *Maybe this was a good idea. My grandparents would love it.* "Let me get the big flashlights."

"And maybe something to jot some notes on too," he added, taking one of the flashlights she offered. She searched the nearby desk for a notebook and pen.

"Elvis, guard the place while we're gone." Cassidy followed Levi outside. "Do you have any photos of the old place before it burned down? Maybe if this works out, I could decorate it like the original."

"I'm sure I have some somewhere. I did all kinds of jobs there as a teen, and I helped your granddad with security and bartending for a while. I'm sure I've got some snapshots somewhere. But depending on when they were taken, they might be Polaroids or maybe even slides. We didn't take pictures every day back then like your generation does. Folks your age have never had to wait for film to be developed."

Before Cassidy could ask any more questions, a door slam distracted them. Austin closed the door of a silver Mustang and strode across the grass. It took him only a few steps to close the distance between them. "Morning, Cassidy. Mr. Jenkins. Pretty day out here."

"It is. How are things going at the brunch?" she asked, shielding her eyes from the sun with her hand.

"We're packing up. Only a few folks trickled in. There's a ton of food over there if you want something. Annie's planning to take the leftovers to the food bank over in Staunton. She hates to let stuff go to waste." He hesitated and moved a couple of pebbles with the toe of his boot. "I, uh, wanted to thank you for the tour of the cave and give you my resume."

He handed her a couple of sheets of paper. Glancing at them, she slid them into the back of the notebook. "Coincidentally," she said, "that's where Levi and I are headed right now. He had some ideas for the place. Wanna join us?"

"Sure." Austin's face lit up, and he suddenly looked like a kid with a new toy.

As the trio walked through the grotto, Cassidy said, "Levi, Austin has bartending and procurement experience. I showed him the cave the other day, and he has an interest in working with us if we decide to convert it into a venue."

Levi nodded and led the way down the path and around the wooden barrier. "I think it's feasible. It's clean. There's great air flow in there. You've got multiple exits. And I don't think anything will have to be reinforced structurally. We'll have to put in sensors to monitor the air quality for safety. You know, buildup of carbon monoxide and stuff like that. Just to be on the safe side." He gingerly climbed over the stones and flipped on his light. "The opening is wide. We could figure out a way to secure it or build a lobby or something outside that would let you close it off when not in use. It's too wide to put a door over the opening. Or maybe we could come up with something to block off the front to secure it inside the cave. That way, we could preserve the natural rocky entrance. We'll see what we can do."

Before Cassidy or Austin could comment, Levi continued: "To get it up to code, you need plumbing and electricity, a security system, a backup generator, and some things that would make it accessible, mainly the egress. That path is a bit dicey for folks to climb over. We'll have to make a well-lit path up here and clean out all the underbrush. But with a little landscaping, it'll look nice."

"I know it's a ton of work, but that doesn't sound as bad as I'd imagined. I was thinking about making this a place that people could rent, and Austin suggested that we schedule smaller concerts and shows here. It wouldn't be a regular bar, but a neat place that would enhance our revenue stream as an event location," she said.

"I think it would be cool. I saw a cave in Tennessee where they have concerts. The acoustics are incredible. I think folks would want to have events here," Austin added.

"This part is big enough for tables and chairs or a dance floor." Levi swept the beam of his flashlight across the space near the entrance. "I think your best bet is to put a bar over there against that wall, since it's longer, and the stage over there. You could even use a portable stage if you wanted to use the space for different types of events." Levi arced his light like a spotlight on the walls in front and to the side. "It's naturally cool in here, so there's probably not much need for AC. It'll need some heat in the cooler months. We should factor in the price of the duct work in the costs."

Cassidy made notes as Levi talked. He continued: "I can call a couple of my buddies, and I'll work up some numbers this week. I think it's doable. You've got a good idea here. It wouldn't take long to turn this into something special. And with your marketing magic and the gals' decorating skills, you'll have it booked in no time."

A little flutter inside made her smile. Cassidy had always wanted to carry on her grandparents' work. A new place for parties and musical events continued both their legacies and their passions. "I love it. Let's see what the numbers look like."

"I did some construction jobs in high school," Austin said, touching the rocky walls. "Mr. Jenkins, if you need an apprentice, I can help."

"We can always use an extra hand. And let's see what kind of designs Cassidy and the Pearly Girls come up with. I bet it's a doozie." Levi fell silent and walked up and down the tunnels that jutted off the main room. Then his voice drifted in from somewhere in the back. "You know, we may be able to save money by building on, either in the front or the back. We could put the kitchen and the bathrooms in a new area, and that would save on having to retrofit the stone walls. Blasting and drilling in there would not be fun. This tunnel is shorter than the other. Maybe it becomes the route to the facilities and the emergency exit. This is doable. Cassidy, I'll get you some estimates by next week. Just don't find any more bodies in here. We've had enough of that to last a while." They could hear him snickering as he made his way back to join them in the larger space.

Cassidy could feel the flush covering her cheeks. She pretended to look at the space, hoping no one noticed. "I'm excited about this. Austin, I'll let you know what we decide. Are you sure you want to work here even if it isn't a full-time bar? I try to book our venues as often as I can, but it wouldn't be like managing a bar that's open every night to the public." She paused and glanced over at him.

"I think it would be fine. That way, I can help Annie if there's downtime, and I can also finish my degree."

Cassidy felt another flutter starting in her core. *All the pieces are falling into place. I know I have to see what the estimates are, but this feels like a sign to move forward.*

"Thanks for the consideration," Austin said. "I'm excited to be involved from the beginning."

The trio stepped out into the sunlight, and Cassidy blinked to focus her eyes. Her phone dinged with a string of alerts. "Levi, we may need to look at some kind of booster in there for cell phones—and Wi-Fi too. People will want to use their phones."

Levi shrugged. "If you say so. Not sure how these devices became so critical to everyone's being. But we can figure out a way to get better coverage down here."

Cassidy smiled and patted his shoulder. "Thanks. Any ideas on themes for the place?"

"Maybe a modern take on the honky-tonk. You know, with a hip vibe," Austin said.

"Speaking of that," Levi added. "I found something in the barn the other day when I was setting up for the reunion. I didn't have a chance to explore it further, but it may help you all with your decorating. Come on. I've got to lock up the barn when Miss Annie is done. We can take a peek while she's cleaning up."

The trio clambered over the rocks and cut through the garden.

"It's in here," Levi said, guiding them from the back door. Cassidy flipped on the overhead lights and followed Levi to the loft steps. The space under the loft looked dark and spooky. *Maybe I should do something with this spot too. It's a seating area, because I couldn't figure out what to do with it.* Maybe it could be a second bar or a coat check room? She tried not to think about the gory thoughts and the prickly feeling on the back of her neck that crept up every time she thought of Britt.

Levi flipped on a big flashlight and moved deeper into the space under the loft. "It's back here. All these years, I didn't know anything was back in this space. The other day when I was moving tables, I spotted a loose board. When I tried to pry it up to fix it, I found a trapdoor."

Cassidy felt the butterflies awaken inside her. *A secret passage. Girl, your imagination always goes to pirates, treasure, and secret rooms. You read way too many adventure books and watch too many episodes of "The Curse of Oak Island."*

"I think it was a root or storm cellar at one time. We don't get too many bad storms around here, but many of the buildings had places to shelter in in the early days. Or it could have been part of the bootlegging operation. Root cellars were great for storage before iceboxes and AC. Who knows?" Levi poked the floor with his boot and then pried up a board. He tugged on the wood, and part of the flooring swung up like a hidden door. He aimed his light in the space below.

A jolt of electricity surged through Cassidy. *I can't wait to see what we find down here. Please don't be snakes or giant bugs.*

"I haven't had a chance to really explore the spot. I wanted to show the Pearly Girls too." He climbed down several wooden steps. He swung his light around. Crates and boxes lined the walls. "I opened this one."

Austin stepped forward and helped him lift the heavy wooden lid off of the crate as Cassidy flipped on the other flashlight. "It's full of framed pictures from your granddaddy's place," Levi said.

A chill enveloped Cassidy, and it wasn't from the temperature in the root cellar. *All this stuff was destroyed in the fire. How could it all be boxed up and stored here? Like someone intentionally moved it to preserve it ahead of the devastating fire.*

"Wait. Look at this," Levi said. He stepped across the small-ish space to the other wall where something was covered in tarps and what looked like old bedsheets. He moved one of the tarps and stirred up a cloud of dust.

"Hey, this is too cool," Austin said, touching the shiny surface.

"It's the infamous bar top," Levi whispered. "I thought I'd never see this again." He ran his fingers over the smooth surface.

"We could incorporate this into the new place. This is amazing!" Austin said, stepping closer to look at the signatures.

"But, how..." Cassidy sputtered. She wanted to share in the excitement, but this discovery made her question everything she'd ever been told about the fire. "How did all this stuff get down here and nobody ever knew about it?"

"I have no idea. I watched the building burn," Levi interjected.

All kinds of thoughts swirled in Cassidy's head. *Was the fire set intentionally? Were they planning to remodel? How come no one found all this stuff when they renovated the barn?*

"Wow," she said, climbing the steps. Before she could clear her mind and get a bead on what Levi had discovered, Anastasia and Kelly popped their heads into the darkened space.

"What are you all doing down there?" Kelly asked, staring down into the open space in the floor.

"What is that?" Anastasia asked.

"A root cellar," Cassidy said. "Levi was showing us some more storage space. It's very dusty and buggy. We'll be up in a minute."

"Ewwwww," Kelly squealed. "We'll wait up here. That gives me the willies, just thinking about big hairy spiders."

Austin popped his head up through the open hole in the floor, and Kelly and Anastasia dissolved into a fit of giggles.

"We didn't know you were here, Austin. It's so good to see you," Kelly cooed as he climbed out of the root cellar. "You'll make sure we're not attacked by any creepy bugs or rabid bats."

Cassidy and Levi followed. The former cheerleaders fawned over Austin as Levi closed the trapdoor with a loud bang. "Call me if you need anything. I'm headed over to the maintenance shed."

"We have news," Anastasia said, dusting off Austin's arm and shoulder. "You had something on you. I hope it wasn't a spider. You might want to shake out your hair and shirt."

"I'm fine. It was nothing," Austin said, taking a step away from the two attentive women.

Putting on a pouty face, Anastasia continued: "We've made an executive decision we think everyone will like."

"Yes," Kelly interrupted. "Since the events are already planned and paid for, we're going to go ahead with next weekend."

"That means we'll all get a chance to try more of your awesome drinks," Anastasia said, patting Austin's arm again.

"The committee will contact our classmates this week and drum up attendance. And we're rescheduling the fireworks. I think Vince will want to have some sort of tribute for Britt, so we'll see you all next Friday for the sock hop."

"Toodles," Anastasia said. "Austin, you need to dress up as Elvis or Fabio. It'll be perfect."

"Fabian," Kelly corrected.

"Whatever. That's before my time," Anastasia said, before stomping off toward the dance floor.

"Bye," Cassidy waved at the two women. *Well, at least I don't have to do any refunds. The murder, the cave, the hidden stash of honky-tonk memorabilia. This is all a lot to process. And Britt's murder is the ugly specter hanging over everything.*

10

MONDAY MORNING

"Yikes. I hope there are no creepy-crawlies down there," Ruth-anne said, following Roxie and Kate to the back of the barn. "The thought of it gives me the heebie-jeebies." She did a full-body shiver that looked like some kind of shimmy dance, with some foot stomps thrown in for good measure.

"You're not even in the root cellar yet," Kate said. "And you're already psyching yourself out."

"Dust is several inches thick down here. I didn't see any bugs," Levi said, pulling up the trapdoor under the loft. "There's nothin' in here that'll bother y'all." Dust particles shot skyward and danced in the light as he lifted the heavy wooden door.

"Who knew this was here? An old, forgotten root cellar," Aileen said, staring down into the dark space. "But it does look creepy down there."

"How did you find it? It's in such an out-of-the-way place," Ruth-anne said, as Levi waved his flashlight across the opening, revealing the creaky wooden steps that led to the darkened area below.

"I noticed a loose board the other day. When I went to repair it, it was nailed to the others. It was a door built into the floor. I don't remember a cellar in here, but it was a barn full of cows when I was younger, so I probably just never noticed it before."

"I bet they stored hooch down here," Roxie said, descending

behind Cassidy. "It's bigger than I thought. You could use this for more storage. Look at all this space! It would make a great hiding place if you ever needed one."

A scratching sound near the back wall caused all the women to freeze. Ruthanne eased over to a nearby crate and picked up a hammer that sat on top. Cassidy strained to hear the noise again. *Great, now I need to call an exterminator.*

"Time to get a barn cat," Aileen said.

"A cat'll take care of things. That or a black snake," Levi said.

Ruthanne squealed. Aileen reached forward to pat her on the shoulder, but Ruthanne took a deep breath and let out a blood-curdling scream. The hammer clattered to the floor.

The Pearly Girls rushed around her, and Cassidy peeked around shoulders and elbows to try to see what was going on. *I hope it's not a snake—or Jimmy Hoffa.*

"Look," Ruthanne said, regaining her voice. "Is that what I think it is?" She rushed over to what was sticking out from under the tarp. "It's the bar. It's the famous bar. Look at all those signatures." Ruthanne tugged at the tarp to reveal more of the countertop with all kinds of doodles and autograph graffiti on it. "Yes, that's really it." Her voice quaked as she stared at the find. She covered her mouth with both hands.

"I never thought I'd see that again," Kate said. "Would you look at that? Cassidy, this is the mother lode of music memorabilia. Look, Tammy Wynette and Glen Campbell."

"Hey, over here. This is almost as good," Aileen said. "These crates are full of pictures from the old place. Your grandpa had so many of them. He never had to ever worry about painting the place. It looked like he had wallpapered every inch of space with framed images of every country star imaginable. You've got a wealth of history in these crates."

Cassidy slumped against the cool wall. *Everything I've heard about the honky-tonk wasn't necessarily true. I'm thrilled to uncover the original stuff. Maybe it's another sign to move forward with the new plans for the cave. But why is all this down here under the barn? Was the fire not what they said it was?*

Ruthanne let out another shrill squeal that caused everyone to rush over to a large stack of crates.

"My lands, Ruthanne. This better be good. You're going to give us all a heart attack with all that screaming," Roxie said.

"Oh, my stars. Oh, my stars. Not again." Ruthanne's voice cracked again as she pointed to something on the floor that looked like a pile of clothes. "Not another one." She sniffed to hold back the sobs. "It *is* another one!"

Cassidy and Levi aimed their flashlights behind the crates. Cassidy's breath caught in her throat when she saw a pale hand draped limply over a woman's forehead.

It was Darcy Branch, who lay in a heap in a pose that made it look like she was sleeping—except she wasn't breathing. What was she doing down here?

Clutching the flashlight to keep from dropping it, Cassidy gasped. She grabbed her phone and punched in 911 as she walked toward the stairs to get more connection bars on her phone. Before the dispatcher could finish her spiel, Cassidy blurted, "Hi, this is Cassidy Jamison at Celebrations at Ivy Springs. I need you to send the police and an ambulance right away."

"What happened?" the dispatcher asked. "Emergency units are on their way. Is the person breathing? If not, can you start CPR? I can talk you through the compressions."

"She's cold and not breathing, and she's been here for a while. My team and I were looking through the storage area under the barn, and we found her behind some crates. I have no idea how she got down here or what happened."

"The ambulance is a few minutes out. When they get on the property, where should they go?"

"To the barn. I'll have someone flag them down," Cassidy said.

"I'm on it," Kate said.

"I'll go with her," Aileen said as she scurried up the steps after Kate.

Ruthanne continued to stare at Darcy. "She's the one who left town and became the writer. Her aunts were so proud of her. Who would want to kill her and Britt? None of this makes any sense."

Roxie nodded slightly. "I heard the other cheerleader gals complaining that she took off and didn't help with the reunion. They were grousing because she was smarter and more famous than any of them. They were still doing their mean-girl thing."

"Is there any immediate danger?" the dispatcher asked, jolting Cassidy back to the emergency call.

"No. I don't think so. No one else is around except my team. I think I hear a siren. I'm going to hang up now. Thank you."

Ruthanne and Roxie followed Cassidy up the old steps, and Levi brought up the rear. The tiny group stood around the trapdoor and stared into the inky darkness below. *This explains why her car is in the lot. So maybe the lipstick was hers too? Darcy, who did this to you? How could another guest end up dead at my place? This reunion is turning out to be a disaster. Definitely not the epic party Britt had in mind.*

Stomping and shouts interrupted Cassidy's thoughts. She turned to see three EMTs rush into the barn.

"Where's the victim?" one of the medics yelled from the doorway.

"Down in the root cellar," Levi said, pointing with his light. "She's over in the corner behind a crate. Up against the wall."

Levi handed his flashlight to the first guy, and the two emergency workers hustled down the steps, followed by a deputy. Detective Zac Turner appeared, with Aileen and Kate on his heels.

"Morning, Cassidy, ladies, Levi. We'll be back up in a few minutes to get your statements. Please hang around here. We need to talk to everyone," Detective Turner said as he flipped on his own flashlight and double-timed it down the steps.

Cassidy let out a long sigh that fluttered her bangs. She sank into a nearby chair. "Two women on the reunion committee are dead. Who did this?"

Aileen patted her shoulder. "It's not your fault. Those girls have been scrapping since middle school. I'm sure Britt had an enemy list as long as my arm."

"She ticked off every contractor who ever did work for her, and I overheard some of the gals chattering in the bathroom about how they had hated her since high school. She had a reputation for a sharp tongue," Roxie said.

Ruthanne lowered her voice. "I heard from MarthaJo over at the bakery that while Britt was trying her best to twist Darcy's arm to do an article on her and her job as a hoity-toity Internet influencer, that Darcy was actually having a fling with Vince."

"I heard that too," Roxie corroborated. "But I heard that Britt tried to blackmail Darcy into doing the article. She said she had some dirt on her, which caused Darcy to leave town all those years back."

"Britt had no luck with men, even when she was a flirty cheerleader. She always picked the ones who knew they were handsome or wealthy and had the morals of an alley cat," Kate added.

The conversation halted when Detective Turner's head popped out of the space in the floor. "Okay, ladies and Levi, go through how you found her," he said, joining them at a nearby table and dusting off his polo shirt.

All the Pearly Girls spoke at once, and the heated talk echoed through the empty barn.

A shrill whistle cut through the air. "There! That's better," Kate's voice was heard to say. "He can't possibly get the skinny on this if y'all are yammering at the same time. Levi, you go first, since you found the stuff originally," she continued, pointing at the lanky man. "Then we'll each add what we know."

The group did a round-robin retelling of the morning's events. When Detective Zac was satisfied that he had all the details, he walked over and glanced down in the root cellar again. "The forensic team will be over shortly. We're going to need the space for a while."

"That's fine," Cassidy said. "We don't have any other events planned until Friday. Do you all need anything while you're here?"

He shook his head, and then asked, "Anybody have any last thoughts or things they remembered about Ms. Branch or Ms. Mahoney?"

"This may explain why her key and car are in the parking lot," Cassidy said softly. "And the lipstick and the motel key."

"Anything else you can think of?" Detective Turner asked.

"What happened to Britt and Darcy?" Aileen whispered. Then she covered her mouth with her hand like she was trying to keep any more questions from seeping out.

"Not sure," the detective said. "Britt's death was made to look like a stabbing, but she didn't have any injuries that could be tied to a knife or other sharp object. This one did. We'll have to wait until the autopsies are done. But Ms. Branch may have been dead longer than Mrs. Mahoney."

Ruthanne gasped and sank into the nearest chair. "That is so awful. Who could do such a thing? Both girls were townies, even though Darcy had moved away a long time ago. Her aunts and cousins live around here. And she was kind of a big deal with her books and her journalism career."

"We'll be checking into their lives. Both of the killings seemed personal. If you hear or find anything else, let me know. I know you all have work to do, so you can go. One of us will check in before we leave." The detective retreated down to the root cellar.

"That's our cue," Kate said, herding the rest of the gang toward the main doors. "There's nothing else we can do here."

"I'll be in the shed if you need me," Levi said. "I need to knock down some of those weeds near the grotto."

Cassidy followed the Pearly Girls to the office. When she opened the back door, Elvis bounded out and danced around everyone's feet. "I'm going to take him for a quick walk. Be back in a few."

"I'm sure folks will be blowing up our phones as soon as word of this leaks out," Kate said. "You may get some big press attention on Darcy. Let us know if you have a statement you want us to use for talking points."

"I didn't think about that," Cassidy said. "I have the one we used last summer. I'll go and do some edits and check with the detective to see when it's okay to post it." Cassidy headed for the door, and Elvis followed, ready for his next adventure. "Be back in a bit."

"The story's already leaked," Roxie said, holding up her phone. "Somebody must have been listening to the police scanner."

"Come on, Elvis. A quick lap around the garden, and then we need to get some work done." Without waiting for his leash, Elvis darted off toward the barn. Cassidy had to jog to catch up to him.

A forensic tech stepped outside with several bags and bins. "Hi," Cassidy said to her. "Word of the second body is already out on social media. I was wondering if it was okay to put out some kind of statement."

"Let me secure these in the van, and then I'll check with the detective," the young woman said.

Elvis took full advantage of the wait time to sniff around the barn and do his own investigation of the flower beds.

Cassidy jumped when Detective Turner poked his head out of the barn. "Are you getting calls already?"

"Not yet, but it's a matter of time. Roxie saw some posts on social media about another murder in Ivy Springs. I need to put out some kind of message."

"Wait until we do the notifications to the next of kin. I'll text you. It'll be late today."

Cassidy nodded. "Will do."

"Need anything else?" he asked.

She shook her head, and he disappeared back inside the barn.

Cassidy scooped up Elvis and carried him back to the office.

Zac said Darcy was killed before Britt. These two deaths had to be related. Did Britt kill Darcy and then herself? No, that didn't make sense. Britt wouldn't have been able to stage herself as Lady Gaga. Someone killed Darcy and then Britt. Wait a minute, was Darcy in the root cellar all this time? She stopped walking and closed her eyes, trying to remember what had happened. *Nobody noticed her when they were down there earlier.*

Too many unanswered questions bothered Cassidy as she slid into her office chair and turned on her laptop. Zac thought that Darcy had been stabbed, but that Britt hadn't been. He did say that both killings looked personal. *The reunion is ground zero for some deep-seated rage. There are so many different pieces missing from this puzzle. I need a way to make some sense out of this before someone else gets hurt. Or worse.*

LATER MONDAY MORNING

Cassidy's neck and shoulders hurt from hunching over her laptop and her notes for so long. She felt light-headed; and, to make things worse, thoughts of Britt and Darcy kept ping-ponging around in her head and taking center stage.

"Hey, hon. Are you okay? You look awfully pale," Ruthanne said, stopping what she was doing. "Let me get you a ginger ale to settle your stomach."

"I'm fine. Just thinking about who could do this to both of these women." Cassidy opened her laptop and pulled up a spreadsheet. "Thanks," she said to Ruthanne, who handed her an aluminum can.

"Okay, here's what we know," Roxie said. "Britt left her first husband Mac because of all his affairs. But they still seemed friendly. That sounds fishy, but who knows. I saw them at one of the events, and it looked like old times. She's married now to the older, wealthier Vince who has had one midlife crisis after another until he settled down with his young hottie Britt. He left his wife of twenty-some years for the former cheerleader. Mac, the once-hunky quarterback, hadn't moved on." She counted off facts on her bejeweled fingers. "And Vince was fooling around with the successful Darcy."

Aileen moved behind Cassidy and leaned closer as she watched her type. Roxie continued: "And then there's Darcy. She was always smart and quiet. Not like Britt's crew. Darcy was a hard worker, determined to make something of herself and to get out of this town. Those cheerleaders tormented girls like her. I'm so glad Darcy made her dreams come true."

"I looked her up," Kate said. "She's been working for that magazine for several years now. And before that, she wrote for some large newspapers. She lives in New York and rubs elbows with people Britt would give her eyeteeth to snap a selfie with. And she's written two best-selling books. I'm surprised she even came back here for this reunion. She doesn't need Ivy Springs anymore."

"Maybe she came back to see Vince," Aileen said quietly.

"I hope that cute detective comes back over here with some details," Ruthanne said, winking at Cassidy.

"Stay out of the gossip mill. We're lying low, remember." Kate turned her head and glared at Ruthanne.

"I forgot. Operation Knitting Ninja." Ruthanne's face blushed, and she covered her mouth with both hands like she had leaked some state secret.

"I knew it!" Cassidy said. "Y'all were acting weird, and then the town gets yarn-bombed. It was you all in your matching black outfits."

"And pearls," Roxie drawled. "Kate saw a video on Instagram, and she showed it to us. It looked like harmless fun. And it gave Ruthanne's giant scarf a purpose."

"I like to knit," Ruthanne said softly.

"Speaking of that, it's in the back closet. I pulled it down off the mailbox the other day," Cassidy said.

"So, that dang ole scarf gave us away," Aileen said. "It was fun to decorate Main Street. I have some pictures. It was definitely colorful. And I think the Ivy Springs pioneer looked good in his new sweater that Ruthanne made."

"The arms were too long, but I've never made a sweater for a statue before," Ruthanne said.

"No posting pictures," Kate said. "We need to lie low until this blows over. We don't need the detective or the sheriff asking any questions."

"I wouldn't worry about it," Roxie said. "Detective Zac has his hands full with two dead bodies and a gossipy town. The knitting prank will be long forgotten by tomorrow. Plus, we didn't damage anything."

"But it could be trespassing," Kate said with a scowl.

"And we now have our own mystery here, besides, you know, the other two things," Ruthanne added, nodding her head. "How in the world did all that stuff get in the barn? I thought the honky-tonk went up in flames during the storm."

"It did, but obviously the contents didn't," Aileen added.

"I don't remember any talk of moving all that stuff out of the bar," Kate said.

Cassidy tapped her lips with her index finger. "Ruthanne, how far back do the books go here? Do you have any from that time period? Maybe there's something about the insurance money or other expenses that might give us a clue."

"Brilliant, Cassidy. Just brilliant. Let me go see. Most of the stuff is in the back room," Ruthanne said, knocking several files off of Cassidy's desk.

"Go, go. See what you can find," Kate said. "I've got this." She picked up the folders and restacked them.

"Ruthanne's always nervous about audits. She saves everything, even if she doesn't have to," Roxie said. "I'm sure she'll be able to find the records."

The gals busied themselves with various projects, including checking their phones for yarn-bombing photos, until Ruthanne returned with an armful of dusty ledgers. She plunked the stack down on her desk. "These go back to the nineteen-fifties. If there's something, I'm sure I'll find it in here." She pulled out her glasses from her curly silver hair and stuck them on her nose.

"Need any help?" Aileen asked.

Achoooo. Ruthanne sneezed as if on cue.

"Bless you," Kate said.

Ruthanne grabbed a tissue from the pink box on her desk. "Nah. I'm not even sure what I'm looking for. I guess I'll know it when I see it."

"Just like porn," Roxie said. When the other gals stared at her, she continued, "It's like that old quote. You know the one."

Aileen replied, "It was from Supreme Court Justice Potter Stewart."

"Yep, I'm sure it's that one," Roxie said, scrunching her nose. Kate rolled her eyes.

The gals found tasks to work on at their desks, and Cassidy returned to staring at her screen. There had to be something in Britt's and Darcy's private lives that led to their murders. *Is the affair at the center of all this?* On a whim, she grabbed her phone and tapped out a text to Kelly, asking if she wanted to meet later for coffee. Maybe she'd be able to shed some light on Britt's inner circle.

Her phone pinged with a quick response, **Brew'd Awakening at 1?**

Perfect. See you then, Cassidy replied. *Okay, now what can I find on the gang from Ivy Springs High in the meantime?*

Around twelve thirty, Roxie broke the silence in the office when she stood and gathered her things. "Okay, I'm ready for lunch. Who wants to go to town? I need to get up and walk around. And maybe do a little shopping."

"You want to go see if anyone took down our handiwork," Kate said with a grin.

"Shhhh! Don't slip and say that around the police. You don't want them to throw us in the slammer again," Aileen said.

"That was one time, and it was because Ruthanne was driving a stolen car," Roxie said with a wink. "And everything turned out okay. The rock star who was with us fessed up and cleared our names. No harm, no foul."

"What about that time in Daytona during bike week, and that other time we had that run-in in Las Vegas?" Aileen asked. "Roxie, I know you remember that trip. That's when you got a tattoo."

Cassidy raised both eyebrows, waiting for more details.

"It's a little one," Roxie said. "No big deal."

"They were fun excursions. Nobody went to jail except for that big mistake, but all charges were dropped," Ruthanne added.

"But we still had to spend the night in jail in Harrisonburg because of that joyride," Kate said, wagging her finger at Ruthanne.

"It builds character and gives us cool stories to tell. Who's up for lunch at Planet of the Grapes? They have great ham-and-grilled-cheese sandwiches," Roxie said.

"And wine," Aileen added. "I'm in."

"Me too," Kate said, rising. "What about you two?"

"I want to keep going through these books," Ruthanne said, pushing her glasses up and rubbing her eyes. "I feel like I'm on the verge of finding something. I hope it's not just wishful thinking."

"I'm going to take Elvis for a walk and get him settled in the apartment before my meeting with Kelly at Brew'd Awakening," Cassidy said.

"And sleuthing. We need details." Aileen pulled her sunglasses and keys out of her bag.

"Make sure you swing by the barn, too, and find out what's going on with the foxy detective," Roxie added. "We want all the info when we see you next. Toodles."

Kate and Aileen followed Roxie out the front, and Cassidy rose to grab Elvis's leash. *A walk by the barn couldn't hurt anything.* "Do you want me to bring you anything back?" she asked Ruthanne.

"I'm good. I'll work until I get hungry and then head home. I'll let you know what I find. I feel like Nancy Drew hot on a clue trail." She did a quick jazz hands to celebrate.

"Can't wait to see what you find. Come on, Elvis, let's go see what we can see." He didn't need to be told twice. He bolted for the door and waited impatiently for her to open it. He trotted across the grass and through the garden, where he paused for a moment to check out his fish friends in the koi pond. When he heard a noise, he zoomed off toward the barn.

Cassidy caught her breath when Elvis came to a sudden stop by the open barn doors. The building looked deserted except for the van and the two police cruisers parked nearby. Plans for a quick, quiet peek inside were dashed when Elvis let out a string of barks and dashed inside like he owned the place.

"Hey, there," Deputy Sanchez said, bending down to pat Elvis.

Cassidy cleared her throat. "Hello. Is there anything my team or I can get y'all?"

"We're almost done here. Waiting for forensics to wrap up. The detective wanted to stop by and see you. Let me tell him you're here." He turned and disappeared into the barn's dark interior.

When he returned, Detective Turner paused to pat the little dog on the head. "Hey, Elvis. And hey to you too," he said to Cassidy as he cracked a smile. "We're almost done. You can lock up soon."

"Thanks. I'll let Levi know," she said, pulling out her phone and tapping a quick text to her groundskeeper. "Uh..."

"You want to know about Darcy?" he asked, giving her his best detective glare.

She nodded slowly.

"It looks like she was stabbed and left here in the cellar," he said.

"I didn't even know that space existed until Levi showed it to us yesterday. He said he saw a board sticking up when he was setting up for the reunion. When he went to fix it, he found the hidden door and all the memorabilia from my grandfather's honky-tonk. That's what he was showing us when we found the, er, uh, Darcy. Had she been down there the whole time?"

"Probably. Our best guess is she was killed elsewhere and hidden here," he said, glancing over at the forensic technicians.

"The knife we found. Uh, do you think that was..." *What is wrong with you, girl. Use your words. Why does he make you so nervous?*

"We'll have that knife you found at the other scene examined. It may or may not be related. At first, I thought it was a prop since it wasn't used on Mrs. Mahoney. And it had been wiped of prints and covered in paint."

The butterflies in Cassidy's stomach turned into bats and started banging into each other. *Did the killer hide the weapon at the other murder scene? Was Darcy killed in the garden where I found all that stuff?*

As if he could read her thoughts, he said, "Darcy was killed first. Before we leave, we'll do another walk-through of your garden. That may have been where she was attacked. Where exactly did you find the keys?"

"It was like they were scattered in a row in the mulch. On the left side of the wedding arch." Cassidy closed her eyes for a moment. "I think we found the lipstick, the motel key, and then the car key. We were near the grotto side, walking toward the trellis. They were all off the path in the mulch."

"Thanks. We're going to take a look around. We'll be done here in a bit." He hesitated like he had more to say. Then he quickly added, "We'll close the doors."

"I'm heading out to meet a friend. Levi will check on the barn later." She twisted Elvis's leash in her hand. "Uh, what about Darcy? You said both murders looked like they were personal."

He pulled out his aviator sunglasses. "We won't know for sure until the medical examiner has completed his work."

Cassidy let out a puff of air.

"Our best hypothesis right now is Ms. Branch was stabbed, and Mrs. Mahoney was strangled. But that's not information to share." He nodded slightly and headed for the parking lot.

"Bye." Cassidy finger-waved over her shoulder and nudged Elvis toward the office. *Every time I think I've made headway with him and we're having a normal conversation, he reverts to police mode. He's exasperating at times. I think the Pearly Girls are exaggerating what they think they see in him. He and I have a good police-citizen relationship. That's it.*

12

Cassidy found a parking spot on a side street and locked her red Wrangler. She hustled around the corner and found an empty table in the cozy coffee shop. Scents of cinnamon, vanilla, and strong coffee tickled her nose and made her long for a sweet caffeine hit.

"Hey, girl. I haven't seen you in a month of Sundays." Marcie Chen waved to her from behind the glass display cases. "What can I get for you?" The svelte woman pushed a strand of dark hair away from her face and pulled on a pair of rubber gloves.

"Hi, Marcie. I'd love to have one of your vanilla bean iced coffees."

"With lots of syrup and cream and, of course, whipped cream?" she inquired with a wink as she pulled on a metal lever on one of the giant devices on the counter.

"Of course. And I think I'll have one of those peanut butter cookies too. Everything in here smells so good. Heavenly."

Marcie smiled. "Mom's been on a baking kick. She's trying out some new twists on some old favorites." She swirled the whipped cream on top and handed the cup to Cassidy.

"Thanks. This looks yummy."

"How are things going at your place? Well, you know: besides the Britt thing," Marcie whispered. She grabbed a pair of tongs and dropped a cookie the size of a dessert plate into a white bag. Shifting to a more neutral topic, Marcie said, "I enjoyed the outdoor concerts last summer. I hope you do those again."

Cassidy tapped her debit card on the machine. "I'm hoping to expand our musical offerings this year. I'll send you a schedule when I get the dates confirmed." Cassidy dropped her card and receipt into her purse.

"Cool." Marcie's glance flicked to the large glass door as two men wandered in, followed by Kelly.

Cassidy waved at Kelly and found a seat in the far corner facing the window. Marcie had decorated everything in cheery yellows, whites, and oranges, with modern artwork on every wall. The interior reminded Cassidy of a bouquet of daisies on a bright sunny day.

While Cassidy scrolled through her Instagram account, Kelly slipped into the orange chair across from her and dropped her large black bag into the empty seat next to her.

"Hey," Kelly said. "I hope you haven't been waiting long. The bus was early for my littlest kiddo. I had to drive him to school, and I was late for everything after that. It kinda had a domino effect on the rest of my day." The slender Kelly, usually in designer clothes, looked a little rumpled this morning in mom jeans and an oversized white shirt. Her normally blown-out hairstyle was replaced by a limp ponytail. She blew on her steaming coffee and then looked down at her fingernails.

"No problem," Cassidy said. "I'm so glad you could meet me here. It's been a little hectic around my place. The police finished with the, uh, the scene." Her voice drifted off as she chose her words carefully, trying not to upset Kelly.

Kelly sniffed and rummaged through her bag for a tissue. "I'm processing it all. I can't believe Britt's gone, and now Darcy. I mean, this is Ivy Springs. No one here even locks their doors. And now there's a crazed lunatic running around." She sniffed again and continued. "I thought we were going to meet as a committee to decide what to do, but Anastasia took over. So I guess we're moving ahead with the rest of the events, with a memorial ceremony for Britt and Darcy in your garden. I hope you don't mind."

"We'll be glad to help any way we can," Cassidy said. *Wow. Zac hasn't even talked to the family yet, and word has spread all over town about Darcy.*

"I have no idea who will turn up. I think everyone is kinda over the whole reunion thing by now. The grand bash was Britt's idea." Kelly wiped her eyes and sipped her coffee. "This didn't turn out like it was supposed to. I wish we'd never planned this whole thing."

"Any idea who would do this to Britt?" Cassidy asked in almost a whisper.

Kelly shook her head. "Everybody loved her. She was always the star and the center of attention. She wouldn't have it any other way. Britt was a natural leader. People always wanted to be around her. She spent her whole life being in the thick of everything, and she didn't like it when she wasn't. At times, she could be pretty mean, but she really did care what other people thought of her."

"How was her relationship with the gals on the team?" Cassidy probed.

Kelly did a slight wave. "I dunno. We've all been friends forever. Darcy didn't run with our crowd, but she blossomed into a mega-popular celebrity writer everybody wanted to talk to. I was thrilled when she said she'd help us. We didn't treat her the best in high school. She kinda ran with the nerdy crowd." She looked up at Cassidy and paused. "No offense," Kelly added. "I thought this would be our chance to make amends."

Ignoring the insult, Cassidy asked, "What about Anastasia?"

"What about her? She was always underfoot and vying for

attention too. You know, Britt's second fiddle. She was never in the spotlight she craved. Her dad was loaded, and her parents were older. They doted on her constantly, like a pet or a plaything. Can you say *spoiled*? If you ask me, she has the expectation that people will give her stuff or let her get her way—usually to shut her up. She is soooo annoying. We were never that close. I always called her Britt's mini-me. She followed Britt around and tried to insert herself into everything. She had to look like Britt, talk like her... You get the picture."

"She seems to have stepped in to fill the void on the reunion committee," Cassidy said.

"Large and in charge. She likes being the center of everything too." Kelly looked over her shoulder and lowered her voice. "I always thought she was jealous of Britt. She was too sweet and tried constantly to stay in her good graces. She kissed Britt's whatever whenever she could."

"What about Britt's husbands? Was there anyone in her life who would want to cause her harm?"

"Ha!" Kelly said a little too loudly. She glanced around again to see if anyone was watching. "Are you kidding? Britt could wrap men around her finger. She divorced Mac years ago for his philandering ways, but they're still close. He even fixed her AC unit when it went out last summer. He jumps when she calls him. And don't get me started on Vince. He's old and rich. She was his midlife crisis. Well, one of them." She waved her hand glibly and looked around the coffee shop like she was expecting someone.

Cassidy leaned forward slightly, hoping Kelly would continue.

She did: "Vince is smart, distinguished, and very well off. He liked having arm candy, and he spoiled her, and she was more than willing to take and take. He gave Britt anything she wanted. But recently, she found out he had been having a string of affairs. Britt slipped and mentioned to us that he was bored with her and wanted someone who could carry on an adult conversation."

Cassidy's eyebrows shot up behind her bangs. "What did Britt do?"

"What could she do? She had a prenup; and if she left, she had pretty much nothing. I think she sucked it up and stayed. But she griped about him constantly, and when she saw him with Darcy, I thought she was going to have a stroke. Pure rage."

"Why did she let her on the planning committee if there was that much bad blood?"

Kelly made a face. "Deep down, Britt will always be Britt. Darcy is popular and famous, and she was dying for Darcy to mention her in an article or something. Britt thought the publicity would help her build her social media following to impress Vince and prove that she was a legitimate businesswoman."

"Interesting." Cassidy's thoughts bounced back to Vince. "How did Darcy and Vince get together?"

"It's Ivy Springs." Kelly let out a long puff of air. "Darcy was back last year settling her father's estate, and Vince was the family's insurance agent. I think business turned to pleasure. You know, drinks to discuss the estate led to, well, other things. He was looking for the intelligent-librarian type. We were all surprised." Kelly did a half-shrug and pushed her coffee away. "It's been nice talking with you. I've got to get to my yoga class. Anastasia or I will text you later in the week with our plans for next weekend." Kelly glanced at her phone. "I've kinda lost interest in the whole reunion deal, and we still haven't heard from Vince about the funeral. I'm sure Britt would have wanted an extravaganza and a big pink coffin. Something folks would talk about for years."

"Thanks for meeting me today. It was good to see you again. And I'll talk to you soon about next weekend." Cassidy picked up her bag and her trash.

Kelly rose and tossed her cup in the trash can near the door. Without saying anything else, she breezed out the door.

Cassidy slipped out behind her and stood on the sidewalk. Soaking up the bright sun, she let the warmth flow over her as she breathed in the mountain air, tinged with lavender and pine scents. She closed her eyes and took several cleansing breaths. *Britt was popular, but she did have her detractors. Why do I keep thinking about the Darcy-Vince-Britt thing? Could love or lust be at the bottom of all this?*

She felt a presence near her, and her eyes flicked open. "Oh, hi, Detective Taylor. I'm enjoying the sunshine before it turns cold." She felt like she was babbling. *Why does he make me so nervous? It's that cop stare of his. And I always feel like I have to explain what I'm doing.*

"It's Zac," he said. "I'm grabbing some coffee from Marcie for the team." He reached for the door.

Now we're back on a first-name basis. It won't last long. His friendly vibe switches to full-on interrogation mode in a matter of seconds—and, most of the time, I don't know what I did to trigger the change.

"So, your task force is hard at work," she said, hoping to prompt him to provide more details about the murders.

He nodded. "We're chasing down lots of leads and interviewing folks. Darcy and Britt had a wide circle of acquaintances. It was good to see you," he saluted with two fingers and disappeared inside the coffee shop.

That was abrupt. So much for getting any information out of him.

On the ride back to work, her thoughts bounced around like a pickleball on a tournament court. Converting the cave, the murder investigations, Austin, and Zac. *They both are handsome. Girl, you need to focus. You sound like a love-sick tweenie. Wake up. When I get back, I need to check out the stuff in the barn again. I bet I could spiff it up and blend what we found in with my design ideas for the cave.*

A new idea popped in Cassidy's head, and she swung a U-turn and headed out of town. Once on the outskirts of Ivy Springs, she passed both of Sid Pro Quo's motels and turned into the gravel driveway of Gibson's Towing next to the junkyard. She drove behind a chain-link fence topped with razor wire. A bright red Dodge Charger and a giant flatbed filled the spaces in front of a small beige building that looked like it hadn't been updated or painted since the nineteen-seventies.

Cassidy parked next to the Charger, hopped out, and scanned the area. Several empty cars sat on this side of the fence, and piles of rusted metal provided the backdrop. A low rumbling sound from the junkyard next door drowned out all other noises.

She pulled on the glass door, and a blast of warm air and a strong mix of oil and some cleaner greeted her in the empty waiting room that was full of mismatched plastic chairs. "Hello! Anybody here?" she yelled. She took a couple of steps toward a beige counter. Every inch of the shelf behind it was crammed with dusty football and baseball trophies.

Rustling began in the back and got louder. "Hey, how can I help you? Need a tow?" Mac asked, setting a mug on the front counter that was already covered in dried coffee rings.

"Uh, hi, Mac. I'm Cassidy Jamison from over in Ivy Springs."

"I remember you from the party at the barn."

"Yes," she said, eyeing the former quarterback. Other than the wrinkles on his ruddy face and a receding hairline, Mac looked the same as she remembered. "I wanted to stop by and make sure you're okay. Britt's death was so sudden."

He looked stunned. Then he shook his head a couple of times like he was trying to clear his thoughts. He sniffed and replied, "I never thought it would end up this way. I always hoped we'd get back together one day." He leaned one elbow on the front counter.

"I'm sorry for your loss. Were you and Britt close after high school? I moved out of town and lost touch with people." *That sounded lame before I even got the words out, but I didn't want to lead with "Did you kill your ex-wife?"*

"Yeah. We talked and texted on a regular basis. She called me to fix stuff like her car and the AC. I was always her go-to guy," he said with a chuckle.

"Oh, my staff found some car keys and a hunting knife after the reunion dinner. Did you hear anyone say they lost anything?"

"Uh, no. Wasn't me. My hunting stuff is at home or in my old truck," he said, looking like he was tired of the conversation.

Not sure if she should press him further about the knife, Cassidy paused, and he continued. "I hunt and fish every chance I get. Keep most of my gear in my trophy room at home. I'll check it tonight, but I have no reason to think anything's missing." His phone buzzed, and he looked at the screen. "Uh, I gotta go. Gotta help some lady with a flat. If you ever need a tow, call me. Hey, maybe we can get dinner sometime," he said, stepping around the counter. He held the door with one hand and handed her his business card with the other.

Cassidy tried not to look surprised at his offer of a date. "Thanks," she said, heading for her Jeep as he paused to lock the glass door. Shaking her head in wonder at how much time could change people, she climbed in and headed for home. In school, she would have been over the moon if he had asked her out. Now it wasn't even a consideration. Turning up the classic rock station and cranking down her windows, she enjoyed the breeze as she sped along the curvy roads back to the office.

She pulled into an open spot in the front lot between Celebrations' van and Ruthanne's Mini Cooper. She pushed thoughts of Mac and his invitation to the back of her mind and concentrated on the possibilities of the cave. A tingle of excitement zipped around inside her. Despite all the trauma around the murders, the idea of repurposing the cave seemed to be doable. She smiled at herself and locked the Jeep. *This seems like the right thing to do.*

Voices near the porch distracted her. "Hey, Cassidy, come here if you've got a sec," Levi hollered.

"Good afternoon," she said to her groundskeeper and Vern, the contractor.

"You know Vern Dwier. He came to look over your cave to see if he could help us."

"I've known Cassidy since she was a little tot running around Evelyn's place," Vern said, shaking her hand. "You've got a nice facility here, and I've got some ideas to get your cave up to code. I'll work on my proposal and quote and set up some time next week to go over the options."

"Thank you so much. It's good to see you, and I'm excited about the project, especially since we found some of my grandfather's memorabilia," Cassidy said.

"That's interesting," Vern said, wiping his brow with the back of his hand. "I'd thought everything was lost in that ole fire."

"We did too, so this was almost like a sign that we need to show it off again," Levi said. "Thanks for coming by." He shook his friend's hand, and Cassidy waved her goodbyes.

Inside the apartment, Elvis bounded from the living room to greet her. "I wasn't gone that long," she said, picking up the wiggly dog, who licked the end of her nose. She carried the chihuahua downstairs and into the quiet office.

"Is Levi still out there?" Ruthanne's head popped out from the doorway.

"No, he headed over toward the barn when Vern left," Cassidy said.

"I need to tell him the grass is getting a bit tall near the patio. Elvis was whining at the door, so I took him out, and the grass was up to his little shoulders. He wasn't too happy about trekking around in it. It tickled his tummy." Ruthanne giggled. "Oh, hey, come see what I found." She waved both hands and shooed Cassidy into the office. "See? See?" Ruthanne said, tugging at her arm before Cassidy could focus on what was causing all the excitement. "I've been poring over the books. Back in 1984, your grandfather got a check from the insurance company for the fire."

"So, he collected the insurance money. I wonder if he ever thought about rebuilding. Where did the money go?" Cassidy asked, leaning over Ruthanne's shoulder to see the entry.

"That's the interesting part. About two months later, I found something surprising." Ruthanne tapped her pen on a pile of ledgers next to her.

A little quiver formed in Cassidy's stomach, excitement coursing through her. "Oh? Does it explain what happened?" Excitement suddenly turned to panic at the thought of the possibilities of insurance fraud or arson. Giving her head a quick shake as if to rid herself of the dark thoughts, Cassidy refocused on what Ruthanne was pointing to.

"No, but it might be a clue," Ruthanne said, slipping on her reading glasses. "See this entry on this page? Your grandparents donated all the money to the library. It was when the town was campaigning for the building fund. I don't remember hearing anything about a big donation, but I had young kids in those days. So I probably wasn't in tune with everything that was going on in town. Your grandparents must have kept it quiet."

"Okay, my family didn't profit from the fire, and they never rebuilt. But how did he know to move all that stuff ahead of the fire?" Cassidy's voice faded as she stared at the ledger until the black and blue numbers blurred.

"I watch too many murdery shows on TV," Ruthanne said. "I can almost hear Keith Morrison narrating the soundtrack in my head. This all sounds a little suspect to me. Maybe get Aileen to sweet-talk the sheriff and see what he knows? I wouldn't like to think it was premeditated. It has to be a coincidence. Right?" she said with a sigh.

"I don't want it to be bad either. But all that stuff in the root cellar turned what I thought I knew about the property upside down. Maybe I'll swing by the library later to see what I can find."

"I'll keep looking through the books, but so far this is all I've uncovered. I've got to head out and do some errands. And we're meeting our knitting group over at Planet of the Grapes later for a chat," Ruthanne said.

"Are y'all plotting round two?" Cassidy asked.

Ruthanne giggled. "Nope. I think that was a one and done. It was fun, but we were so worried that we were going to get in trouble. And it was more work than any of us expected. More than any of us imagined. They covered it on the local news and on Facebook. Some folks were even taking selfies with the decorations. What a hoot! You have any big plans tonight? Please tell me you'll call Austin or Detective Zac." Ruthanne's eyes twinkled like one of the characters on a Saturday-morning cartoon.

"I've got some things to take care of here, and I've been so busy lately. I promised Elvis some quality time," she said with a smile.

"All well and good, but you need to get out more with people your own age. All you do is work and hang around with us," Ruthanne said, straightening the ledgers on her desk. "You need me to do anything before I head out?"

"Nope. I'm going to work on the calendar and see where we have open spots where we can look for bookings. Then Elvis and I may go into town too."

"Good, I guess. Did you hear we're getting an ice cream shop?"

"We need one, but it's opening in the wrong season." Cassidy frowned.

"I eat ice cream all year round," Ruthanne said. "A new couple in town is subdividing the old Meat and Greet space. One side will be called the Dairy Godmother, and the other will be the Atomic Sushi."

"What a combo, but both will do well here. I'm glad we're getting some new places. Ivy Springs is blossoming. And that means more opportunities for partnerships with our fellow businesses," she said with a wink.

Ruthanne picked up her purse and patted Elvis. "See you all tomorrow for the staff meeting. Toodles."

"See ya." Cassidy busied herself with the schedule. "Hey, Elvis. There aren't as many open spots this winter as I thought there were. We're doing well. How 'bout we head to town and celebrate?"

He yipped and booked it to the back door.

After she got Elvis settled into the front seat, Cassidy inched the Wrangler out of the parking lot. The leaves would be showing their colors soon, and the roads would be jam-packed with those out to enjoy the mountains in autumn.

"Pizza, Elvis?" His ears jutted skyward. "Sounds good," she replied. "The weather's good for a table on the patio."

Locating parking on a side street, the pair trekked to Feeling

Saucy. Snagging the last table near the metal fencing, she opened the menu as Elvis settled in at her feet.

"Hey, there. What can I get you two?" Pete Russo asked, ambling up to her table. The stocky waiter with the physique of a wrestler smiled and handed her a menu.

"I know what I want," she said, returning the smile. Little Petey had grown a lot since she babysat him. "I'll take a personal-sized cheese and sausage with a root beer."

"Sounds good. That'll be right out. And Elvis, I've got a couple mozzarella sticks back there with your name on them." He picked up the menu and swung by another table on his way inside.

A shadow covered her table, and Cassidy looked up from her phone. "Hi, Detective—uh, Zac," she said. "Twice in one day."

The detective towered over her table, and Elvis revved up his greeter mode. "Just out for a stroll this evening, and I saw you sitting over here. Uh, I hope I'm not interrupting something."

"No, Elvis and I stopped in for a bite. Would you like to join us?"

The muscular detective pulled out a chair and folded his tall frame into the spot across from her before she had finished her sentence.

"Are you on a case?" she asked, eyeing his jeans and maroon casual shirt with a zipper at the slightly open collar.

"Always got several cases going; but no, I'm only on call tonight, for a change." He glanced at the sidewalk behind her.

When he didn't say anything more after a long pause, Cassidy replied, "That's good." Before she could press him on the details of the investigation, Pete popped up from out of nowhere.

"Hey, Zac. What can I get you on this fine evening?"

"A small supreme and a Coke should do it. Thanks."

"Be back in a flash. Elvis, here's some water. You need a beverage too." The chihuahua wiggled and lapped at the ice water in the metal bowl.

"So, anything else interesting going on at your place?" Zac asked when Pete disappeared again.

"Well, we kinda have our own little mystery now," Cassidy said.

Zac looked up with a puzzled look. "You didn't find anything else, did you?"

Shaking her head, Cassidy replied, "Not related to Britt or Darcy. For years, I heard that the honky-tonk had burned down and everything was lost. But Levi found the bar top, and crates and crates of framed memorabilia, in the root cellar where we also found Darcy. I was kinda stunned. I thought all that had been destroyed years ago."

"You should figure out something to do with it. The sheriff said your granddaddy's place was full of local history."

Before she could reply, Pete set two steaming plates on the table. "Let me know if you need anything else." Jamal Baskerville, the lanky teen behind him, handed him a drink for Zac and a refill for Cassidy. Then he slipped Elvis a mozzarella stick.

"Thanks, man. This smells good," Zac said.

"Yes, and Elvis says thank you too. He's a little busy devouring his snack," Cassidy added.

The conversation trailed off as the pair dug into their pizzas and watched the people milling around, enjoying the crisp evening air. Despite the slight chill, shoppers crowded the sidewalks on both sides of Main Street.

Cassidy savored the cheesy garlicky flavor. She popped the last bite in her mouth and pushed the plate to the center of the table. "This was good."

"So, what are you going to do with the memorabilia?" Zac asked, looking at her with his hazel eyes. The golden specks that dotted the edges were almost mesmerizing.

Cassidy chided herself for getting distracted. "We had a contractor come out this week and look at the cave to see what it would cost to turn it into a venue. Austin thinks we could have small concerts or comedy acts there when we're not hosting an event."

His friendly grin faded, and Zac furrowed his brow as he turned his head to watch the passersby.

"What, you don't like the idea?" she asked, wondering what had brought on the quick change in his demeanor.

"No, that's not it. I was thinking of something else. Never mind. I think that would be cool."

"I want Levi to build a bar that we can use to hold the historic counter from the honky-tonk with all its signatures. Somebody put a coat of Polyurethane on it, and it seems to have aged well. You can actually still read most of the famous autographs."

"Sheriff Howell has fond memories of the old place. He mentions it from time to time when he talks about the good ole days in Ivy Springs. He has lots of stories about what went on there and the acts that came to perform."

Cassidy felt a wry smile creep across her face. "That's interesting. He and I have never had any long conversations. I guess he's different around his coworkers. I mean, not so official."

It was Zac's turn to smile. "Not really. He's always brusque, but he does have a sense of humor that comes out every once in a while."

I've never seen a humorous side to the sheriff. Maybe I should chat him up sometime about the honky-tonk and the fire. He might have an interesting take on things.

13

The rest of dinner was unusually quiet. Then Zac got a text, and the alert seemed to echo across the patio. "It's work. Dinner was fun. Gotta run." He tossed enough cash for both dinners on the table and jogged down the street. *Well, at least I can say I had dinner with someone, even if he did run away unexpectedly.*

"Okay, Elvis, we should head out too." She added more money to make a hefty tip and waved to Jamal. But when she tried to guide the dog back to the Jeep, Elvis had other ideas.

Not ready to head back home, Elvis trotted down the sidewalk, and they wended their way around the clusters of shoppers and tourists in front of the eclectic stores and restaurants. *It's nice to see people out and about on a weeknight. The boutiques, galleries, and all the new eateries have good crowds.*

Cassidy and Elvis strolled down the sidewalk until they reached the edge of the business district. A sprawling neighborhood with mature trees sprang up out of nowhere. The Victorian homes in this area reminded Cassidy of dollhouses, with all the gingerbread trim and the pastel colors. Several were being renovated for bed-and-breakfasts, thanks to some rezoning. The small-town charm, the tree-lined streets, and the perfectly manicured flowerbeds provided the ideal backdrop for tourists who wanted a cozy getaway within walking distance to town.

After an enjoyable stroll through the neighborhood, Cassidy and Elvis made their way back to the Jeep. The chihuahua hopped into the passenger seat as Cassidy buckled in. On the way home, her phone blew up, with a continuous series of pings. Resisting the urge to check the string of texts, she sped along the open country road, taking pleasure in navigating the curves, and pulling through the Celebrations wrought-iron gate in record time. Elvis danced in his seat as she paused to check the texts from the Pearly Girls that seemed to have multiplied during the short ride home.

The gist of the long discussion was that appetizers and drinks had led to another yarn-bombing expedition. Ruthanne and Aileen were leading the charge to decorate a senior facility for fall over in Mint Springs. *I guess their secret's all over social media, so they aren't sneaking around anymore and trying to hide their identities. From the pictures, it looks like they were having a party and recruiting more knitters for future escapades.*

Cassidy smiled and helped Elvis out of the Jeep. Not yet ready to head inside, he led her on a jaunt to the garden's koi pond. Cassidy stood by the wedding arch and watched the sun drop behind trees on the ridge across the valley. The sky's orangey reds turned a purply gray color, and the night sounds took over the garden as a cool breeze rustled through the trees.

"Come on, Elvis. It's getting chilly, and we've got some work to do."

Inside her apartment, Cassidy streamed some smooth jazz and settled at her dining-room table. The dueling mysteries in her head battled for her attention. Detective Zac didn't share much information, per usual. *He likes to play it close to his bulletproof vest. Now I want to know where he went in such a hurry. Maybe he got a lead on the murders.*

While her laptop booted, she pulled out her folder and spread the contents across the table. Hopping up, she rummaged through her desk drawer for a stack of colorful sticky notes and a black Sharpie. "Elvis, I think I need to see a visual to make some connections."

Not interested in the neon notes or the details of the murders, Elvis curled up on the couch for an after-dinner nap.

Cassidy spent several hours making a column of facts for Britt, and one for Darcy. As in life, Britt's space stood out front and center with twice as many colored squares. Most of what she found online for Darcy were her professional credits, work at *The Washington Post*, and a couple of online magazines. She had also authored two nonfiction books. Cassidy couldn't find anything related to her life in Ivy Springs, though. Her biography appeared to have been carefully crafted and focused exclusively on her credentials. No mention of any kind of a social life or her earlier days growing up in the valley.

An idea flashed in her head, and she pulled up a website she had used last summer that had digitized versions of high school yearbooks. A couple of clicks later, she was thumbing through four years' worth of Ivy Springs High School digital yearbooks.

Time flew by as she got lost in the years of photos and a parade of memories. Cassidy stood and stretched to ward off the kinks when her back started to ache. She hadn't uncovered anything unexpected in the pages and pages of candid photos and school pictures. Darcy didn't appear very frequently, only in shots for the school newspaper and the drama club. Britt and Kelly were everywhere, and Anastasia seemed to worm her way into all the cool kid pictures, but she was always on the fringes. From her body language in the shots, it always looked like she was never truly part of the group.

"Hmm. Elvis, Anastasia either was a lucky late bloomer, or she had a good plastic surgeon." Her nose, mouth, and chin had been sculpted by her junior year, and she had dropped at least twenty pounds and lost the glasses and braces. "Interesting. The brassy hair color and style are the same."

After a few more clicks, she had a few things to add to Anastasia's section of the dining-room wall. Cassidy stood back and stared at the rainbow wall that was three-quarters covered with neon stickies. Anastasia's father was a doctor, and her mother was a real-estate agent. She had been immersed in dance, horseback riding, and cotillion since elementary school. After college, she had moved back in with her parents and stayed put in one of the old Victorians a block or so from Main Street. She had never married.

Staring at the wall of notes made Cassidy feel like her eyes were full of sand. Switching gears, she googled her grandfather's honky-tonk, hoping to find something new about her own little mystery.

Buried on the fourth or fifth page of search results, Cassidy found a link to a book about the musical history of Virginia, and the Ivy Springs tonk was mentioned. She let out a little squeal, and Elvis raised both ears.

A surge of excitement spread through her like a shot of tequila. Cassidy downloaded the ebook and scoured the index. The author had an entire chapter on musical traditions along the I-81 corridor, and there were photos of the old wooden structure and one of a band on stage inside the old bar. Another photo showed her great-grandfather, grandfather, and a young Levi posing next to the steps of the wooden building that looked more like a cabin. "Elvis, I'm going to order a hardcover version of this for our lobby. I don't think I've ever seen photos like these before. Come to think of it, my grandparents never talked much about the bar or had any photos around. I remember seeing the charred remains in the woods. The site always had the feel of one of those abandoned places."

She reread the chapter about the Blue Ridge Mountains twice. The author noted that her grandfather's bar was destroyed by fire, and the owners chose not to rebuild. *So, nothing new here, but the photos are cool.*

Cassidy heard a noise outside, and she jumped. Elvis let out a little growl, but he curled back up on the couch when nothing materialized. She paused and tiptoed toward the kitchen window. "I don't see anything, Elvis. Maybe it was the wind. We should turn in. Falling asleep at the dining-room table is not good for my neck or back." She rolled her shoulders and head as she checked the door and flipped off all the lights.

Lying in bed, sleep evaded her. She stared at the pitch-black darkness with only a sliver of light in the tiny gap between the curtains and the window. Thoughts of the murders and the list of suspects kept creeping into her subconscious. *Zac said Darcy was killed first. Someone or several someones killed her and found the hiding place under the loft. Then someone killed Britt, and the killer left the knife under the carpet where we found her. But it was after the police had already investigated. And Darcy's car key and other stuff were found in the garden. Anastasia said the knife belonged to Britt's ex-husband.* Cassidy made a mental note to talk to Mac again. *Was it one or two killers?* That question danced around the edge of her thoughts. *Could one person kill them and then move the bodies without any help?* Both mysteries muddled together in her head. *How did the police handle multiple cases at the same time and keep all the facts straight and still manage to get to sleep at night?*

Cassidy tossed and turned for hours and then woke with a jolt. The sun's rays streaked across the ceiling and the wall opposite her bed. "Elvis, did you hear something?" The mighty mite of a dog yawned and rolled over. "Maybe I was dreaming again. Okay, today let's see what some of my sources in town are saying about the murders. Then I'm going to check in at the library to see what they have in their files about the fire. This is a small town. Somebody has to know something."

She double-timed her morning routine, found a casual outfit, fed Elvis, and slipped on her tennis shoes for his morning walk to greet the koi. Elvis stretched his outside time into a tour of the grotto, cave, and a lap around the barn. All was quiet around the property. Thankfully, the only things they spotted were some new fall flowers and a couple of birds.

Cassidy finally persuaded Elvis to return to the apartment. As he settled in, she grabbed her keys and purse and fired off a quick text to the Pearly Girls and Levi that she'd be in the office after lunch. That started a flood of responses about what the gals were each up to, which Cassidy decided she would take the time to read later in favor of getting her own day started.

She rolled down her windows and cranked up an oldies station in the Jeep. The crisp morning air smelled good. Cassidy had missed the fresh, mountain scents when she lived in the city. Actually, she was so busy there that she hardly ever noticed the breeze, sunshine, or even the changing of the seasons. *I'm glad to be back in Ivy Springs. The mountains feel like they're part of my DNA.*

Finding parking in the free lot next to the Baptist church, Cassidy hoofed it around the corner to her first stop, Brew'd Awakening. Her quest today required a heavy dose of caffeine and sugar.

Marcie Chen looked up from behind one of her coffeemakers that spewed steam into a small cloud. "Good morning, Cassidy. You're out and about early this morning. What can I get for you?" she asked with a happy wave.

"Everything looks wonderful." Cassidy glanced at the glass case full of breakfast delights. "How about a vanilla bean iced latte and one of those apple turnovers?"

"Great choice," Marcie said. "Mom pulled the pastries out of the oven just a few minutes ago."

Before Cassidy could ask Marcie any questions, Deannie Sullivan, owner of Bearly Collectibles across the street, sidled up to the counter. "Hey, y'all. Good morning. Cassidy, how are things at your place? I heard about what happened. How awful. Are you and the gals okay?" She wiggled with an exaggerated shiver. "Sorry to bring up dark thoughts and the murders," she whispered. Before anyone could comment, Deannie continued, "Hey, Marcie, can I have one of your killer dark roasts and a fudge tart? Oooh, I guess my choice of adjectives wasn't the best. Sorry."

"Be right up. Here you go, Cassidy," Marcie said, handing her a white bag and her iced coffee.

Deannie looked over her shoulder and around the store to see who else was around. "The deaths of Darcy and Britt were shocking. Britt was a regular in my store. She collected the Boyds Bears figurines, so she was in whenever the new shipments arrived. I'll miss chatting with her about her collection."

"Anybody know Darcy?" Cassidy asked, hoping for any tidbit she could find.

Both women shook their heads. "She had already moved away by the time I got here. I heard snippets about her from time to time. The town's proud of their famous journalist," Marcie said, handing Deannie a steaming cup of coffee and a paper bag.

Sensing that the conversation had run its course, Cassidy waved to Marcie and made her way out, with Deannie on her heels. Their paths diverged on the sidewalk, and Cassidy found an empty bench across from A Novel Idea to enjoy her breakfast. Cars drifted by on their way into town, and a couple of joggers and dog-walkers passed by. Everyone smiled and waved a greeting. *Not like mornings in a busy city where everyone was in a constant rush all the time.*

After the last bite of the gooey breakfast treat, she wiped her fingers on a napkin and found a nearby trash can. On a whim, she doubled back and opened the heavy oak doors of the bookstore, bells jingling to announce her arrival. Cassidy breathed in the smell of books. A sense of wonder and peace spread through her. The store, filled with rows and rows of floor-to-ceiling shelves, had books and gifts on every available flat surface.

"Hey, Cassidy," Ahni Rao called from somewhere in the store.

"Good morning, Ahni. Where are you?" Cassidy craned her neck down several aisles, looking for the owner with the lilting voice.

"Back here in Romance. We got a big order in, and I'm restocking."

Cassidy made her way around bookcases and found the petite woman stacking new releases on a nearby shelf. "There you are. I couldn't see you from up front."

Ahni laughed. "Don't think I'm clairvoyant. I can see the front of the store in those." Ahni pointed to the mirrors in the corners. Dusting her hands off on her jeans, she continued, "There. I think that looks pretty good. Romance is always popular. Hopefully, they won't be on my shelves long. What can I do for you?"

"I wanted to see what you had in your Local History section," Cassidy said, flipping through some of the new titles.

"Over there. Second shelf by the front window. Left side." Ahni pointed down the aisle. "They sell well to the tourists. Help yourself, and holler if you need anything. If you don't find something you're interested in, I can always order it for you."

"Thanks. I'm doing some research on Ivy Springs," Cassidy said, heading to the front of the store where Ahni had pointed.

About ten minutes later, the storekeeper popped her head around the corner. "Finding everything okay?"

"Yes, thanks. I was looking to see what I could find on my family's old honky-tonk."

"Make sure you check the library's History room. They have a really good collection. I used it when I was doing some deed research," Ahni said.

"That's my next stop. I'll take this one about the musical history of the area and this one about haunted places in the Blue Ridge Mountains," Cassidy said, handing her the two paperbacks and her debit card.

Ahni tapped on her tablet and scanned the card. When the device beeped, she offered Cassidy the card and a "Read Banned Books" paper bag full of her purchases.

"Thanks. Take care." Cassidy pushed on the front door, and the bells on the handle jangled again. Shakespeare, the fluffy store cat, darted out between two shelves, startling Cassidy. "Hey, baby. I didn't know you were nearby. It's good to see you." She leaned over and stroked the Persian's neck as he wound between her legs.

Ahni's cheerful laugh drifted through the store. "He's my greeter. Though he often slacks off on his duties. He has several secret napping nooks in the stacks. Come back and see us soon."

Deciding to leave the Jeep where it was, Cassidy walked down the street and around the corner to the library. A crowd of about ten people stood outside the large glass doors. Checking her Fitbit, she saw she had about ten minutes to kill before the doors opened, and, knowing Marion, the head librarian, it would open precisely on time.

Scrolling through her Instagram feed, Cassidy paused on photos of the gals decorating the senior center. Cassidy smiled. She pocketed her phone when Marion unlocked the door and welcomed the people inside who had been waiting on the sidewalk. Since no patrons gathered around the desk, Cassidy stepped in front of Marion's space. "Good morning. Ruthanne suggested that I pop in. I'm doing some research on my granddad's honky-tonk, and she said there may be something in the archives here."

"And she's right. We have lots of things on our local history. And thanks to your grandparents, who were huge patrons, we had the funding for the conference center and the local history program. Your granddad even donated some photos to the collection. Here, let me show you."

Cassidy followed the woman in the crepe-soled shoes, dodging carts, small children, and bookcases as she threaded her way to the back of the building. Marion flipped the lights on and ushered Cassidy into a smallish room with microfiche readers and three computers lining each wall. "Over the years, volunteers have digitized our collection, so start here on the computer. It's like any other search engine. Kate and Aileen said you were a technology whiz. Call me if you have problems, but I'm sure you'll have no trouble with the software. You can print copies over there of anything you want to keep."

"Thanks so much for all of your help. You mentioned their donation. I found a reference in old ledgers about it, but no other details. I'm curious. When did this happen?"

Marion beamed. "I've been here almost forty-three years, and that was one of the most exciting times. It was fun to be a part of the new library project. Your grandparents made a huge donation, and the town was so grateful. We wanted to name the building after them, but your grandparents were so humble and wanted to fly under the radar, so we didn't make a fuss. But come here," she beckoned her with a little wave like she was giving her a secret signal.

Cassidy tentatively followed the librarian to the inside of the large conference room. "We wanted to honor them and their wishes, so everyone settled on this." She pointed to a small bronze plaque above the door. "They didn't want anything fancy."

"I've never noticed that before," Cassidy said, as a warm feeling radiated through her. "That is so nice. I had no idea." She pulled out her phone and snapped a picture of it for her collection.

"I'll be at the desk if you need anything during your research." Marion waved her hand and hustled back toward the stacks.

Cassidy wiped away a tear that leaked out and hurried over to start her search. She plunked down in a wooden chair and opened the search window. *What a gold mine!* She ended up printing twenty-five pages of articles and photos of her grandfather's place.

Her stomach rumbled, reminding her that it was past lunchtime. Gathering her things, she decided on a quick stop to grab some lunch before heading back. Elvis and the gals were probably wondering what had happened to her. *I don't quite have the whole picture yet, but many of the pieces are starting to fill in some of the blank spaces.*

14

TUESDAY AFTERNOON

After running her errands in town, Cassidy took a break to eat her sandwich in the Jeep. When her phone beeped with three rapid text alerts, she wiped her hands and glanced down at the screen. Austin. *That's odd. We don't have any scheduled events until the weekend.*

> The police are here. They want me to come down to the station.
> For questioning about the two dead women. I texted Annie, but she didn't respond.
> Can you find her? I have no idea why they want to talk to me. Not a good way to start my day.

I'll see if I can reach Annie. Do you need a lawyer? Cassidy asked. *It's almost twelve-thirty. Had he just woken up?*

She waited for what felt like many, painfully slow minutes, but received no response to her question. Starting the vehicle, she told her phone to call Annie. After three rings, she heard a faint "Hello. Annie's Eats."

"Annie, it's Cassidy Jamison. I got a text from Austin. He said the police want him to go to the station for questioning, and he couldn't reach you."

"Oh, my stars. It's because I'm out here near Berryville at a job, and the cell coverage is spotty. Crud. I can't leave. I'm the only one here, and this lasts until three. This is not good. What would they want with him? All he does is work, eat, and sleep. He never causes any trouble." Her voice rose several octaves as she continued to talk.

"Don't panic yet," Cassidy said. "It might be nothing. I can run over to the police station and see what's going on. Not sure if they'll let me see him or not. Maybe they only have some more questions for him. I'll fill you in as soon as I know something," she said, balling up her sandwich wrapper.

"You're the best! I can't thank you enough. Text me the minute you talk to him. I hate not being there to help him," Annie said.

"Will do. Don't worry until we know something." Cassidy clicked the disconnect button. She could feel her heart pounding in her temples. *Why Austin? From what I can tell, he worked hard the entire time the reunion was going on.*

A murky thought crossed her mind and sent a shiver down her spine. *Was there something deep-seated that I missed about him? Here I am, almost ready to hire him for the new project. Okay, get a grip, girlfriend. Your mind is going to the dark side. The police could just want to ask him some questions. Trust your instincts.*

She let out a long breath and put the Wrangler in gear. She headed two blocks over to the sheriff's office, but finding parking at the government center at lunchtime took longer than the entire ride. She hustled to the front door of the brick building with the wavy nineteen-sixties awning over the sidewalk. She took a couple of deep breaths to calm down before she pulled on the glass door. The faint scents of antiseptic and burnt coffee tickled her nose when she stepped inside. Hoping her hair wasn't wild from the drive over, she patted it down and steeled herself for her mission.

She pulled out her phone and scrolled through Instagram to distract herself from her anxious thoughts as she waited for the line to inch forward to the information desk. When it was finally her turn at the counter, Maura Tinsley, a deputy who Cassidy remembered from high school, said, "Hey, Cassidy, it's good to see you. It's been a minute, hasn't it? How can I help you?" Maura pushed a strand of dark curls out of her eyes.

"It's good to see you too. I didn't know you worked at the sheriff's office."

"Three years. I came over here from the tax office. It's way more interesting over here. You never know what's going to walk through the door," Maura said with a wink. "What brings you by?"

"My friend, Austin Taylor, was brought in for questioning. His sister is out of town, and she asked me to stop by and check on him."

"Austin. Oh, yes. He came in an hour or so ago. He's in the back. I'm sure he's fine. Sheriff Howell is with him," Maura said with a slight smile.

"Is Detective Turner available?"

"Let me check. Last I saw of him, he was in the interview room too." Maura cradled the phone's receiver with her shoulder and punched several buttons. "I'm sorry. He's not answering. He's probably tied up. Do you want to leave a message?"

"Maybe I'll wait a bit and see if I can catch him when he's done." Cassidy chewed on her bottom lip.

"Okay, but it could be a while. His meetings are looooong, and if he's not here, then he's always out on the road. He's hard to catch," Maura said, shifting red folders on her desk.

Settling in a plastic chair next to a side table full of outdated magazines with crinkled covers, Cassidy sat so she could see the office area behind Maura and the door.

Scrolling through the major news sites and the local ones, she read all the stories she could find on Darcy and Britt. Not surprisingly, Darcy's death got more coverage than the former cheerleader, even on the local sites.

By the time she had shifted in the chair for the fiftieth time, she heard a "Cassidy, what are *you* doing here?" from across the room. Zac, with a coffee mug in his hand, covered the distance between them in a few strides. "I didn't expect to see you here. You okay?"

"I'm fine. I got a text from Austin, Austin Taylor. His sister Annie is my caterer, and she's out of town and very concerned about her brother. She asked me to stop by and check to see if he needed anything." *Like a lawyer.* She paused to stop herself from babbling and drew a long breath in through her nose, hoping that would calm the staccato beat of her heart.

Zac's bright grin faded like the sun when storm clouds roll in, and she couldn't tell what was going on behind those hazel eyes. After an uncomfortably long pause, he said, "We had some questions we needed his help on. He'll be out soon. Nothing to worry about."

A wave of relief rushed over her. *Okay, so Austin's not under arrest. And it sounds like he'll be free to go soon.*

The detective, now in his stern business mood, stared at her.

"Oh, that's good. Annie will be glad to hear it. I guess I'll wait here until he comes out to see if he needs a ride."

Without another word, the detective nodded and headed for the door to the back offices.

Well, that was a little weird. He went from friendly to Oscar the Grouch in less than two seconds. Shaking off the exchange with the detective, she texted Annie with what she knew and promised a follow-up when she had more information.

She waited about another hour until the door opened and Austin stepped out into the waiting room. "Hey, I didn't expect to see you here," he said.

"I talked to Annie, and she's up in Berryville. She asked me to see what I could find out about why you're here and let her know. Are you okay? What did they want to know?" she whispered.

"Oh, yeah. Fine. The sheriff and Zac had some questions about the two murders and what I'd seen at your place. Have you had lunch yet? I'm starving. I missed breakfast."

Cassidy nodded. "I have, yes. But if you want to grab something, I could get something to drink."

"Cool. Let's go see if Marcie has any sandwiches left." He held the glass door for her. "My car is over there. You want to meet at the coffee place?" *I guess the police let him drive himself in. They weren't looking to take him into custody. That's good news.*

"See you in a bit." Cassidy headed for her Jeep and another trip to Main Street.

After finding a seat at a small table in the corner, Cassidy took a sip of her iced chai and looked across at Austin, who pulled off his sunglasses and set them on the table. "So, what exactly did the police ask you?" she asked.

"They had a lot of questions about Britt and Darcy. And they wanted to know what I remembered about both of them last weekend—like who they were hanging around with, if I ever saw Darcy with Vince, and if anyone had any altercations with the victims. They also asked a fair number of questions about Mac. I don't remember ever talking to him. Maybe I got him a drink. I don't remember."

Cassidy leaned forward, waiting for more details. After a long pause, she asked, "Well, did you have answers for them?"

"Not really. I had a couple of conversations with Darcy and several with Britt. She hung around the bar more. I didn't think any of the convos were that big of a deal. They were mostly about their drinks or the weather.

"There was one thing the detective seemed to be interested in.

One time, Britt and Darcy were at the bar with some other women. Britt and her bunch did most of the talking. Then the chatter stopped, and they all left, one after the other. Not to go back to their seats or something. They all took off out the main doors, but they went individually. It was like about five minutes apart. It caught my eye, and I remember watching them all slip out like they were waiting their turn to be the next to leave. It looked odd. It was like Darcy, that guy Vince, Britt, and some other gal were all leaving, but they didn't want to be seen together."

Cassidy furrowed her brow. "So, explain that again."

"It was like they were together, but not really. I remember seeing Darcy pick up her purse and head out the barn doors, and Vince was minutes behind her. Then the other blonde woman on the reunion committee ran over to Britt, and they had a lively conversation, and then Britt flew out after them. The other woman waited a bit and then she left too. It was weird."

"Who was the other woman?" *Could that be the night Darcy went missing?*

"I dunno. She was blonde," Austin said, taking a bite of his pimento sandwich.

They're all blonde except Darcy. "If you think of who it is, let me know."

Glancing down at her phone, Cassidy noticed several missed texts. "It's Annie. I didn't send her an update." Slightly embarrassed that she had forgotten to respond, she tapped a quick text.

Thanks, popped up on her screen. **I haven't heard anything from Austin either. Tell him to check his phone.**

"She said to check your phone," Cassidy said.

He nodded and polished off his sandwich. "Yep, she's been blowing it up. I guess I should have told her I was done, but I was hungry. When I got the call, I wasn't sure why the sheriff's office needed me to come in. It turned out to be a big nothing. But they did tell me not to leave town." He shrugged and scrolled through his phone.

"I need to get back to work. I'm glad things worked out for you."

"Thanks for coming down here. I appreciate it," he said with his megawatt smile. "See ya around. Hopefully soon."

I'm glad he wasn't called in for more than a few questions—but they still told him not to leave town.

15

"Cassidy, you got a minute?" Levi asked, knocking the dirt and grass off his boots on the mat at the back door.

"Hey, Levi. I haven't seen you in a while. How are things?" Ruthanne asked, stacking the old ledgers in a pile on the desk. "Cassidy, I'm taking these to storage. I didn't find out anything else about the fire."

Levi looked surprised for an instant and then changed the subject. "Vern stopped by with his proposal. He got it back quicker than I expected, so I flipped through it. I think you'll be pleased." He handed her a manila folder, and she thumbed through the stapled pages until she got to the total cost.

"This is interesting. His projected numbers for all the construction aren't anywhere near what I thought they'd be." She sank in her chair and scrutinized the drawings he had included.

The bells on the front door jangled, and Elvis yipped and tore through the office to greet Roxie, Aileen, and Kate.

"Whatcha looking at so seriously?" Roxie asked, dropping her purse and an old photo album on the table.

"Vern brought over his estimates and plans for the cave," Cassidy replied.

The three huddled behind her, staring over her shoulder. "So, what's the total damage to move forward?" Kate asked.

Before Cassidy could reply, Ruthanne breezed back in. "Oooh, what's everyone so interested in? Let me see." She and Elvis scooted closer for a better look.

"The plans for the new venue. This is so cool. Can you imagine going to a show in a cave. I can't wait. The acoustics will be faaaaaaabulous," Aileen said.

"Your grandparents never knew what to do with it. Evelyn said your grandfather wanted to turn it into a tourist attraction for cave tours, but it wasn't as deep or spooky as some of the others in the area, and it never seemed profitable or the right time to do it," Kate said.

"Plus, there are so many other caverns around with stalagmites and stuff that are more interesting. This one just looks like an underground room with rocky walls," Ruthanne said. "But lucky for you, that is perfect for what you want to do with it."

"We could do an epic Halloween party down there," Roxie added with a wink.

"Levi, if this is a firm estimate, I think it's doable. Ruthanne, what do you think? Now, we would have to spread out the payments," Cassidy said, staring at the stack of papers in front of her.

Straightening her reading glasses, Ruthanne peered over Cassidy's shoulders. "Hmm. That's definitely doable. That's a good bottom number. I'm pleased as punch. When you said you wanted to do this, I thought it was going to be a multimillion-dollar project. This is relatively affordable. And it wouldn't take long to recoup the costs if you can keep it booked. I can do a quick projection for you if you want an idea."

Cassidy nodded. "Yes, please. That would give me some targets. And if I can land one or two more of those music tours, we'd have a nice nest egg for the project," she said, tapping her bottom lip with her finger.

Levi nodded. "It's a very clean site. The biggest expenses will be the air-filtration system and the add-ons for the bathrooms and the entrance. I think we can do this, gals."

"Okay," Cassidy said. "Quick vote based on what we've seen here. Do we move forward?"

All hands shot in the air. "Elvis votes *yes* too," Aileen added, picking him up and waving one of his little paws in the air.

"Then it's unanimous. Levi, could you let Vern know to send over the contract and the rest of the paperwork? I'll get the lawyer to take a look at it, and we should be good to go. We'll have to come up with a timeline. I don't want the construction to affect any of the events we've already scheduled."

"Will do," Levi said. "We can contain it to that side of the property. It won't affect the garden, barn, or amphitheater. We'll need to do some landscaping and decide if you want a path from the current parking lot or not. You'll need a maintenance road somewhere for deliveries."

"Levi, you're on a roll," Aileen said. "This is so exciting."

"We need a cool name for the place," Kate said. "This is going to be such a popular addition to the property."

"So true," Roxie said. "Who else can provide a cave for someone's next shindig? You'll be the talk of the valley. Oh, I went through my old photo albums last night, and I found some of the honky-tonk if you want to borrow them."

The small crowd around Cassidy's desk moved to the table as Roxie flipped through the old photos, many in black and white that had yellowed with age.

"Oh, look. There's Jack and Evelyn in front of the infamous bar," Aileen said.

"Cassidy, you look like your grandma in this one," Ruthanne said, pointing to another photo of Evelyn in a swing.

"And there's Roxie with Willie Nelson and George Strait. Is that Glen Campbell? Look how young they look. Oh, look: the Polaroids are starting to fade," Aileen said.

"Oh, my stars, that's Roxie with Conway Twitty, and John Denver's in this one. They look so handsome. Wow. This is going down memory lane. And there's Waylon Jennings." Ruthanne bounced up and down and pointed.

"These are great," Cassidy said. "They'll help with the theming of the new venue. You're right, we need to give it a fun name. And we need to work on some design themes."

"How about The Underground?" Kate asked. "That could be a little nod to the bootlegging that went on around here, too. Or what about The Lair?"

"How about The Abyss?" Roxie asked.

"I like them. Let's start a list, and we'll see which one grows on us," Cassidy said, mulling over the names in her head. *The Lair's catchy, but The Abyss has a mysteriously dangerous vibe to it. Should I have an Abyss right next to the serenity garden?*

"I'll leave the photo album here. Gals, go look through your stuff and see what pictures you have of the old place," Roxie said. "We'll get on some design ideas. There is so much we can do with the past and the present. And all the loot Levi found in the barn."

"I think it would be neat if you could give new life to the stuff we found," Levi added.

"We need to go through all those crates and see what we have for decorations," Kate said. "We'll come up with some color ideas. I think you should go modern with the furnishings and vintage with all the memorabilia."

"This'll be as cool as the Batcave," Ruthanne said. "Too bad that's probably trademarked. That would be a neat name."

Cassidy laughed. "I want to tie into the history of the property." Her thoughts flitted to the honky-tonk and then the fire. That whole story still bothered her. She cleared her throat and asked the question that had been niggling at her brain for a while: "While you all are here, can you fill me in on some things about the old place? I have some questions."

"We'll try. We were wee children during its heyday; by the end, we'd all gotten married and started having kids. Plus, our mothers didn't like us hanging out there," Aileen said.

"But we did anyway," Roxie whispered gleefully.

"But we weren't regulars," Kate added, her glance darting from Roxie to Levi. Ruthanne looked at something on the counter while Aileen twisted a button on her blouse.

What are they not telling me? "Well, what else?"

"Not much to tell," Ruthanne said. "We were all sad when it closed for good."

"I always hoped it would reopen," Aileen said.

"It was about the only place to go to see good live music in a tri-county radius," Kate added. "It'll be nice to bring that back. I mean, your concerts in the amphitheater are fun, but this will be more intimate and a definite nod to the past. I'm enchanted with the whole idea of using a cave."

I might as well ask. They're beating around the bush and trying to telepathically send some message to each other. Here goes. Let's talk about the elephant in the room. "Okay, but one thing doesn't make sense to me. If it burned down in an accident, why was all the stuff stored in the barn before it could be destroyed?"

The conversation came to a grinding halt, and everyone stared at his or her hands or shoes. The silence, which probably only lasted a few seconds, was deafening and felt like an eternity.

Elvis broke the spell when he jumped at Levi's pant leg. The groundskeeper leaned over and picked him up. He looked around at each Pearly Girl.

"Go ahead, Levi. Spill it, and we'll fill in what we know," Roxie said in a low tone.

Kate let out a long "pffffft" sound as she sank into one of the chairs in the kitchenette.

Levi patted Elvis's head and stared off into the distance. After another long silence, he finally said in a soft voice, "Your grandfather got some news from the doctor. It wasn't great, but they said they could do treatments over in Staunton." He patted Elvis again. "He and your grandma decided they were going to close the tonk down. He told everyone he was closing for renovations to the place. Just temporarily, until they could figure out how his treatments were going. I think he always had hope that he'd get better, but he was sick for a long time. He was in remission a couple of times, but that danged cancer kept coming back. Your grandmother was really worried about him, and she didn't want him to have the added stress of running the bar while he was recovering."

Levi paused. Before anyone could comment, he continued. "Your granddaddy and grandmom packed up the memorabilia and pulled out the bar. He loved everything about that place—all the signatures on the bar, the old photos, and all the good memories. He was going to store it until he figured out what he wanted to do next. It was a strange time. I never asked him what he did with all of it, and he and your grandmother never talked any more about it. I thought it had gotten lost or forgotten as time passed."

Cassidy was on the edge of her chair. She had known about the cancer, but this was news to her. Thoughts of an intentional fire were dancing around the edge of her consciousness. *Please let it not be true. There were charred remains on the property, so there was definitely a fire.*

Mentally willing him to continue his story, she locked eyes with Levi. Finally, he added, "Your grandpa left it closed for a couple of weeks. He thought the renovation story would buy him some time in case circumstances changed. But it was summer, and we had a bad string of thunderstorms. One hot and stormy night, the place got hit by lightning, and it caught fire. There was nothing anybody could do. Back then, all we had was the volunteer fire department and one truck. That building went up like matchsticks before anyone was roused out of bed to notice it." Levi paused and patted Elvis again. "He was sick for a long time. The cancer and the fire changed everything."

"The chemo worked off and on, but he battled several rounds of cancer over the next few years," Kate said.

"He was never his old self," Levi said. "He was tired all the time. And he didn't want to rebuild if he couldn't give it his all."

Kate patted Cassidy's shoulder. "Your grandparents were torn about the insurance money. The building and the kitchen stuff did burn in the fire, but he didn't feel right about keeping the money when he had already decided to shut it down."

"It was about the same time that the town decided to build the new library, so Evelyn and Jack gave the insurance money to the building fund," Aileen whispered.

"I found the entries for the donation," Ruthanne said, glancing at her desk where the stack of ledgers had been.

"And Marion showed me the little plaque at the library," Cassidy added.

The Pearly Girls nodded. "Jack didn't want to be recognized for it," Roxie said. "But after he died, the library committee finally got Evelyn to agree to the token of remembrance. They deserved it. They made it possible for Ivy Springs to have a nice library."

"Your grandparents were instrumental to the expansion," Aileen said. "Back then, things were tight all over these parts. That money made a difference in so many lives in this town. Look at how popular our library is," she said, glancing down at the photo album. "So, you should be proud. Not only were they integral to the music scene around here, they also made the library and its resources available to everyone."

Cassidy closed her eyes for a moment. The warmth of knowing what had happened and what her grandparents had done surged through her. Then the sadness of how it all had ended dampened her mood. *Well, one mystery solved, and at least it wasn't something nefarious.* Her eyes fluttered open.

"How come no one remembered all the stuff being saved from the honky-tonk?" Cassidy asked.

"Life got busy. Nobody talked about it, so it kinda faded into the background," Levi said quietly.

"I didn't know it was packed up," Ruthanne said. "I thought it all burned."

"Plus, your granddaddy was sick, and people were worried about him. They weren't talking about the bar," Kate said.

"This seems like fate. I guess we have no choice. I say we move forward with the cave project and incorporate the saved stuff into the designs," Cassidy said.

A loud whoop went up from the gals, and Levi smiled, setting Elvis on the floor. The little dog joined in the festivities, excited about whatever everyone else was cheering about.

Not wanting to ruin the moment, Cassidy weighed the last question that was niggling at the back of her brain. When the gang paused from cheering and dancing, she ventured, "There's one more thing I've been thinking about."

"What?" Ruthanne rushed over and patted her on the back. "You look really intense."

"Levi, Austin, and I were in the barn's root cellar, the day before you all came down and we found Darcy. How did we miss finding her that first time?"

Levi shrugged a shoulder. "The day we were there with Austin, we were so busy looking at that one crate and the bar top by the stairs. We didn't go over behind those other crates where she was."

"The day we were all there, I moved over to that back wall to see the other crates. That's when I spotted poor Darcy." Ruthanne shuddered and grabbed the chairback to steady herself.

"I think it's possible she might have been down there the whole time," Levi said quietly.

"I'll check the cameras again, but I didn't see anyone skulking around," Cassidy said.

Before Cassidy could continue, Detective Turner stuck his head in the doorway. "Sorry to interrupt, folks." The conversation ceased, and all eyes stared at the detective. "Good afternoon. Cassidy, the sheriff wants the forensic team to go through the garden and the barn again. Can you let us in? Not sure how long we'll be."

"I'm headed over that way. I can unlock it for you," Levi said.

When he disappeared through the back door, Roxie said, "Wonder what they're looking for this time?"

"I had an appointment this week at the beauty shop, and I heard some of the deets. Gloria said the police brought Vince and Mac in for questioning, and the sheriff worked them over pretty good. Earleen said she thought they were closing in on the murderer, and it might be more than one person." Aileen pursed her lips as her eyes widened.

"You can't believe all the chatter that gets stirred up in this town," Roxie said.

Ruthanne's hand shot to her mouth. "Do they really think one of Britt's husbands had something to do with the murders?"

Aileen shook her head. "Who knows, but they're looking for something." She pointed with both index fingers at the barn.

"Well, Detective Zac sure knows how to be a buzzkill," Roxie said, rolling her eyes. "I'm going to go play with some interior designs. I've never done any sketches for a cave before."

"I think we should try a bootlegging, rough-outlaw theme with an old country and western flair," Kate said.

The Pearly Girls gathered their sketch and design books and headed for the conference room.

"Oooh, we're going to outlaw country," Ruthanne said.

"It wouldn't be the first time," Roxie yelled from the other room.

Cassidy smiled and pulled up her camera app to see if she'd missed anything on the night Darcy disappeared.

16

THURSDAY MORNING

Cassidy grabbed a banana and a yogurt, stuffing them into her messenger bag as Elvis danced at the door. "Okay, let's go for your morning commute before we see what's shakin' in the office." Today, he led the way to the barn.

The weathered red dairy barn dominated the landscape, with the view of the valley behind it. *The mountains seem to go on as far as the eye can see.* She scanned the perimeter of the property and stared at the tree line. "Come on, Elvis. The reunion committee will be here later to set up for their big sock hop tomorrow. I hope they have more people show up than they did for the events last Sunday. This didn't quite turn out as Britt and her team had planned. And I never did get the chance to talk to Detective Zac before he left yesterday. I got so wrapped up in the brainstorming with the Pearly Girls about the new place that I lost track of time."

Thoughts of Britt and Darcy kept worming their way to the forefront of her mind. The plan was to settle in at her desk to get some real work done, like looking over the bookings they had for the rest of the year. But her afternoon took a U-turn when she pulled out her notes on the murders again. There may be some truth to what Aileen had heard at the beauty shop. What if the police were looking at key men in the women's lives? But what did Austin have to do with it, except that he was working all the events? And if it were Vince, why would he kill his wife *and* his girlfriend? That doesn't make sense. And then there's Mac, always the happy-go-lucky, good-time guy. *I don't think he has it in him to stab someone and then strangle his ex-wife. He was always the big man on campus in high school. What if the motivation for the murders wasn't love, but jealousy? That puts a whole new twist on things.*

"This is making my head hurt. Time for some caffeine." Cassidy filled Elvis's bowls and plunked a pod of something called Death-wish Coffee in the coffeemaker. *That should be potent enough to ward off the groggies.*

After the coffeemaker spewed out the last of the deep brown liquid, she added creamer and sugar. Stirring a little vortex in her mug, she debated about reaching out to Zac. "Here goes nothing." She pulled out her phone and tapped in a text to him. **Didn't see you all leave yesterday. How are things going?**

"See, Elvis? Nice and friendly. And it doesn't sound like I'm fishing for information or poking around in his investigation."

"But you probably are," Roxie said, making a beeline for the coffeemaker. "That blend smells good. Ruthanne said she ordered some different kinds of coffee from a new distributor. Oooh, Zombie Apocalypse. I'm going to try that one."

"I was checking in with the detective to see how it went yesterday. It's curiosity. Nothing more."

Roxie raised a perfectly arched eyebrow almost to her honey-colored bangs. "Sure. Whatever you say. You two need to stop dancing around it. Everyone around you two can feel the electricity between y'all. Except you two. Wake up and ask him out."

Cassidy could feel the warmth rushing to her cheeks. Luckily, at that precise moment, her phone alerted.

Distracted by the incoming text, she glanced down. **Meet me at the pizza place for lunch at 1? I've got some more questions.**

Leaning over her shoulder, Roxie said, "Of course you'll go. Lunch dates are always fun."

"He has some questions to ask me," Cassidy said, dismissing it as a date. "About the murders. It's business."

"Sure. You haven't figured out yet that he goes out of his way to find ways to talk to you? Call it what you want," Roxie said, waiting for the coffeemaker to stop hissing.

"He wants to know what information I've gleaned, mostly from the four of you. Y'all have way better social lives than I do."

"And that's precisely why you're going to meet him for lunch. You gotta start somewhere. And don't forget to hire that cute Austin for the underground bar. He'll make a great addition to the team." Roxie retrieved her mug and stirred in some creamer. "And it never hurts for interested gents to have a little competition." She winked and sauntered off to the conference room.

Cassidy nodded and tapped her reply to the detective. "It's just lunch," she yelled.

"Sure," Roxie yelled in a sing-song voice. "Sure," she called again from the front.

"It's a meeting that happens to be at lunch," she muttered to Elvis. He turned his head to the side and stared at her. "Not you too," she whispered, blowing a kiss to the chihuahua.

A little after twelve-thirty, Cassidy called out, "Roxie, I'm going to take Elvis home and head out soon."

"Okay, I'm almost done here. I'll lock up. Have fun on your date," Roxie called from the conference room.

"It's a professional meeting," Cassidy whispered again and gathered her things. After Elvis settled on the couch in her apartment, she changed outfits and touched up her hair and makeup. "It never hurts to look your best for a business meeting," she said to the mirror.

The trees flew by the car window on her way down the mountain. *Today must be my lucky day.* Cassidy pulled into a spot in front of Feeling Saucy. The lunch crowd had started to thin out, and there were plenty of on-street spaces and open tables on the patio. She hopped out of the Jeep and looked up and down Main Street. No sign of Zac yet.

When she opened the door to the family-owned pizzeria, garlic and other spicy smells tickled her nose and made her stomach growl.

"Hey, long time no see! What can I get you?" Sal Russo bellowed from behind the counter. The meatball of a man with tomato-sauce stains on his apron came around the counter. "Sit anywhere you like! Here's a menu."

"Can I actually get two?" she said, sitting in a booth. "I'm expecting a friend in a bit."

He raised one eyebrow. "Of course. Can I get you something to drink while you wait?"

"An unsweetened iced tea will be fine. No lemon."

"Be back in a flash." Sal hustled back to the kitchen and burst through the swinging door with enough force to leave it in motion for a few seconds after he cleared it.

Cassidy perused the menu and checked her Instagram feeds. She had moved on to Facebook by the time Zac slid into the booth across from her. "Sorry I'm late. An interview went longer than I expected."

"Hey, Zachary." Sal's voice boomed across the restaurant as he approached with Cassidy's drink. "What can I getcha?"

"I'll have a Coke with one of your loaded specialty pizzas. Pile as much as you can on it. The more, the better."

"You got it! And Miss Cassidy, who looks lovely this afternoon, by the way, what can I get for you?" Sal asked.

Cassidy could feel the warm flush in her cheeks. "Thanks. I'll have one of the personal pizzas with cheese and pepperoni."

"Perfect choice. And for you, I'll even make it with extra cheese. Be back before you miss me," Sal said, turning on his white sneakers that squeaked as he shuffled to the back.

After a long silence that felt like an eternity, Zac finally cleared his throat. "We finished at your place. I don't think forensics will need to come back, but I may have a couple of plainclothes officers there this weekend to see what's going on during the rest of the reunion events." He glanced up at her and replied quickly, "Don't worry. They'll blend with the guests. And there shouldn't be any marked police cars in your lot."

Cassidy sat up straighter on her side of the booth. "Why?"

He looked at her over the red plastic rim of her cup. "Just to see what's going on."

"Who are you watching? I mean, should I be worried that someone on my property is dangerous? Do I need to warn my staff? Should I cancel the events?" She felt her heartbeat throbbing in her temples.

"You should always be vigilant and aware of your surroundings," he said.

He has his public-safety announcement memorized. "I try to be careful, but I don't want to put my staff and the caterers in any danger. Or any of my guests." She glared at him across the table.

"I don't think anyone is in any danger. We want to be on-site during the last of the events to see how people interact. That's all," he said in a low tone.

"Which people?" she said a bit too loudly. *What if I misjudged Austin? Was he overly anxious about the job? Did I get dazzled by his smile? Did I totally miss some serial-killer vibe? I'm usually a better judge of character than that. Or is it someone from the reunion? I feel like I constantly need to look over my shoulder.*

"We're only observing. It will be one of my female deputies and a state trooper. Nobody will stand out." Zac paused and waited for what seemed like forever. When she didn't respond, he added, "I wanted you to be aware that they are there. Again, we don't anticipate any issues. We are in the middle of ongoing investigations. Normal stuff in my world."

But not in mine. "Thanks. Should I be worried about Austin or any of the other vendors?" she whispered.

"I don't think so. We want to see some of Britt and Darcy's friends up close." He stopped abruptly and stared out the front window for what felt like another eternity.

Before Cassidy could think of something else to ask, he fumbled with his phone, scrolling through something. "Something interesting happened last night. Seems dispatch got a call about some vandalism about two o'clock this morning."

She knew she had a puzzled look on her face until he held up his screen. All the signs and fence posts in front of Sid Pro Quo's no-tell motel were covered with long knitted garlands.

Cassidy nodded her head. *The gals were at it again. What is it with this yarn-bombing?* Though it did improve the look of Sid's chain-link fence around the swimming pool that looked like a science experiment.

"Sid Proctor wasn't too happy. He thinks there's a menacing gang running around town creating havoc. He said he was going to press charges for trespassing. If you see any roving gang members, please pass the information along."

Cassidy opened her mouth, but closed it again when Sal approached with two steaming pizzas. "Right outta the oven," he said.

"Be careful: that cheese is molten. Let me know if youse guys need anything."

"Will do. Thanks. It looks delicious." Cassidy spread her napkin in her lap.

The conversation tapered off as Zac poked his pizza with a fork to release some of the heat. Cassidy dug into her food as soon as the steam had escaped the layer of thick cheese.

After two mini-slices, Cassidy slid her plate forward. "How was yours?"

"Good. I like the junk pizza. It gets unwieldy with all the toppings. But when it's a mess, it's good."

It's now or never. I need to prod a bit more about the investigation. Let's see if he shares anything. Swallowing hard to get rid of the lump in her throat, she asked again about her friends: "Are you all watching Austin and Annie?"

Zac's eyebrows furrowed, and his mouth turned into a straight line.

Afraid to poke him anymore, she counted to thirty. The silence and his stare were almost unbearable.

The detective stretched forward. "Right now, neither of them is on our radar. We're looking at close friends and acquaintances of the deceased. But that's not to share."

Surprised that she'd gotten that much information, Cassidy decided to try her luck again. "Did you find out how Britt died?"

He nodded slowly and paused.

She leaned forward, hoping he would continue.

He took a swig of his drink and swallowed slowly. "Darcy was stabbed with a knife. Probably the one you found in the barn near Britt, but we don't know for sure yet. The medical examiner is doing some final tests, but it looks like Britt was strangled with something like a belt or a strap."

Cassidy's mind immediately jumped to the murder of Johnny Storm last summer during the concert series and the awful way he'd been strangled with a garotte made from a bass string and a couple of drumsticks. *Poor Britt. And poor Darcy. Both murders felt personal, not something random. Someone was really angry at both of these women.*

From the moment she left the pizza parlor, Cassidy found herself replaying her conversation with Zac over and over in her head. *Austin's off the hook. Whew. A person of interest sounds so ominous. I think he'd be good for The Lair or The Underground, or whatever we call it.* But the thought of a killer still running around felt like a dark cloud hovering over everything.

Grounding herself, she pushed thoughts of the murderer out of her head. *Don't obsess about stuff you can't control.* Cassidy parked in the lot and hurried to her apartment with an armload of bags from her morning errands. At least her fridge and pantry would be stocked for a while. An empty spot in the back of the parking lot caused her to stop and do a double take. Darcy's car had finally been towed. Cassidy's light-as-a-feather feeling lost some of its altitude when her thoughts flicked again to Darcy and Britt. *Was there one murderer, or two? And why would someone kill them at a party? Maybe an opportunity had presented itself? Okay, time to look closer at the guests.*

After checking on Elvis and putting away the groceries, she changed into her sneakers and jog-walked to the barn. Fifties tunes drifted through the open doors.

Anastasia stood in a chair, pointing upward at a banner that two men were draping over the railing of the loft high above the dance floor. "Go up on that end. Up. Up. Up. That's better." She snapped her fingers and pointed left and then right.

Cassidy looked at the banner. "Rydell High"?

Anastasia paused with one arm in the air and turned to stare at her. "Like in *Grease*. We're recreating the sock-hop scene. It was Britt's favorite movie, so this will be a tribute to her. And it's perfect because it's full of all kinds of costume ideas." She stared at Cassidy like it was an obvious fact. Cassidy searched Google and thumbed through images of actors in 1950s costumes. Pompadours and ponytails.

Anastasia waved her arm and continued: "For my outfit, I nixed the Pink Ladies getup. I'm going with Sandy's catsuit from the carnival scene. Can't wait for everyone to see it. This is going to be a great event. The Pink Ladies remind me so much of our group. Speaking of that, ask the caterer if she has a fancier tablecloth for our memory table." Anastasia pointed over her shoulder. "And where is that caterer? She should have been here by now." Anastasia continued to shout instructions to the two men in the loft.

Cassidy wandered over to a small table near the door, where a tiny photo of Darcy with straight bangs and braces in a black plastic frame sat in the shadow of a 24 x 36 monstrosity with a gilded frame that looked like it came from Versailles. In the photo, which looked like an oil painting, Britt posed in her perky cheerleader outfit. Next to it were smaller framed photos of Britt with a cat and Britt being crowned homecoming queen.

"Don't you love it?" Anastasia said, almost skidding to a stop behind Cassidy. "I wanted to do some kind of tribute to our fallen sisters. I think it looks fabulous. Kelly got the photos of Britt. Though the table kinda looks empty on the other side. I should have gotten some of those battery-operated candles. Do you have any?"

"I'll see if we have any in the supply closet," Cassidy said, not making any effort to rush back to the office.

Kelly and two other women wandered over to the table and stepped closer to Anastasia. Kelly dabbed her eyes with a crinkled tissue.

"What a monstrosity of a picture," a woman in a form-fitting magenta top said, rolling her eyes.

Anastasia turned and stared daggers at her.

"What?" the woman asked. "I never knew people actually bought those giant portraits."

The third woman stared at her own baby-blue sweater and picked at some mysterious piece of lint.

Kelly opened her mouth but closed it again without commenting.

The eye-roller said, "Come on, Anastasia. I wasn't knocking your nice tribute table. It was just a comment about that." She pointed at the framed portrait on the easel. Changing the subject, she continued: "This area looks nice the way it is, but I think we need to move the DJ's table to have enough room on the dance floor for the dance-off."

"Good idea," Anastasia said. The sneer on her face softened. "Hey, I know what else we could add. Why don't we put the trophy for the contest winner on the table with the photos. That will complete the look. Plus, it's tall enough to balance out the picture frame." Anastasia rushed to the kitchen area and returned with a giant gold-colored statue with a pair of ballroom dancers perched on the top.

Cassidy's eyes widened, but she swallowed her comment about the humungous trophy. *I hope the winner's car is big enough to transport it home. Wow! Where would you put that?*

"There. That looks wonderful. Too bad we don't have Britt's tiara from homecoming. Maybe somebody can swing by the florist and get some white roses." Anastasia turned, as the eye-roller and the lint-picker scurried over to the loft before they were sent to town for flowers.

"Not sure we can get the right flowers on short notice. I think we need to focus on tonight's event. We need to set up the registration table," Kelly said. "And then someone should check on the caterer. She should have been here by now. She does know she's supposed to be here, right?"

"I'm on it," Anastasia said, twirling her finger in the air. "You. Can you check on those candles? They would be a nice touch."

"Sure," Cassidy said, following Kelly to the registration table.

"We're not doing the fancy name tags tonight." Kelly set a pack of "my name is" stickers and some black markers on the table. "Most of the folks took the printed ones home the first night, and they'll probably forget to bring them back. If they come back..." Her voice drifted off as she flipped through a folder. "This didn't turn out like any of us planned." When her voice quavered, she hurried off toward the restrooms.

Cassidy picked up the registration folder. *Bingo. A list of all the guests and checks by the names of those who attended last weekend.* She quickly snapped a photo of the four pages and pocketed her phone. *That's a start.* She returned the folder to the spot in front of the chair and straightened the tablecloth.

"Hey," Anastasia yelled from the kitchen. "Can I get some help in here? Now!"

Several of the committee members migrated toward the kitchen. "The caterer needs help unloading stuff. Let's get a move on and get this place ready for a party." Anastasia blew through the door and zipped around the main room, firing off orders to the DJ's assistant, who happened to walk into the wake of Hurricane Anastasia. "Heyyyyy," she yelled again. "Kelly, wasn't there supposed to be a photo booth tonight? Get on the phone and see where he is.

The guests will be here in an hour. Kelly. Kelllleeeeeeee! What is going on around here?"

Cassidy slipped out the main doors as Anastasia continued to bark orders to everyone in sight. Glancing at her Fitbit, she saw she had time to check on Elvis and grab something to eat before all the cool kids arrived for the party. She wondered how many T-Birds and Pink Ladies would show up. *I hope the Pearly Girls stop by. I'm sure they won't be able to resist the lure of a party and our own true-crime drama. If they do show up, I'm going to grill them about the decorations they left for Sid Pro Quo.*

About an hour later, the sun slipped behind the mountain ridge, and the sky turned from pinky orange to plum. Cassidy made her way to the barn, where Bill Haley and the Comets' "Rock Around the Clock" blared through the barn's main doors.

Inside, she stood behind the registration table, where the gal who'd rolled her eyes earlier sat filing her nails. Cassidy waved at the woman, who nodded slightly and continued to work on her nails.

Several couples and singles sat at three tables near the edge of the stage. About thirty people filled the cavernous barn, and that included the catering, photography, and DJ's staff. Kelly and her husband, dressed like bobby-soxers, stood next to the photo booth.

Cassidy followed the sounds of loud giggles to the bar, where the Pearly Girls, in their standard cashmere sweaters and pearls, surrounded Austin, in his black leather jacket and overly gelled pompadour.

"Oh, Austin, I want one of those pink lady drinks too," Ruth-anne said.

"Me too," Kate and Aileen added.

"And show us your Elvis moves. I want to record it this time," Roxie cooed, stirring her bubblegum-pink drink with a flamingo swizzle stick. "You've got the look and the moves down. Can you curl your lip?"

The DJ played "Jailhouse Rock," and Austin/Elvis did his best imitation of the King, which drew a group of mostly women to the bar. So far, Austin had provided all the evening's entertainment. Cassidy eased her way out of the knot of cheering guests and looked around for a quiet spot to lurk. A tap on her shoulder caused her to whirl around.

"Sorry. Didn't think you heard me when I called your name," Zac said. The detective, looking casual in his black jeans and an olive-green pullover with fresh-from-the-shower damp hair, stood next to her. The ends of his blondish hair curled up at the base of his neck. His gaze scanned the room repeatedly. *Always watching. Always the cop.*

Cassidy shook off the dreamy thoughts. "See anything noteworthy?" she asked, trying to figure out what had caught his attention.

"Your bartender can draw a crowd," he remarked. "He's good for business."

"He's got the Pearly Girls mesmerized."

"And they fit right in with their Jackie O and Audrey Hepburn duds," he said with a slight grin.

Before Cassidy could comment, Anastasia, in a black jumpsuit with huge lapels, rushed over. "Did you get those candles? The only ones I found in one of the drawers were birthday candles."

"No, I didn't have any of the battery-powered ones," Cassidy said. "We can't have real candles in here. It's against the fire code. I think your table looks nice as it is," she said, glancing over at the trophy.

Zac cut his eyes to the monster trophy and gaudy frame. He raised an eyebrow but didn't comment.

Before either of them could say anything, Anastasia interrupted again: "It's almost time for the hokey pokey. We have two dance instructors here who will be teaching old-timey dances from the fifties. It'll be like that old show *Happy Days*. Detective, you're welcome to join in the festivities." Her glance darted around like she was having difficulty focusing. "Enjoy yourselves. Cassidy, I told your staff over there to grab one of the tables. They seem to be the life of the party tonight. I am glad someone is having a good time." She turned on her red heels and tore off toward the stage, where she tripped over her own foot and stumbled. Catching herself, she wobbled for a second. Zac stepped forward to steady her, and she pulled away like his touch burned. "I've got this," she said, stomping off.

Cassidy raised both eyebrows. When Anastasia was out of earshot, she said, "Miss Independent. She took over after Britt's demise. Sort of."

"Sort of?" Zac's lips formed a straight line.

Cassidy lowered her voice. "I'm not sure she's having as much success. People tend to ignore her. She comes across as a screaming banshee sometimes. Britt was brash, but people looked to her as the leader even though she was not the kindest person around. I think Anastasia's main desire is to be popular, but for some reason she's always on the fringes of the group."

He nodded. "I need to go speak to the state trooper outside. See you before I leave."

"Save me a dance," she whispered to his back.

"I can arrange that," Roxie said.

Cassidy jumped, and she covered her mouth with her hand.

"Don't worry about it. Nobody except me heard you. He's cute, and you should ask him out. We can help nudge him along if you want," she said with a Cheshire Cat grin.

"Uh, no, thanks. I can manage," Cassidy said, hoping her cheeks weren't bright red.

"Like I said. We can move things along. That's our superpower. Hey, did you see Austin's Elvis moves? You have to hire that guy. He will be fabulous for the new venue. If you get tired of standing, come and join us over there. We've got a table front and center with the perfect view of the bar." Roxie pointed toward Austin with her blood-red manicured nail. She did a little finger wave that Austin returned with a grin.

"Thanks. I'll swing by." Cassidy glanced around to see if Zac had returned. *Lots of empty tables and no detective. I think the murders scared folks away.* She walked around the tables to find a good spot to watch the dance floor and the bar.

Around ten-thirty, the small crowd trickled out of the barn. The DJ continued to play party favorites in the hope of enticing the remaining few to wander out on the empty dance floor. The tall trophy stood guard with the garish frame on the tribute table. *I guess the dance-off was a bust.*

Giving up, the DJ started packing his gear, and so did Annie as Austin served the remaining guests at the bar. Within fifteen minutes, all the guests had left. Anastasia blew into the empty main room. "Has anyone seen Austin or Annie? Where'd they go? I thought everyone understood we stayed until midnight." She tore off in a walk-jog toward the DJ. "Are you packing up, too? You have not played all the sets I gave you."

He raised both hands like he was surrendering. "What? There's no one here."

"What did you say?" Anastasia screeched.

The DJ turned around and continued to pack his gear as Anastasia stomped her foot and caught the hem of her black pantsuit on her heel. After she spent several seconds yanking on the shoe, she finally freed it and stormed off toward the bar.

Within fifteen minutes, all the reunion folks had left the barn.

Kate and Aileen helped Cassidy check all the spaces to make sure there were no stragglers, and Ruthanne locked the doors.

Convening near the tables, Ruthanne asked, "Do we need to clean up anything?"

Cassidy shook her head. "Anastasia's crew will get their decorations later. We'll leave the chairs and tables in place. Hey, we get a little break tomorrow."

"No reunion events? That'll be nice," Kate said, dusting off her hands.

"All the events are in town or at the golf course tomorrow," Cassidy said.

"Maybe things will start getting back to normal. Did you see that photo of Britt?" Ruthanne asked.

Aileen smiled. "I hope Anastasia doesn't forget that giant portrait or the even bigger trophy. That reminds me, Britt used to give the school staff and faculty all autographed copies of her photos every year. But thankfully, none of the pictures were that size."

"Let's go, ladies. I say we call it a night. Everything that needs to be turned off is off," Kate said.

Cassidy followed them out the front and set the alarm. She trailed behind the Pearly Girls. "Where's Roxie?"

"She left with that retired teacher. They're headed over to the Grapes of Wrath. None of us were up for extending the evening or crashing her date. Plus, we all had a late night last night," Aileen said.

Cassidy waited and waved as the gals climbed into their cars and headed home. *Interesting. I forgot to bring up the yarn-bombing escapades. Hey, isn't that Austin's silver Mustang? Did he leave with Annie, or one of the gals who was flirting with him at the bar?*

The sun peeked through Cassidy's bedroom window, making interesting splashes on the bedroom walls. A shrill bird's call sent her to the window for a peek. No bird in sight, but Austin's silver Mustang sat alone in its row in the front lot. Grabbing her phone, she checked the time and then fired off a quick text to Annie about Austin's car.

Not getting an immediate response, Cassidy continued with her morning routine that Elvis watched from his comfy perch at the end of her bed. "Come on, pup. I need to grab something for breakfast, and I'll feed you downstairs."

She blew through her office-opening tasks and filled Elvis's bowls to his satisfaction. Still no update from Annie. Sinking into her office chair, she pulled up her camera feeds and scrolled through, starting with the Friday morning clips. At about one-thirty Friday afternoon, Austin pulled into the front parking lot and locked his Mustang. He glanced at his phone and walked toward the barn. She switched cameras and caught him going in and out of the barn, helping Annie unload the van. But there were no other clips of him leaving. She skimmed through the feeds a second time to make sure. *I guess he got a ride with someone. Maybe he went out to celebrate after work? It's just odd that there's no clip of him leaving.*

She scrolled through her emails and opened her event calendar, but her thoughts kept bouncing back to Austin and where he might have gone. *Why does this bother me so much? With all the stuff that's been going on around here, anything out of the norm makes me edgy. Austin doesn't seem like the kind of person who would run off and not tell anyone. And Annie usually calls me back right away. Take a breath. If you don't hear something soon, then let Zac know. It's probably nothing.*

The front door opened, and Elvis seized the opportunity to be the Celebrations greeter.

"Hey, puppy," Aileen said from the front room. "What are you doing up here all by yourself?" Aileen, laden with a shopping bag, a purse, and a beach bag, hustled in through the doorway, managing to scoop up Elvis, who was basking in all the attention along the way. "So, what's shakin'? What's new in your love life?" she asked, tickling the chihuahua.

Cassidy tried not to roll her eyes. "That's funny. Elvis says to tell you he's single. And by the way, you sound like Roxie."

"Who sounds like me?" Roxie called from the porch as Ruthanne and Kate popped their heads through the doorway to see what they were missing.

Huddling around the coffeemaker, Aileen said, "I was asking about Cassidy's social life. I mean, since she's had two very handsome gentlemen take an interest in her lately. She's got her pick of beaus. Hey, you didn't tell us about your lunch with the deeee-tective."

"Well, do tell," Roxie said. "And my advice is to go out with both of them."

Cassidy could feel the heat rising in her cheeks. "Austin is friendly, and I'm considering hiring him to *work for me* when we get the cavern venue ready. That's it. Nothing more. He's a talented bartender, and I think he'd be a good addition to the team. He is very good at entertaining his patrons."

"I bet. And, what about the fearless Detective Hottie?" Roxie waved her bejeweled hand for Cassidy to hurry up with the details.

Cassidy could feel her temperature rising. "We chat from time to time about his cases, especially the ones with ties to my property. I'm helping him. You know, like any good citizen would."

"What did Shakespeare say? I think she protests too much," Roxie added with a wink.

"Yep. I noticed that too," Kate said. "We've all seen how moonie-eyed Zac gets around you. He goes from mister hard-boiled detective to someone who's crushing on you."

"Crushing?" Cassidy's mouth formed a small "o."

"That's my granddaughter's term, but it seemed appropriate for this occasion," Kate replied.

"He's trying to solve two murders. It's all part of his investigative techniques," Cassidy insisted. "Sometimes, he asks for my help. He's being a good detective."

"Of course he is," Ruthanne added. "But there's more to the story. He spends a great deal of time at this place. More than he does at any other business in this town. And as cute as Elvis is and as cool as we are, Zac is definitely here to see you. Believe me, we've noticed."

"So, tell us more about your interest in our local law enforcement," Roxie said with a grin.

Cassidy's phone rang, and when she glanced down and saw Annie's name, she said, "I've got to take this. Excuse me. Hi, Annie, what's up?" Cassidy strode toward her desk, grateful to escape the Pearly Girls' onslaught of questions, but she could feel their stares as she plopped in her chair.

"Cassidy, sorry I didn't respond quicker. I've been driving around all morning. I am beside myself. I haven't seen Austin since he helped me load the van last night. He was going back inside to get his phone charger and then head home. Last night when I got home, I was super-busy with unloading the perishables and things I needed. I didn't even realize he wasn't home. Austin lives in the guest house behind our garage, so I don't always see him come and go. When I noticed he wasn't there, I ran over and checked his place. His bed hadn't been slept in. This is not like him. I have no idea where he is. I hopped in my car, and I've driven around to every place he might be. Cassidy, I can't find him."

Cassidy clicked on the camera app and peeked at the live shots of her property. The silver Mustang sat in the same spot. "His car is still here," she said. "I reviewed yesterday's feeds earlier, and I saw him get out of the car, but there were no shots of him leaving with anyone. And no one's been near his car."

"This is so not like him. Austin flirts, but he has no interest in the barflies. He never leaves with the gals he meets. He's always joking about the things they leave him with his tips. Car keys, hotel keys, love notes... All that's not his style. He's working on his MBA online at night, so he's a hundred percent dedicated to finishing school. When he starts talking about a girl who he likes, that's when I know it's serious. He meets hundreds of women at work every week. I'm sure it would break their hearts, but being attentive is part of his job. He doesn't do hookups. I would put money on it." She let out another sigh.

"I'm sorry I don't have any more information for you," Cassidy told her. "If he picks up his car, I'll have him call you." A sinking feeling grew in the pit of her stomach.

"Thanks. When I find him, we'll figure out how to get his car from your place. And that's after I give him an earful for scaring me half to death. Sheesh. He's gonna hear about this." Annie disconnected, and it was Cassidy's turn to let out a long puff of air. She tapped a quick text to Zac about the car and what Annie had said about her brother.

He replied in seconds, **Thanks. I'll keep an eye out. Let me know if he turns up.**

A little before lunch, Aileen laced up her tennis shoes. "Kate and I are starting our daily walking routine today. Anyone want to join us?"

"I'm headed out in a few too," Roxie said. "I've got a date with Martin. We're going to a couple of wineries this afternoon."

"You and that teacher have been seeing a lot of each other lately," Kate said.

"All in good fun. He's heading back to Florida on Monday. Gotta seize the moment. Ta-ta. Y'all have fun on your walk," Roxie said.

"You too," Ruthanne called after her. "I'm heading out soon. I need to meet my book club over at A Novel Idea. We're planning what we want to read for the next three months. It's our romance quarter. Va-va-voom. I'm voting for spicy." She wiggled her eyebrows as she packed her purse.

"Have fun. We're going to go lap the grotto and the field around the barn." Kate held the door for Aileen. "Getting our steps in. We like to move it. Get a mooooove on. Let's get moooving." She made up her own song as she marched out.

When everyone had cleared out of the office, Cassidy picked up Elvis's leash, and he dashed to the door. "Yep, a walk sounds like a good idea too. Then we'll go see what we have at home for lunch. Maybe soup and grilled cheese?"

Elvis yipped his agreement on their way to the patio. He darted out through the partially open door, energized by the time outside and the fall temperatures. A cool breeze sent a shiver through Cassidy, and she pulled her cardigan tighter around her. "I guess the warm leftover summer days are over. Fall is here, and the leaf peepers will be out in full force as soon as the colors start popping out on the trees." Autumn was always a favorite time for Cassidy. The valley and the surrounding mountains showed off their fall colors, and it was a time for all the fun traditions like apple-picking, hayrides, football games, and bonfires.

A shrill scream disrupted her trip down nostalgia lane. "What was that?" Elvis tore off toward the grotto. Another earsplitting scream echoed across the grounds, and Cassidy broke into a run.

"This is like last summer. I can't believe it," Aileen said, pointing to the mulched rose bed near the back of the garden. "Kate, hurry up over here. I need a nurse. I hope."

Cassidy stepped closer for a better look. A black sneaker sprouted from a black pants leg in the mulched bed. The leg and an arm jutted out from under one of the knockout rose bushes. Cassidy flashed back to the murder of Johnny Storm in the serenity garden last year. She sucked in a deep breath. "Austin! Is he breathing?" Cassidy's stomach felt like it was rising and falling sharply as if she were on an out-of-control roller-coaster. *How can this be happening again? And how did Austin end up in Levi's flowerbed? Please tell me he's breathing.*

Kate kneeled down and checked his pulse and his airway. "Call 911. I stopped to tie my shoe, and lo and behold, Aileen finds a body. Tell the dispatcher he's breathing on his own, but I can't rouse him. He keeps drifting off. Tell them to hurry with the ambulance."

When the call connected, Cassidy blurted, "This is Cassidy Jamison at Celebrations at Ivy Springs. I'm in the garden, and there's an unconscious man. He's breathing on his own, but he won't wake up."

"In the garden on the back of the property?" the dispatcher asked.

"Yes. Where we have outdoor weddings."

"Got it. Police and an ambulance are on their way. They're estimating they're about three minutes out. You should hear sirens soon."

"I'll go wave them this way," Aileen said, hustling off toward the parking lot.

"Thank you. I'll have someone waiting to show them where we are." Cassidy stifled a sigh. She tapped the red button and exhaled loudly. *I seem to be calling 911 a lot lately.*

"Austin, can you hear me?" Kate yelled in his ear. He groaned and rolled over.

"Stay still," Kate commanded. "Help is on the way. They'll be here in a minute."

Cassidy shifted her weight from leg to leg, and Elvis plopped down in the grass. After what seemed like an eternity, EMTs ran into the garden, heading toward the kneeling Kate. She rose and stepped out of the way as they swooped in. Butch Chalmers, sporting the uniform of an Ivy Springs deputy, rounded the corner and headed toward the group huddled around Austin.

The team worked on Austin for what seemed like forever. Cassidy, Ruthanne, Kate, and Aileen stood in stony silence, trying to pick up any clue about what was going on as the EMTs worked on Austin.

A soft touch on Cassidy's shoulder made her jump and swallow a squeal.

"Sorry," Zac said. "I didn't mean to startle you. I guess you found the bartender. What happened?"

"Kate and I were on our walk. I went over to sniff the last of the roses, and I saw a tennis shoe sticking out," Aileen said. "I totally freaked out. All I could think about was last summer." She clutched both of her hands like she was hugging herself.

"And she screamed like a little schoolgirl," Kate added. "I checked his pulse. He was breathing but kinda out of it."

"Any idea why he was in your garden?" Zac asked, looking at Cassidy.

Cassidy shook her head. "I was trying to figure out why he'd left his car here. I guess we know why now."

"Have you called his sister yet?" She shook her head, and he continued: "Tell her he's breathing. I'm not sure what hospital they're taking him to. I can find out for her."

"Sentara Martha Jefferson in Charlottesville," the EMT yelled.

Cassidy nodded and punched Annie's contact. After three rings, she got her voicemail. "Hey, Annie. This is Cassidy. We found Austin unconscious in the garden. He's breathing, but they're taking him to the hospital in Charlottesville to check him over. Sentara Martha Jefferson. Detective Turner is here with me. Call me when you get this message." She disconnected and took several deep breaths to calm the bats that were flying around in her stomach.

"Anything else unusual?" he asked, scanning the area.

Cassidy paused and watched as Deputy Chalmers walked in concentric circles around the flower bed, searching for evidence. "Did he just join y'all?" she asked, indicating the deputy.

"Yep. He finished the academy recently and signed on with us. Did you notice anything unusual about Austin the last time you saw him?"

"No. I checked the cameras before I called Annie about the car. I saw Austin arrive, and there were a couple of shots of him working near the barn. I never saw him leave," Cassidy said.

"Who was he with?" he asked.

"Annie, and everyone at the reunion who ordered a drink. He always had a crowd at the bar."

A dark look crossed the detective's face, but he seemed to

recover quickly. He jotted something in his black notebook and nodded. Then he turned and joined the deputy in his search. One of the EMTs returned with a gurney. Cassidy watched as they lifted Austin onto it and wheeled him out of the garden.

"I hope he's okay," Aileen said. "This is too much. What else is going to happen around here? This reunion is jinxed."

"Why in the world was he in the garden?" Kate asked. "Or is this because of something more sinister? Did he see or hear something he shouldn't have? We know he talked to just about everyone at the reunion. Why would someone want him out of the way?"

"Or did he meet someone out here?" Aileen asked.

"If he did, it went bad," Kate added.

"Annie said he went back to the barn, where he had forgotten his phone charger. If he were leaving after retrieving it, the garden path isn't the closest way to his car," Cassidy said.

The three women and Elvis stood by quietly, watching the police continue to search the area.

First two dead bodies, and now an injured bartender. Something niggled at the back of Cassidy's thoughts, but she couldn't quite put her finger on it. It was like something hiding in a foggy mist. *What was his connection to Britt and Darcy? And what had happened to him when he was getting his phone charger?*

19

After the EMTs and police left, a pall fell over the group. Not having anything else to do in the office, Aileen and Kate headed home. Cassidy and Elvis finished their walk and trudged back to the apartment.

Cassidy's phone binged as she unlocked the back door. **I'm at the hospital in Cville. Austin has been moved to a room for observation. Thanks for leaving me the msg**, Annie texted.

Cassidy stared at her phone for a couple of beats. How could all this be happening here at what was supposed to be a fun high school reunion? Shaking off the dark feelings and the guilt, thinking that maybe she could have done something to prevent some of it, she unhooked the dog's leash. "Elvis, let's get you situated, and I'm going to do a road trip to Charlottesville and see how Austin is. Maybe he's awake and remembers something."

She scooped up her purse and headed back out the door again. "Why did they take him to Charlottesville when there are closer hospitals?" she asked herself aloud, climbing into the Jeep and locating a radio station with peppy music for the forty-some-minute trek to the other side of the mountains.

The '90s throwback tunes made the ride fly by. Cassidy drove over and around the mountains and took the hospital exit into the city. Charlottesville looked like a huge metropolis compared to Ivy

Springs. She laughed at the comparison after living in Washington, D.C., for so long. None of the cities in the Blue Ridge compared to a major metropolitan area like the nation's capital.

She found parking in the deck and hurried across the walkway to the main hospital. **Where are you?** She texted Annie. **I'm in the lobby.**

Near the emergency room in an observation room, Annie texted.

Be there in a sec, Cassidy replied.

"May I help you?" a perky greeter asked from behind the large desk in the open foyer. Her blue vest sported all kinds of buttons and pins with funny sayings, and her purply-tinted hair shone almost as brightly as her smile.

"Hi. My friend Austin Taylor was admitted a little while ago. His sister said he's in an observation room near the Emergency ward."

"Not sure if you can go in to see him. It'll depend on his condition. But to get to Emergency, turn left at the first hall and go to the end. It dead-ends into a nurses' station. They can help you there."

Cassidy waved her thanks and hurried in the direction the woman had pointed. The industrial floor and the off-white tiles on the walls, along with the antiseptic smell, created a scene that looked like any one of a number of TV hospital settings.

At the end of the hallway, one nurse juggled several file folders and a telephone behind a shared desk. The nurse held up one finger to signal that she would be done in a moment.

Before she could talk to the nurse, "Cassidy, Cassidy. We're over here," came from down the hall. Annie waved both arms from a doorway to the left. "I'm so glad you could come. I've been one hot mess since last night."

The nurse who was on the phone glared at Annie but continued her call.

"Is it okay to go in?" Cassidy whispered when she stopped at the doorway to his room.

"I say it's okay," Annie said, pulling her inside. Austin lay under white sheets and a thin blue blanket. He was plugged into several monitors. Despite all he had recently been through, he still looked model-cool propped up on two pillows. His blondish brown hair looked tousled in a hipster way, and his ice-blue eyes focused on the golf tournament on the TV above him. "Hey, Cassidy. What are you doing here?"

"I could ask you the same thing. You gave us a scare when your car was in my lot this morning. Nobody knew where you were."

"Sorry about that. It's all a little fuzzy. I wish I knew all the details. They said I was in your rose garden. I remember going back for my phone charger. I'd left it behind the bar. Anastasia and another gal with short brown hair asked me if I knew where their friend Kelly was. We walked around, flipping on lights and checking for her. They searched the main room, and they asked me to go and check the hallway and the loft." He paused and reached for the water bottle on the nearby table. After a couple of sips, he continued. "Sorry. I'm thirsty, for some reason."

"The doctor said you were dehydrated, and you have a concussion," Annie interrupted.

"Yeah. But I'm also hungry. I'll be glad when they're done with whatever they're doing. I want to blow this popsicle stand and get some real food. Did he say when I can leave? Not counting the dull headache, I feel fine. Except hungry. They're not feeding me anything here."

"They want to make sure you're okay," Annie said, plopping down in the seafoam green chair next to his bed. "And we'll have to see what you can have to eat. You may need to take it easy for a while."

"I'm fine. It was a bump on the head. I got way worse playing football and rugby." He tried to sit up, and his monitor beeped. Annie hopped out of her seat in perfect mother-hen fashion.

"You're staying put until the doctor says you can go," Annie said, pushing him back against the pillow. She gave him a side-eye that he didn't argue with.

"So, what happened in the barn last night?" Cassidy asked, hoping to get some more information.

"I was going down the back hallway, and I heard a noise. I hollered in both bathrooms and got no response. And I didn't see anyone. So I walked back toward the loft area. I remember the lights going out, and I felt a cool blast of air like a stiff breeze."

"What was it?" his sister asked.

"I dunno. I don't remember much after that. I remember thinking I should ask Cassidy if her place was haunted. It was spooky. And then something hit me in the head. I guess it wasn't anything paranormal," he said, rubbing his neck. "That's all I remember until I woke up here, and the nurse kept yelling at me. Annie, go see when I can get out of here. I don't need to spend the night if I promise to take it easy at home."

"If they let you out, you're staying at my place, so I can keep an eye on you," his sister muttered. "If I leave you to your own devices, you'll be out washing your car, heading to the gym, or something."

"Speaking of that, we need to swing by Cassidy's and pick up my baby," he said with a half-smile.

"You can leave it there as long as you need to," Cassidy said.

"'Preciate it. But I want to get out of here," he said, as Annie disappeared into the hallway.

"Is there anything you need?" Cassidy asked.

"A quarter pounder with cheese and some fries."

"Sorry. If it's food or booze you're wanting, you'll have to get Roxie or one of the other Pearly Girls to smuggle that in."

"I like your team. They're fun. And I would sure love the chance to come and work for you," he said with his best puppy eyes.

"We're going to move forward on the cave venue. The construction costs were not as bad as I expected. I'm not sure how long it'll take or when we could even open. But I'm willing to give you a try if you're still interested. We'll have to talk details when I have a better idea of the budget and the bookings timeline."

"Sounds good," he said, showing boyish dimples on either side of his bright smile. He shook her hand vigorously. "It is going to be the coolest thing this town has seen. Nobody has anything like it around here. You could do concerts, parties, comedy shows... Heck, you could even do things like poetry slams and open-mic nights. I know you'll be able to keep it booked. I look forward to the opportunity to show you how I could help grow your business." He shook her hand again and then let go abruptly.

"The gals were brainstorming names. Everything from The Underground to The Lair to The Batcave came up."

He grinned again. "I don't think you can get the licensing for the last one, even though it's cool. I like The Lair."

"I do too. As a kid, I was always looking for hidden treasure down there. And it was rumored that my family used it as a place to hide their bootlegged hooch."

"That's it, then. You've got to do a nod to your family's moonshining activities and the old honky-tonk."

Not sure how much time she had left before the nurses shooed her out, Cassidy tried again to jog his memory about the night in the barn. "So, you were with Anastasia and some gal you didn't recognize. Anyone else around?"

"Uh-uh. Annie took the van back to her place, Levi said he'd be by later to lock up. It was just those two women from the party left in the barn. The other gal acted like she was bored and ready to leave. Anastasia seemed jumpy, and she yelled at us like a drill sergeant, trying to hurry us along. I was ready to go too."

"Hmmm. Kate and Aileen cleared the building, and we locked up before I left. You said Levi was there?"

Austin nodded. "The back door to the kitchen was unlocked. I went in for my gear. Anastasia and her friend were inside. Levi popped his head in and said he'd make sure to lock up everything when we were done."

"Did you notice anyone else?" she asked.

"Nope. We did a walk-through. It was just the people I mentioned," he said. "We never did find Kelly."

Before Cassidy could ask any more questions, Annie returned with a doctor and two nurses. "That's my cue to skedaddle. Let me know if either of you need anything."

Who was with Anastasia last night? And where was Kelly? Did someone on my team miss people left in the building? If someone conked him on the head, how did they get him outside? He's not a small guy. It would take two people—or a wheelbarrow—to move him to the garden. Cassidy retraced her steps through the hospital corridors and across the walkway to the parking deck. *There are way too many questions I don't have reasonable answers for.*

The unanswered questions about Austin and the murders swirled fiercely around her head and dampened her mood. Pushing them temporarily aside, she tried focusing on the cave. She really hoped it would be a hit with guests. Would The Lair be a good name? Several other names for the venue bounced around in her head. *I want to pay homage to the past, and Kate's suggestion seems to be the name everyone is drawn to.*

As she climbed into her Jeep, thoughts of the reunion and the attacks crept back in and battled for her full attention. She paid the parking fee and headed west for the long ride home.

The fact that Anastasia and a woman were in the barn after Cassidy locked it bothered her. None of the activity showed up on her security-camera feeds. So, the attacker—or attackers—would have had to go out the back and follow the tree line to stay out of the cameras' range. *I think it's time for more cameras. And I need to see if Mateo's night guard noticed anything out of the ordinary.*

20

SATURDAY AFTERNOON

After grabbing a late lunch from a drive-thru, Cassidy sped home and ate with one hand on the wheel and the other in the bag. She balled up the wrapper as she pulled into her parking lot and dashed up the stairs to her apartment to check the cameras again. *Now that I know what I'm looking for, maybe I'll see something that's hiding in plain sight. And I need to widen the timeframe for my search.* She typed a quick text to her security contact to see if any of the guards had reported anything out of the ordinary.

After poring over hours and hours of footage almost frame by frame, Cassidy stood and stretched. Kelly had left with her husband at about nine-thirty, so unless she had sneaked back in, she wasn't on the property. There was one shot of a woman in all black with a ponytail, walking around the side of the barn to the main door. Was that Anastasia? Or was it the mystery woman who was with her? She put all of the clips in Dropbox for Zac and dashed off a quick text to explain that they were related to the night Austin was attacked.

After feeding Elvis, she showered and found a navy pantsuit with a red camisole. "You hang out here, baby. I'm going to crash the reunion dinner at the country club and see how things are going. Maybe I can learn something that will help wrap up this case before the weekend is over and everyone heads home. At this rate, this thing could take years to solve, and that thought drives me nuts. Darcy and Britt need justice. This whole thing seems to be one dead-end after another. And I don't get the sense that the police are making much progress either. I don't want people to think of Celebrations at Ivy Springs and then immediately conjure up tales of two unsolved murders. Wish me luck tonight. Maybe I can shake something loose."

The chihuahua turned his head slightly and settled on the lap blanket at the end of the couch. "You want me to leave Animal Planet on for you?" She switched the TV to his favorite channel. "Be back in a bit."

Cassidy hiked down the back stairs and out toward her Jeep, glancing toward Austin's lonely Mustang on the other side of the empty lot. She rolled down the Wrangler's window, enjoying the crisp evening air and the winding roads en route to the golf course. *If I get there at cocktail hour, I might be able to mingle and chat up some folks before dinner is served. Maybe they'll be more relaxed and willing to spill some details. I'd be grateful for any clue.*

As the road switched to a steeper incline, her thoughts of work and her never-ending to-do list wormed their ways back into her consciousness. *Hey, Mateo never did answer me.* She made a mental note to call her security consultant later.

After having her choice of spaces in the lot in front of the clubhouse, Cassidy waited for the Aerosmith song on the radio to end before she climbed out of her Jeep.

The focal point of the golf club was the colonial-era home with the wraparound porch and tall white columns. The house had been expanded over the years; when the property had been converted to a golf course, the house had been gutted and rebuilt to host events for members and guests, but they'd left the historical façade. She locked her purse in the Jeep and made her way up the slate pathway to the massive front porch that was large enough for thirty or forty people. Purple, orange, and umber mums burst out of large ceramic pots along the wooden porch's perimeter.

Light jazz wafted from the speakers in the porch ceiling. She pulled open the giant oak door and gazed across the empty foyer. To the left, a library that served as a place for members to socialize looked dark. To the right, a bar and dining room with lots of empty tables sat in semidarkness. Following the peppy music that didn't match the empty, somber ambiance, she spotted Kelly and some of her friends at a table near a long L-shaped bar. The cherry wood gleamed under the pendant lights, and the brass fittings gave it a classic look. Long rows of glass shelves filled with bottles of different-colored liquors faced the guests. The hanging glass pendant lights and the full-sized mirror that ran the length of the bar focused the light on the bartender and created a halo around him and some interesting designs on the walls. A handful of guests in casual outfits huddled around several of the tall high-top tables that dotted the room's perimeter.

She ordered a ginger ale and smiled when the bartender waved off her attempt to pay. She took her drink and walked up to Kelly's table, where two other blondes and a guy in a lavender polo shirt sat around the table, a dozen or so empty glasses covering most of the wooden surface.

"Oh, lookie here," Kelly said, waving her hand—with an enormous diamond ring—around. "If it isn't Cassidy. How are you? Pull up a chair. I was telling Meg, Joyce, and Ken here about what's been going on. This has been a reunion to remember. I guess Britt got what she wanted, except the ending was a big fizzle. It didn't turn out the way anyone expected," she slurred. She waved her hand again and almost knocked over two highball glasses.

"Whoopsie," one of the blondes said, pushing the empties toward the center of the table. "What happened to the waitress?" Looking over her shoulder, she continued: "With all these empty chairs here, there's no way the kitchen's backed up. It seems like they could get someone out here to clear and bring the next round." She grabbed four glasses with the tips of her fingers and moved them to the next table. She continued to relocate the empties until they cluttered the other table.

"Thanks, Meg, for clearing for us," Ken said. "That's better. Now, what were we talking about? Oh, yeah, all that murdery stuff. For cheerleaders, y'all like to walk on the dark side. We could use another round here. Joyce, do you see the waitress anywhere?" he asked, glancing around the room.

Joyce, who sat across the table scrolling on her phone, looked up. "Nope. She went in the kitchen and never returned."

"We should tell Anastasia," Kelly said. "She should take care of it. She wants to be in charge now. Maybe she'll see what hard work really is. But, no matter what she does, she can't take Britt's place." She sniffed and wiped a tear, smearing her dark eyeliner.

"Don't start crying again. All we can do is remember the good times," Ken said, patting Kelly's shoulder.

"Anastasia'll never know what hard work is. Her dad was rolling in it, and she got whatever she wanted. Always. She never earned anything," Kelly wailed. "Her daddy bought her everything she ever had. He paid for her spot on the cheerleading team by promising the school new uniforms. She couldn't dance either, and remember, he got her a solo in the big pageant. And don't get me started on her shrill caterwauling during that phase where she wanted to be a singer. Sooooo, Daddy Dearest paid for lessons and got her the lead in the musical. He even flew her to New York to try out for

American Idol. What a joke." Kelly rolled her eyes. "She is such a brat, and now she's acting like she was Britt's best friend. She didn't know Britt talked bad about her behind her back."

"Oh, that's so true," Joyce said. "I went outside last weekend to take a call. I couldn't hear over the DJ. Anyway, while I was outside, I heard a catfight. I tiptoed over to hear better, and it was Britt giving it to Anastasia. She said something like 'Oh, no, sister, you're not pinning this on me. I say a lot of things when I'm upset. That doesn't mean I told you to do anything. Maybe I should make some phone calls about you.'" The woman paused and glanced at the alerts on her phone. She looked up to find everyone staring at her. "Oh, I couldn't hear what Anastasia said after that, but there was a bunch of cussing and hissing. Too bad we'll never know. But I'm sure it was good." Joyce waved her hand like she was shooing away a bug.

"Anastasia always seemed so angry," Meg added. "Nobody wanted to cross her. I think people gave in to her just so she wouldn't threaten to tell her daddy. Back in the day, even the teachers were scared of her. I know *I* steered clear of her. She was a class-A bully. I don't know what Britt ever saw in her." Her painted-on eyebrows shot skyward.

"You can say that again," Kelly interjected. "Whatever trouble she got herself into, her daddy managed to make it go away. But Britt never crossed her, and Anastasia followed her around like a puppy. I never figured that whole relationship out. It was weird."

"It's because Britt got some kind of sick pleasure out of bossing around a rich girl," Ken said. "She was always into mind games."

"I bet Anastasia had something on Britt, and I bet it was juicy." Meg's lips formed a sly smile.

"Well, hello, Anastasia," Joyce said loudly. "It's so nice to see you. This is such a lovely venue. Too bad more people didn't show up for the festivities. Maybe they left town after last weekend's fiasco."

"How many are we expecting tonight?" Meg asked, glancing around the cavernous room with about thirty seats filled.

"We had a few regrets from those who couldn't attend this evening. I guess life got in the way; too bad. Their loss. A couple of our classmates had to catch flights back home, but we should have a decent-sized group with the locals. Maybe they're waiting to make an entrance." Anastasia studied the table next to them and opened her heavily made-up eyes wide. "I see you all have started the party early. Kelly, are you okay?" She waved her blood-red talons at the collection of empty glasses and shook her head slightly.

"I'm fine," Kelly said. "Britt's death hit me harder than I expected. I probably should have bailed on tonight too, but I didn't want to leave you hanging since you inserted yourself in the lead role, and I figured you'd need help from the squad. And I owe it to Britt."

All eyes were on Anastasia. Ignoring the slight, she squinted, and then her sightline focused on someone across the room. "I had to when no one else bothered to step in or step up," she said, gritting her teeth. After a beat, her face softened. "Oh, hi, Cassidy. I didn't notice you there. Uh, you're welcome to one of the empty seats in the dining room if you want to join us for dinner, since you're already here. The red dots on the name tags are beef, and the yellow ones are chicken. Just wait until everyone is seated, and you can appropriate a spot of one of the no-shows."

"That won't be difficult," Joyce said under her breath.

Pausing for a moment to stare across the room, a flush crawled from Anastasia's neck to her cheeks. "No way! What is that? Who put all their empty glasses on the memory table?" She stomped off to near the door, where the Britt-and-Darcy tribute stood without the giant dance trophy.

"It's weird, if you ask me," Ken whispered. "It's like she revered

Britt even though she had to know the queen bee treated her badly. I'm stunned her world didn't crumble when you-know-what happened. She's always been an odd duck. I can't figure her out. She has always been either way up or way down in the dumps. Can you say mood swings?"

"She's enjoying her time in the spotlight right now, even if it is for a very small audience. She never really did fit in. And she thought Mac loved her," Joyce scoffed.

The group watched as Anastasia angrily stomped over to the memory table. She gathered empty glasses and small plates and dumped them on the end of the bar. Then she clanked a spoon on a glass. One of the burly guys at the bar let out a long whistle, and all conversation stopped.

"That's better," Anastasia said. "It's dinner time. Please grab your glasses and find your seats in the dining room for our magnificent feast. The planning team has carefully put name tags on every table. Before you leave, make sure you stop by and sign the memory books for Britt Rogers Mahoney and Darcy Branch. Their absence here has left a hole in so many lives. We will truly miss them." Anastasia paused and glanced around the room. "And after dinner, we'll have time for tributes if anyone wants to say anything before we continue the festivities. But for now, let's go find our seats."

Someone groaned in the back, and a ripple of laughter moved through the small crowd.

"Let's get a move on before the chicken gets cold." Anastasia pointed a long finger toward the other side of the room.

"Come on, Cassidy," Joyce said. "You can sit with us. Our husbands bailed. They couldn't take any more reunion nonsense. Booooo-ring! I think the guys headed into town to the nearest bar that wasn't here. You can have one of their seats."

"If we were smart, we'd join them," Meg added.

"And I don't have a plus one, so you can sit next to me. Taking a date to your high school reunion is like the kiss of death," Ken said, draining the last drops of his drink. "You never know who's going to tell embarrassing stories. Or what if any of your exes show up? No, thank you. This boy's stag tonight. But I'm not ruling anything out. I always keep my options open." He winked mischievously as he rose and pushed his chair in.

The group picked up their glasses and followed Kelly, who wobbled on her pink sparkly stilettos to the main dining room. The tables had place settings for about a hundred people.

"Wow. There are a bunch of no-shows," Meg said, plopping down next to Ken.

"Who made the seating chart for this?" Joyce said a little too loudly. She picked up her name tag from a table in the back and moved over to where the others sat. "You okay with beef?" she asked Cassidy. "If not, I think we'll be able to find you a chicken. From the looks of who showed up, we could all have two or three meals each."

"Doggie bags for everyone," Ken yelled.

Meg laughed. "Hey, I say we go gung-ho tonight on the extra desserts. We could take a couple back to our rooms for a midnight snack."

"Or in case we get the munchies," Ken added with a giggle. "Or it could be breakfast if you get lucky."

Anastasia stood near the front with a microphone. "Come on, everyone. Find your seats. I know you all are hungry, and some of you need to get some food in you. I have a few announcements before we get started.

"I'd like to thank Britt Rogers Mahoney for having the creativity and the energy to plan this fabulous reunion. People will be talking about it for years. We will never forget her dedication and devotion." A low murmur moved through the crowd, but it didn't seem to faze Anastasia. "And I'd like to thank the rest of the team who brought you these amazing events. Me, of course, and Kelly Mason Todd, Joyce Underwood, and Meg Stafford for all the long hours they put into this."

"And Darcy Branch," some guy yelled from the back.

"And yes, Darcy." Anastasia glared at the crowd. After an uncomfortable pause, she continued: "I know tragedy hit our community hard recently, but let's use tonight to celebrate the good times. We'll have dinner, and then, as I said before, I saved a space on the agenda for you all to say a few heartfelt words about Britt."

"And Darcy," the guy yelled again, and laughter pealed through the room.

"And Darcy," Anastasia said quietly. "Oh, the announcements. Don't forget the online auction. There's still one more day to place your bids. We have some valuable prizes. And the proceeds go to some scholarship fund. The link's on the school's website."

Meg yelled, "Our school's athletic fund."

"Yes, the Ivy Springs Athletic Fund," Anastasia mumbled. "And tomorrow, there is meditation or whatever in the garden back at Celebrations at Ivy Springs, and a fancy tea to round out all our festivities. So, without further ado, let's enjoy the first course of our feast."

Conversation died down, as the waiters in all-white swooped in with bread baskets and salads.

"Oh, look. Another hoity-toity food presentation. I bet dinner is one little medallion of meat surrounded by two carrots and some asparagus designed to look like a lean-to," Meg muttered, putting her napkin in her lap.

"What do you care?" said Ken. "All of y'all are always on diets. You'll move stuff around your plate with your fork and poke at it occasionally. Who are you trying to fool? I went to school and to cheer competitions with all y'all. I know your secrets."

"Not me," Joyce said. "I'm hungry. I say we should order a pizza. That wouldn't go over well, but at least it would be edible. Plus, I'd love to see the look on Anastasia's face when the delivery guy walks in. That'd be a hoot. Just like *Fast Times at Ridgemont High*. Look at my salad: it looks like they went out and weeded the garden. I swear those are dandelions."

Cassidy poured the lemon-scented dressing on her greens and speared a cucumber. Before she could probe further about Britt and Darcy, a Rubenesque brunette hustled to the table and plopped down next to Joyce. "Sorry I'm late, guys. But what counts is I made it. Have I missed any drama?" she asked.

Ken turned toward Cassidy. "Cassidy, this is Angela Radcliffe—"

"Angela Martin," the brunette interrupted. "I went back to my maiden name after ditching that creep."

"Ooops. I forgot. I can't keep up with y'all's love lives. It's a cross between *Days of Our Lives* and *General Hospital*," Ken said. "Cassidy, this is Angela *Martin*. She works in advertising in Atlanta. Angie Poo, this is Cassidy, who owns the other venue with a barn."

"Nice to meet you," Angela said from across the table. "It's been fun visiting town for a bit. It's changed since back in the day. Been a blast to hang out, but I'm kinda glad I'm heading home tomorrow. Oh, Cassidy, cute place you have there. I loved the barn and garden. Too bad about Britt and Darcy. It looks like I've got some catching up to do. I need a drink," she waved her hands to attract a waiter.

"Cassidy is used to being the center of all the crime action," Meg added with a half-smile. "She had a big-time rock star murdered at her place last summer, and it put little ole Ivy Springs on the map as the locale for Johnny Storm's untimely demise. Cassidy, you should have your own podcast. You'd be a hit."

"I wouldn't worry too much about it," Angela said to Cassidy. "Any publicity is good publicity. And people have short attention spans. They probably won't remember it in a couple of years. But think about it. Podcasts are hot now. That might be right for your promotional efforts."

A couple of years. Is this how my place is going to be remembered?

Before Cassidy could reply, Joyce interrupted, "Angie Poo; I haven't heard that name in years. It looks like you'll be playing the part of Steve Taylor tonight if you sit here." Joyce waved around a place card. "I hope you like beef. Stevie doesn't know what he's missing."

"What?" Angela said, trying harder to flag down a waiter.

"You remember old Steve. He was that good-looking soccer player," Ken said.

"Steve ordered beef. If you don't want that, find a yellow name tag," Meg said.

"I think I ordered dinner at this thing when I registered," Angela said. "Who knows where my name tag even is. It's not that crowded, I'll stay here. Hey, I want a drink. I'll be back in a minute." She jumped up and made a beeline for the bar at the other end of the room.

When a waiter zipped by on his way to another table, Joyce yelled, "Hey, we need one more water and salad thing over here." He nodded and continued on his original trajectory.

Angela returned, carrying an orangey-yellow drink with a paper umbrella in it. "That's better. First things first." She took a long sip of her drink, adding, "And I don't actually care about dinner. I'm a vegetarian now. I can't believe they didn't offer that as an option. What year is this?"

"Ohhhhhhh, they did," Kelly said. "I don't think this

meat-and-potatoes bunch was too interested. In fact, I don't see any tags with green dots on them."

"Hey, girl. How are you holding up after Britt's, well, you know," Angela said, staring at Kelly. "I know you two were close."

"Not as close as Ana-stayyyja thinks she was," Ken said, looking down his well-sculpted nose.

"I'm fine. This whole reunion has worn me down. I need a vacation," Kelly said. "And I'm retiring from committee work after this. I'm spent. Britt and Anastasia sucked the ever-lovin' life out of me. I am so over it. Tomorrow cannot come soon enough. I'm done."

"What happened? Everybody seemed to bail. See what two murders will do for morale. Major downer," Angela said. "I heard in the bathroom that Britt's second husband, the rich one, was stepping out with Darcy. Can that be true? I mean, Britt always had her choice of men. She swooped down and claimed Mac, and never let him get too far off his leash. Well, except those couple of times. I guess she wised up over the years. As much fun as Mac was, we all know the high school years were his glory days, and he'd spend the rest of his time on this orb trying to relive the fame of being the star quarterback. Doesn't he own a towing service or something these days? Anyway, good for Britt. She moved on to a more established partner. A real adult with money to take care of her."

"But it seems the rich old guy had a thing for the naughty librarian—or in this case, the popular journalist. I heard the thing he and Darcy had going was more than just a fling," Ken said, opening his eyes wide.

"Vince, Britt's husband number two." Joyce held up two fingers and wiggled them around. "Yep, that one has sold insurance here for years. If rumors are to be believed, he met Darcy when she came back to town to settle her father's insurance policies and other estate stuff," Joyce added.

"And one thing led to another," Meg added. "I heard from a gal at church that it has been pretty hot and heavy. They were talking about moving in together. Vince would fly out to meet Darcy when she was covering stories in different cities. And Britt thought he was traveling for business," she added with an exaggerated surprised face that made the parentheses on either side of her mouth show.

Cassidy listened intently, trying to soak up all the gossipy tidbits. *I guess it would be tacky to whip out a piece of paper and start taking notes.*

The conversation veered to other topics through the main course and dessert. All the possible motives bounced around in Cassidy's head like lottery balls, as her tablemates chattered about fashion and their love lives. *If even a couple of the rumors are true, then that strengthens the motives of several people and earns them a top spot on the suspect list.*

"Hey, Cassidy," Angela said. "Did I hear that gorgeous bartender of yours was hospitalized? Is he okay?"

News travels fast in Ivy Springs. Cassidy nodded slowly. "He was attacked, and one of my staff found him in the garden. But he's been released from the hospital."

"Oh, good. He was such a faaaab-u-licious bartender. But I really think he missed his calling. He should have been a model or a shrink," Angela added, stabbing her fork into the chocolate raspberry lava cake.

"He's definitely eye candy. I'm surprised one of these cougars hasn't trapped him yet," Ken said. "And it wasn't like they weren't trying."

"Any idea what happened to him?" Anastasia said, lurking behind Kelly and Joyce.

"Uh, no," Cassidy said. "He said he didn't remember anything from that night. Maybe he tripped over something and hit his head." *That excuse sounds flimsy even to me.*

Anastasia made a harumphing sound. "You should invest in more cameras and security at your place, and maybe some better landscaping or lighting." She glanced around the table and then added, "Your business is getting quite the reputation around town. I'm surprised all those crazy podcasters and reporters aren't beating down your door. Anyway, you all enjoy your desserts."

Cassidy chewed on her bottom lip, pausing a moment to decide whether it was worth it or not to snap back at Anastasia.

Anastasia interrupted the monologue going on in Cassidy's head. "Ladies, we're getting ready to start the tribute section of the program. Kelly, you're going to say something, right?"

"I dunno," Kelly said meekly. "We'll see. I am a very private person. And I've got a raging headache."

"But you owe it to Britt. I think Vince will be here later. I'm sure he'll want to say something. And of course, Mac always has something to say." Her stare seemed to be laser-focused on Kelly. "Suck it up and say something nice about Britt."

Before anyone could reply, Anastasia flitted to the next table. Kelly threw her napkin onto her plate and picked up her purse. She hustled out without saying anything.

"Excuse me. I need to make sure she has a ride home," Meg said, hopping up to follow the taller blonde. "We don't need any more accidents around here..."

"Attention. Attention," Anastasia barked into the microphone. "Now is the time for anyone to come forward to say a few words in memory of our fallen classmates—or to just remember the good old days." She paused and scanned those who still remained in the audience. "Where'd Kelly go? Anyone else on the committee besides me want to say anything?"

The only sounds in the room were a low rumble of chitchat and the air gushing through the heating ducts.

After a long, painful pause, Anastasia said, "Okay. We'll all mourn privately, then. Oh, don't forget the auction, and you all need to swing by and sign the memory book for Britt."

"And Darcy," the same guy yelled from the back of the room.

Anastasia looked around the room and glared at the inhabitants at a table in the back.

"Thanks for coming. Finish your meals and your desserts. The bar will be open for another hour in case you want to mingle." Anastasia returned the microphone to its stand and hustled out of the dining room.

"Thanks for inviting me to dinner. I enjoyed talking with you all," Cassidy said, rising.

"It was nice to meet you," Angela said. "Hey, didn't you go to Ivy Springs too? You look familiar."

"She was a freshy when we graduated," Joyce said.

"You were just a baby," Ken cooed.

"Weren't you in the band or something?" Joyce asked.

"Newspaper staff," Cassidy said. "And drama club."

"At least it wasn't that geeky AV club or the Dungeons or Dragons thing," Angela said, searching through her Chanel bag. "It was nice to meet you."

"Thanks. Y'all have a safe trip back." Cassidy wended her way through a maze of empty tables and past the bar. Loud voices from the end of the foyer caught her attention, and she couldn't help herself. She detoured to the closest door and headed toward the noise, tiptoeing to the end of the hallway and pretending to admire an oversized flower arrangement in an ornate vase. Anastasia leaned close to a woman in a black suit. Her outstretched index finger was inches from the other woman's nose.

"I don't care what you do with the food. And I'm not apologizing for the attendance. We've already paid the bill," Anastasia fumed, and her eyes flashed like there was a storm brewing behind them. "And what do you care? You still got paid. Deal with it. That's your job! Send the leftovers home with your staff—or throw them out, for all I care."

"That is what I'm trying to tell you. The dinner was partially paid for. You will be receiving a bill for the remaining portion, including the food that was not served," the woman in black said calmly.

"Are you kidding me? Who negotiated this stupid contract?" Anastasia's voice rose several decibels, and she stomped her foot. "Fine. Whatever. Send it to the reunion committee. I can't be bothered with that now." Anastasia stepped closer toward the woman. With barely an inch or two of space between them, Anastasia glared down at the other woman, who didn't flinch.

"Who do I send it to?, is what I'm asking," the woman said in a lower tone.

"Send it to the school. They'll get it to the proper folks. Or send it wherever you sent the others." Anastasia waved her hand like she was shooing the woman away.

The exasperated woman threw her hands up and walked off. *I feel for her. Nobody wants such a difficult client. Thankfully, I got paid in advance. I hope Annie did too.*

Before Cassidy could plan her next move, Kelly stormed down the hallway, carrying her shiny pink shoes.

"Hey," yelled Anastasia. "That rude woman said the dinner bill wasn't paid. What's that about? I'm not responsible for any of this!" Her volume increased with each sentence. "And you all can bet I'm not getting saddled with the bill."

Kelly shrugged and kept walking. "You wanted to be in charge. Deal with it. It's your job. Figure it out," she giggled.

"Oh, you aren't running out now!" Anastasia bellowed.

"Whatever." Kelly teetered in her bare feet and leaned on the nearest wall to steady herself. Then she resumed her trek down the long hallway.

"I'm not finished talking to you," Anastasia yelled, stomping after Kelly.

"Well, I'm done talking to you." Kelly stopped and turned quickly, causing her to sway even more. "I have nothing more to say. I'm done with all this." After a couple of seconds, she waved her free hand around. "And I'm sick of you bossing everyone around. Who do you think you are? Britt would have hated this, and you know it. This whole thing has been one big flop."

"Quit dissing Britt. You know she worked so hard to make all this happen. She had a vision." Anastasia's voice rose several octaves. "And you, what are you staring at?" Anastasia pointed a bony finger at Cassidy. "This is probably all your fault."

Surprised at the sudden verbal attack, Cassidy stepped back, not quite sure how to respond.

"She would have hated all this," Kelly repeated. "Joyce was right, Anastasia: you've ruined everything. And leave Cassidy out of this. This is all *your* fault. As usual!"

Anastasia let out a growl that sounded like a wounded animal, and she lunged toward Kelly, knocking her to the carpet and landing atop her, the two becoming a tumbleweed of arms and legs on the royal blue carpet.

The two women wrestled around in the foyer for several minutes. Cassidy watched in horror, not sure if she should wade into the middle of it. Anastasia got in a couple of good scratches before Kelly pulled her hand back and whacked her on the forehead with the heel of her shoe.

The brassy blonde groaned and bobbled for a moment. Before round two could start, the woman in the dark suit and two men rushed in to separate the women. "Enough," the woman barked. "Take them to the library and the office and let them cool down." She grabbed Kelly under the arms and pulled her away from Anastasia, who kept swinging her arms in the air.

It took both men to pin Anastasia's arms down and drag her to a standing position. She jerked away from them. "I don't need you to touch me. This is ridiculous. Get away from me!"

"This way, please," the taller man said, pointing to the library.

"It's all her fault," Kelly yelled as she was escorted to the office.

"She started it," Anastasia yelled. "She attacked me. I can't believe how lax your security is around here. You'll be hearing from my lawyer!" One of the men grabbed her elbow and guided her across the foyer. "Let go of me. Don't touch me. I can walk on my own," she yelled.

Cassidy took that as her cue to hurry out the front door. She rushed to her Wrangler without looking back. Pausing to catch her breath, she rummaged through her purse and the glove compartment, looking for something to write on. Finding an old envelope, she spent a few minutes by the light of the dashboard jotting notes about what she had heard this evening. *Maybe some of the pieces are starting to fit together. At least there appear to be some stronger motives now for the murders.*

Cassidy sped home and hardly remembered any of the drive. Thoughts of all the bizarre connections between the reunion folks kept popping into her head. When her head started to throb, she decided to take Elvis for a long walk. Maybe it would help burn off some of the nervous energy that she could feel building inside her.

The pair walked the perimeter of the old farmhouse under the floodlights and out to the edge of the wooded area near the garden. The grotto looked spooky in the shadows, so she guided the chihuahua toward the rose bushes. "One more day of this, Elvis. I was hoping the police would have made an arrest by now, but it didn't turn out like that. I guess not everything is like it is on TV."

The little dog turned his head and marched toward the koi pond. Cassidy switched on the flashlight app on her phone and trotted after him. "All your fish friends are asleep. We can check on them tomorrow."

Still interested in the pond, Elvis inched closer to the landscaping, outlined with rocks.

A twig snapped somewhere in the distance, and Cassidy froze. The little dog continued his exploration. Cassidy strained to listen for other noises.

Chalking it up to the wind or woodland creatures, she tugged gently on Elvis's leash. "Come on. It's been a long night. We'll visit the fish again tomorrow when the sun's out." *And it's not so eerie out here.*

Reluctant to follow, Elvis stubbornly continued his sniff fest around the flowerbeds.

In an attempt to maintain her patience, she counted to ten and mentally worked through her to-do list for the next day while her four-legged pal enjoyed his adventure.

Another snap and the sound of footsteps echoed across the garden. Elvis whipped his head up, growling—now on full alert.

"I heard that too," Cassidy whispered, scooping him up and running toward her apartment. She didn't stop until she'd slammed the door shut behind her and made sure the deadbolt was in place.

Rushing upstairs, she stared out the window, looking for the slightest hint of movement. When her legs started to get restless, she moved on to the bedroom window for another view of the woods. "There's nothing out there, Elvis. It must have been a bird or some other kind of animal."

He turned his head and jumped up onto the end of her bed. Too amped up to turn in, she hurried to the dining room and booted up her laptop. *Maybe the cameras caught something.*

Two peach teas later and nothing on any of the camera feeds, Cassidy pulled out her notes and spreadsheet. After another hour or so, she rose and stretched. She had added all the tidbits from this evening and rearranged her suspect wall. Something had set Anastasia off tonight, and it had turned into a storm when she went after Kelly. *This animosity has been building for years, and I think the reunion pushed them over the edge.*

Cassidy plopped back down in her chair and stared at the wall until her eyes were bleary. *What am I missing? It's like that feeling that it's on the tip of my tongue. It's got to be right here.*

Shaking off the grumpy mood, she padded into the kitchen and put some popcorn in the microwave. Snacks couldn't hurt. *At this point, I'll take any help I can get. I'm usually pretty good at figuring out puzzles and people. This one has me stumped.*

At the sound of the microwave beep, Elvis trucked into the kitchen to see what was going on with the smell of buttery goodness wafting through the apartment.

"I gotcha covered, buddy." Elvis yipped and followed her to the dining-room table. She tossed him a puffy white sample as she slid into her chair.

"Okay, we know Darcy was killed first. Then Britt. Darcy was carrying on an affair with Britt's husband. Britt enjoyed being the center of attention. Everything she did advanced that cause. And there were a lot of folks from Britt's past who were not fans. She is the hub for all these points," Cassidy said, ticking the items off on her fingers. "Then there's Kelly. She's been friends with Britt for years. And Anastasia. At times, she's Britt's biggest fan, but then she dissolves into burning anger in less than a few seconds. And we haven't even mentioned who bonked Austin on the head. That's a tough one. He's a tall guy. If the attacker were one person, he or she would need a way to haul Austin out of the barn. I can't imagine someone dragging a limp bartender—especially someone *his* size—all the way to the garden. It's not feasible. Austin remembers being in the barn, but not anywhere else. So I'm going with 'he was attacked in the barn.'"

She hopped up and moved a couple of the sticky notes around on the wall and added an Austin column. "Well, Elvis, we know it wasn't Britt or Darcy. Sadly, that's about all we know for sure."

Looking back at the wall, she said, "So, was it one or two people? I think two random, unrelated murders would be too much of a coincidence. So scratch that. But, I guess it could be one person.

Or, what if Britt was somehow involved initially. Enraged about being betrayed? Then someone, maybe a partner, killed her?"

Cassidy's head started to throb again. "I'm missing some pieces." She laid her head down on her folded arms on the table and stared at the wall.

When her arms began to tingle, she shifted and opened her eyes. "Elvis, how long have I been asleep? Three a.m.? It's time for bed. We're not getting anywhere. Maybe something will come to me later. And I need to think of a way to get what I learned at the reunion dinner to Zac. I think it might be helpful. But I don't want him to think I'm spreading gossip or things that will cause him to go down a rabbit hole."

Not interested in any more talk of murders, Elvis trotted off toward the bedroom. Cassidy followed and brushed her teeth. She changed into an oversized T-shirt and yoga pants and fell into bed. The soft mattress and cozy comforter pulled her to the edge of sleep, but her thoughts kicked in, keeping her awake. She stared at the dark ceiling for what felt like hours. Elvis had no problem drifting off into a deep slumber, punctuated every couple of minutes with a loud snore.

Images of Britt and her gang flashed across her consciousness like someone quickly clicking through an old View-Master. After tossing and turning for what seemed like forever, Cassidy hopped up and poured herself a glass of milk. *I'm looking at this all wrong.*

Elvis scampered in and made himself a snoozing spot under the dining-room table. "Thanks for the company, baby. Okay. When Austin got hurt, I saw a blonde in black on one of the cameras. That could have been Kelly, Anastasia, Joyce, or Meg. What did Austin do or overhear that caused someone to attack him? Or did he do something that someone didn't like? And then there were the other dramas. Anastasia and Kelly had a knock-down drag-out.

Anastasia and Britt had several dustups. Vince was cheating with a gal Britt was trying to impress. And Mac, the first husband, was still living his glory days like he didn't want anything to change from high school. Is he harboring some deep-seated resentment toward Britt—and life—moving on without him?" Cassidy sighed and stared at the wall.

Elvis darted to the door and growled. The short hair on the back of his neck stood up, making him seem a half-inch taller. "What did you hear, baby?" He barked a response, and she slid on a pair of tennis shoes by the door, grabbing her giant flashlight and phone. Tiptoeing down the stairs, she listened as a faint knocking got louder.

She peeked out and spotted the back of Anastasia, who was hunched over. When Cassidy pulled the door open, Anastasia shoved her phone in her pants pocket. "Oh, I'm glad you're home. And sorry it's so late, but this is important," Anastasia said breathlessly. "I need to talk to you."

Anastasia planted one hand on her hip. "Kelly needs our help. Come with me," Anastasia said with a panicked look. Under the patio floodlight, her hair stuck out in all directions, and her makeup looked smudged. Cassidy hesitated, and Anastasia added, "We made up after the golf-course argument. We had some more drinks after everyone left. I couldn't let her drive home, so I volunteered to drive her. She insisted that we come by your place. She wanted to see where Britt died. She got weepy and ran off into the woods. I can't find her, and I'm afraid something bad will happen. You've got to help me. I don't need this right now!" Anastasia grabbed Cassidy's arm and yanked her out onto the patio. "You gotta help me."

Cassidy steadied herself. "Where did she go?"

"That way," Anastasia pointed off into the distance. "What if she can't live with the guilt of what she's done?"

"What?" Cassidy stopped mid-stride.

"No time to explain. I think Kelly did all this. We've got to help her and talk her out of whatever she's thinking in her addled state. We can't have another death." Anastasia pulled Cassidy in the direction of the barn. "Kelly was always jealous of Britt. She wanted what she had. She wanted to be her, and doing her in finally gave her that chance. I can't believe Kelly's the killer. Come on." This time, Anastasia pushed Cassidy toward the woods.

Cassidy looked around wildly, wondering if her contract security guard was on the property at this hour. No time to notify anyone. *There can't be a third death related to this reunion.* She let out a heavy sigh. "Wait," Cassidy yelled.

"What is wrong with you?" Anastasia hissed. "We've got to find her. We've got to get a move on. Quit stalling."

"Does she have a weapon?" Cassidy whispered.

"I don't think so. Just those wicked stilettos she had on earlier. We've got to hurry before she does something we'll regret." Anastasia gave Cassidy another push that was more forceful than last time. "This way." Anastasia led her toward the grotto. Then she changed her path and headed across the garden to the side of the barn. "I think she was heading this way. She kept whining that she had to go back to where we found Britt. Shhhhh! She may have found a way in."

Anastasia stopped suddenly near the corner of the barn. Cassidy took advantage of the pause and fired off a group text to the Pearly Girls. Hopefully one of them—probably Roxie—was still awake. The only sound Cassidy could hear was Anastasia's heavy breathing. Pushing her luck, Cassidy fired off a text to Zac about what was going on. Hopefully, someone will get her message and send help. *I have to find out what is going on.*

Anastasia's husky voice jarred Cassidy from her thoughts. "I think I see her. Be quiet and follow me. There's no telling what kind of state she's in. Or what she'll try. We already know she can be violent. And she's been on another drinking binge since last night."

Conflicting thoughts banged around in Cassidy's head and crashed into each other. *What did Anastasia say? Her description of Kelly sounded nothing like what she knew about the other woman.* A jolt of fear rocketed through Cassidy. Kelly didn't act the way Anastasia described her. *She's not the one harboring a grudge for all these years.* In an instant, all kinds of things about Anastasia flashed through her head as though she were watching some rapid-fire slideshow. The puzzle pieces snapped into place, and Cassidy shuddered as she glanced over at Anastasia. Cassidy felt a wave of calmness wash over her. *I need to find Kelly and get her away from this woman.*

As if Anastasia could read her thoughts, she turned and grabbed Cassidy's upper arm. Her acrylic talons pressed little dents into her skin. "We've got to help her. Now get a move on." She tightened her grip and led Cassidy around to the barn's back door. The outside light shed a tiny yellow glow in the darkness of the early morning.

"Kelly, open this door," Anastasia yelled, pounding on the door with her fist. "Now! We're here to help you. We know you're inside. I can hear you yelling. Open this door. Now! You have a husband and kids. Think of your family and friends. Whatever you've done, we can fix it." Anastasia continued to slam her hand on the door.

She stopped moving for a moment, and her hair, even wilder than before, stuck out like she had received an electric shock. "I think she said go away. I can barely hear her now," Anastasia said. "Kelly, we're not leaving. Open this door, or we'll bust it down. Come on. We can straighten all this out. Don't be afraid." She paused again. "Do you have your keys?"

"No. I can run back and get them," Cassidy said.

"No time," Anastasia said breathlessly. "We've gotta find a way in. There's a window. Let's see if it's unlocked."

Cassidy pulled out her phone, quickly dialed 911, and slid it back into her pocket, hoping her shirt would muffle the dispatcher's voice. When she heard, "911, what's your emergency?" Cassidy said loudly, "Anastasia, we've got to get help here now before Kelly hurts herself. The barn door is locked. Let me go get the keys. It can't take that much time."

"I told you there is no time. Kelly is drunk and depressed. There is no telling what she will do. She's dangerous, and we don't have much time. We have to find her now!" Anastasia yelled.

Ignoring the dispatcher's questions, Cassidy tried to figure out ways to let the dispatcher know where they were without tipping off Anastasia, who stopped and fumbled with something in her pocket.

WAY TOO EARLY ON SUNDAY MORNING

"I've got this. I know how to get in," Anastasia said with a laugh that sounded more like a cackle. "I learned how to do this years ago when I forgot my keys and had to get back in the house before my mom found out I was out past curfew. And it was usually Britt's fault." She slid a credit card in the crack by the lock and wiggled it. "Darn. It was easier at home." She pulled it out and tried again, this time leaning into the door. "It's still not working. You must have newer locks." Letting out a loud grunt, she banged on the door with both fists and let out a string of curses.

After she caught her breath, she said, "I think I heard Kelly yell again. I guess that's a good sign."

Am I being paranoid? I've got to stay calm and follow my instincts. Something is not right with this woman, and I have to make sure she's not leading me into a trap. But what if Kelly is in danger? I'm gonna have to take a chance.

Cracking glass jolted Cassidy out of her thoughts. "What did you do?"

"When nothing else works, there's always brute force," Anastasia said. "Sorry about your window, but this is an emergency." Anastasia pulled chunks of glass out of the frame and threw them on the ground. "I'm never going to fit through this space. Come here.

You're about the right size. Let me hoist you up, and you can unlock the door from the inside."

Steeling herself for the boost to the window, Cassidy stepped closer and stood on her tiptoes, barely able to see past her nose inside the darkened space.

"Here," Anastasia said, bending over behind Cassidy. She heaved her up on her shoulders and shoved her toward the space where the window was.

"Whoa. I thought you were going to give my foot a boost," Cassidy said, clutching the edges of the sill and trying not to cut herself on any shards.

"Nope. Years of cheerleading and gymnastics," Anastasia said, huffing and trying to keep Cassidy balanced on her shoulders. "I've always been one of the steady girls on the bottom of the pyramid. Again, one of the workhorses. Thanks to Britt."

Anastasia stumbled, and Cassidy balanced herself by grabbing the wall and the window frame. "Oooooompf," Anastasia moaned and shoved Cassidy into the space where the glass had been a few minutes ago. She fell into the dark abyss and landed on one of the prepping tables with her own "oompf."

"Hurry up and unlock the back door," Anastasia yelled. "It's cold out here. And we don't have all night."

Cassidy paused, straining to listen for any noise from Kelly. She flipped the light on and opened the door to the kitchen area, then unlocked the back door, letting Anastasia in.

"What are you doing?" Anastasia hissed. "Now she can see us before we can swoop in to save her. I don't want her to lash out at us. We have to catch her off guard." She flipped the lights off and headed toward the bar area in the main room. "Hurry up. We need to find her."

Cassidy blinked several times, trying to adjust her eyes to the pitch darkness. *If the doors were locked, how did Kelly get in here?* Cassidy thought she heard footsteps, and she paused to listen. *It might have been Anastasia. She's moving along at a good clip, and I have no idea where she went.*

Hearing footsteps on the wooden floors near the restrooms, Cassidy pulled out her phone, hoping the call to the emergency dispatch was still active. She whispered, "I'm Cassidy Jamison at the barn with Anastasia Young. We think Kelly Todd is in here and is in danger. Please send help. We broke a window to get in on the side near the kitchen. The back door is unlocked now. Please hurry." She disconnected the call.

Not wanting to risk Anastasia's wrath, she slid her phone into her back pocket and made her way around the bar toward the space under the loft. She paused every few seconds to listen for Anastasia. The staccato beat in her temples made her head hurt. Taking a couple of deep breaths to calm herself, she pushed on in her quest to find Anastasia and Kelly. *Why do I keep thinking this could be a trap? Something is not right here.* Cassidy's blood felt like it had turned instantly to ice water. *If Kelly's in danger, you have to help her. But the little voice in the back of my head is warning me to be careful. Zac always says, "Be aware of your surroundings."* The thought of Zac brought on a slight smile.

Cassidy hustled back to the kitchen and fumbled around in the cabinets for something she could use as a weapon. Finding the cupboard next to the sink, she felt around for pots and pans. Touching something cold and slick, her hopes rose, until she realized it was a thin baking pan: nothing heavy enough to do any damage. She tiptoed over to the bar area and felt around the countertop. Annie and Austin had taken all the bottles and glasses. On the far edge of the bar, her hands landed on the cool metal of something long and sort of heavy. Ignoring Anastasia's concern about the lights, she flipped her phone's flashlight app on and swept the beam over the bar top. A drink muddler. Her thoughts flashed back to Austin crushing fruit for his fancy drinks. She hefted the industrial-sized tool that was about the size of a small fire extinguisher off the bar and doused her light.

Listening intently for any clue to Anastasia's whereabouts, Cassidy hugged the muddler close to her. The coolness from the metal gave her goose bumps. The floor creaked. *Footsteps, or just the wind? Definitely footsteps. Is Anastasia sneaking up on me?* Cassidy tried to get her bearings straight in the cavernous barn. Sounds seemed to echo off the wooden boards, and it was hard to pinpoint the source. And her pounding heart made it difficult to hear anything else.

"Shut up. Or I'll slap you again. This is all your fault," Anastasia screeched.

More adrenaline jolted through Cassidy's body and compelled her to keep moving. Zeroing in on Anastasia's voice, Cassidy picked her way around the tables and chairs to the loft.

"Get up. Get up now!" The light from Anastasia's flashlight hovered over what looked like a pile of clothes in the back corner. "I'm not going to tell you again," she hissed.

The figure on the ground moved and tried to sit up. "I know why you did it," Kelly meekly said. "And after all we did for you. You've always been a loser," she sneered.

"Just shut up. You don't know anything. None of you really know me or ever did. Now do as I say, or I'll kill you too." She pulled her foot back and kicked Kelly.

Cassidy's heartbeat jumped from bongos to a bass drum in seconds. *I can't wait any longer for backup. I've got to stop her before she hurts Kelly and then comes after me.*

Praying the floor wouldn't creak, Cassidy shuffled closer.

"You won't get away with this. The police already have you as a key suspect," Kelly spluttered. *Why is she egging Anastasia on?*

Anastasia paused for a moment, and Kelly raised her head. Both hands were zip-tied in front of her. "I helped her," Anastasia said with a sob. "I was always there to bail her out. I did the dirty work. I can't tell you how many times I took the fall for her. And then after all that, she turned on me." The flashlight beam bobbled as she started to sob. "And I don't know why."

"Because she was so self-centered. She only cared about Britt," Kelly replied.

Anastasia sucked in a gulp of air and looked around. "I thought we were close. I thought we had something. Britt used me like she did everyone else, and I always did every stupid thing she suggested like a lemming. But no more." Anastasia wiped her nose with the back of her hand and inched closer to Kelly. "I'm sorry to have to do this. You were always the nicer one in the bunch, but I can't have loose ends."

"Why Darcy?" croaked Kelly.

"Britt couldn't stand the thought of Vince leaving her for that nerd. She said it was a matter of time. Vince was bored with Britt and her out-of-control spending. He told her he didn't love her anymore. And there was nothing she could do to win him back. She asked for my help; and, like an idiot, I was always there for her. I would do anything for her. I thought we were in it together. I thought she liked me." Anastasia started sobbing again.

"She needed to stop living in the past and move on with her life. Britt wanted all the fun and drama. She couldn't let go. She never moved on to an adult life," Kelly said, trying to stand up.

Anastasia raised her arms over her head and took a step closer to Kelly.

It's now or never. Cassidy launched herself and let out a yelp that sounded like a sick cow. The noise echoed through the barn.

Anastasia froze and jerked toward the sound. "You should have minded your own business," she screeched.

Cassidy raised the muddler and let out the meanest yell she could muster. She rushed toward Anastasia, who turned at the last minute and deflected the blow with her shoulder. The pair tussled, and Anastasia used her arms to block Cassidy's next swing.

Anastasia's flashlight fell to the floor and rolled across the flat surface. Cassidy felt a whiff of air as Anastasia attempted to land a punch and missed. A second attempt connected with her arm and sent pain streaking up Cassidy's forearm to her shoulder. Cassidy recoiled and dropped the muddler. It clanked and rolled away from the pair.

Cassidy grabbed a hunk of Anastasia's straw-like hair as the taller woman landed on top of her with a thud. The two rolled around the floor, and Cassidy's foot connected with something soft. More groans, and then Cassidy saw starbursts when a fist landed on the side of her face. Her head snapped back and hit the floor. She couldn't tell in the dark if her vision was swimmy, but the pain blasted through her and made her queasy. She gulped air, trying to stave off a wave of dizziness.

With a grunt, Cassidy wrenched her arm out from under Anastasia before the latter could hit her again. As soon as she was free, she scrambled away toward the area under the loft.

Suddenly, the barn was flooded with light. Kelly groaned, covering her eyes with her zip-tied wrists. Cassidy blinked several times, trying to get her eyes to focus after having been clobbered on the head.

Footsteps thundered across the floor, and Anastasia yelled, "Now you've ruined everything!" She scrambled to her feet, sliding as she hustled toward the bar.

23

Some kind of loud war cry or the sound of some weird jungle bird echoed through the barn, and Anastasia and Cassidy froze as the Pearly Girls swooped in, yelling and waving designer bags.

"What is going on in here?" Kate yelled, wearing a trench coat over her pink pajamas with red hearts, and a pair of lime-green running shoes.

"She tried to kill me," Kelly said weakly, slumping back against the wall. "It was her the whole time."

"She's delirious," Anastasia said. "We were here trying to prevent Kelly from harming herself. Ask her. Ask Cassidy." The woman's crazed eyes darted around the room, never landing on anything. She waved her hands around and inched backwards toward the kitchen.

Cassidy tilted her head toward Anastasia, trying to send a message to her team.

Nobody moved. The silence seemed to close in on them, and time seemed to crawl by.

Anastasia broke the silence. "Don't listen to Kelly. She's crazy. She killed Darcy and Britt. And after everything Britt had done for her. She was so jealous. And bitter. She wanted Mac. She wanted Britt's life." Her voice took on a shrieky quality. "And if she couldn't have it, she'd make sure Britt couldn't have it either."

"You're the one who's crazy," Kelly said, lifting her head. "You've always been nuts, but it's gotten worse recently. And Britt never really liked you. In fact, no one ever liked you. You wormed your way into everything. And you made a mess of everything you touched." Talking seemed to deflate her. She slumped back against the wall and heaved a sigh.

"It was you. Trying to always be Miss Perfect. Prancing around like you owned the place and everyone in it," Anastasia screeched.

As Anastasia stepped back toward the loft area, Ruthanne slipped in behind her.

Raising a huge tapestried satchel, Ruthanne stepped closer and let it fly with a whoop. The bag landed with a thud against the back of Anastasia's head, and she teetered and dropped to the floor. Kate and Aileen rushed over. Aileen landed on Anastasia's back, and Kate sat on her legs.

"Roxie, Ruthanne, grab her arms," Kate yelled.

"Get off of me!" Anastasia bucked like a bronco and tried to escape the grip of the sexagenarians.

"What is going on in here?" a baritone voice boomed.

Everyone stiffened and stared at the door. The only sound was the Pearly Girls' heavy breathing.

Sheriff Howell and Detective Zac Turner, along with what looked like scads of deputies and state troopers in tactical gear, stormed the barn and surrounded the group.

"Get them off of me," Anastasia yelled. "They attacked me. This is all a huge mistake. I want to press charges. You all can't treat me like this."

Zac stepped closer and helped Kate and Aileen up. The sheriff relieved Roxie and Ruthanne of arm duty, and then he handcuffed Anastasia.

"Wait! You can't do that!" she whined. "I just told you those old biddies attacked me. Ow! You're hurting me."

"'Old biddies!'" Ruthanne said, waving a fist at Anastasia.

"Okay, ladies," Sheriff Howell said. "We need to get your statements. I know it's late, but we need to take care of this now," he added as Roxie dusted off her hands on her jeans. Every honey-blonde hair was in place, and she looked like she was ready for a fun night on the town instead of the take-down of a murderer.

"Not a problem, Asa. We're always here to help," Kate said.

"I can see that," he said. A slight smile crept across his lips and under his graying mustache. "I can always count on y'all to be smack-dab in the middle of things. And Ruthanne, you've got quite a swing there. What have you got in the bag?"

Ruthanne beamed and hugged her satchel to herself. "Books that I picked up this week."

"The pen is mightier than the sword," Kate muttered under her breath.

A police officer guided each woman to a separate table. It almost looked like a social event with the gals flirting with their police escorts in their RoboCop outfits. Each of the Pearly Girls held court, immediately diving into a detailed explanation of what had happened while the police officers dutifully jotted down the salient points.

A state trooper who Cassidy didn't recognize offered her a seat at a table in the back and introduced himself as Trooper Collins. Without pausing, he launched into a series of rapid-fire questions, and she spent the next hour or so explaining the events that had led her to be in the barn that night.

Just as she had reached the point of feeling completely drained of energy, the trooper mercifully ran out of questions about Anastasia, Darcy, Austin, and Britt, and he excused himself. Cassidy rested her head on her folded arms and watched two troopers half-drag Anastasia, still in handcuffs, out the main doors. "I'm injured," she claimed. "You can't take me to jail. I need medical attention." She writhed like she was doing some weird dance. "That old bat hit me for no reason. I think I'm concussed."

"You deserve a concussion for that comment," Ruthanne muttered from her table near the loft.

Zac approached and stopped beside Cassidy. He looked wide awake and sexy in his black tactical gear. Suddenly aware of how rumpled and tired she must look, Cassidy patted her wild curls down as he slid into the empty seat next to her.

"Your call helped," he said. "You gave us some clues as to what was going on. We didn't know if she had a weapon or not, so we came in with a full team. We've been watching her for a while, but we didn't have enough to make an arrest until now."

"She's very angry. She's been holding grudges for a long time," Cassidy said.

"According to her ramblings," Zac said, "Anastasia said that Britt was so upset about the Darcy-Vince affair that they hatched the plan one night while they were drinking. Anastasia did the deed and hid the body. She said it was all Britt's idea, and then something about Britt ordering her to do it. Then in the next breath, she said Britt hired her to kill Darcy. She wanted a way to get Vince back, and they both decided the best way was to have the journalist out of the picture. Anastasia, who it seemed had been Britt's sidekick since elementary school, had a meltdown when Britt got cold feet and changed her story after the murder. When Britt acted like they had never hatched the deadly scheme together, Anastasia came unglued, especially when Britt tried to pin everything on her."

"There were a couple of times that Anastasia griped about always doing Britt's dirty work. But then there were other times where she was president of her fan club," Cassidy added.

"We heard a lot of folks say that Britt talked awful behind

Anastasia's back. But for some reason, Anastasia seemed to adore her, and she did anything to stay in her favor," he said.

"I remember them always traveling in a pack in high school. They were seniors when I was a lowly ninth grader. But everyone knew who they were."

"Some of the people we interviewed mentioned things that Anastasia did that got her in trouble with the police as a kid. There was a pattern, if you looked closely enough," he said. When Cassidy stared at him, he added, "Mostly pranks that crossed the line, but there was some shoplifting and alcohol pilfering. Then there were some stalking and vandalism charges that got swept under the rug by her father's lawyer."

Cassidy raised an eyebrow, but the revelations weren't all that surprising.

"We'll be here for a while. The EMTs took Kelly to the hospital, and I need to go check on her. You need to get some sleep."

"Oh, we're supposed to have the last reunion event here. Uh, in a few hours," she said, glancing at her Fitbit.

"I don't think we'll be done with the scene by then," he said quietly.

Cassidy chewed on her bottom lip. "If we can get in here to get the tables and chairs, we can move the event outside and have it in the garden. It's either that or cancel it. And I have no idea who to call. Kelly's in the hospital, and Anastasia's obviously out. I need to go see if there are any other names on the contract I could contact. And I have to let the caterer know."

A cloud seemed to settle across the detective's handsome face. He paused a beat and said, "We'll let you know when we're done here, but I don't think it'll be before lunch." He rose and headed toward where the sheriff stood with two troopers.

Well, that was an abrupt way to end a conversation. I guess I'm free to go. She wiped her gritty eyes and decided to swing by the apartment to check on Elvis.

She hustled to the converted farmhouse. The chilly wind from the valley made her shiver. She took several steps across the grass and stopped suddenly. *How did Kelly get in the barn? The back door was locked.*

She heard footsteps and turned quickly to see Kate and Aileen slip outside. "Are you all done with your interview?"

"Yep. We're waiting for Ruthanne and Roxie. It's cold out here." Aileen zipped up her jacket.

"Brrrr," Kate agreed. "I'm going back inside until we're ready to leave."

"Thanks for coming over here so quickly," Cassidy said.

"We zoomed over here as soon as Roxie called us," Aileen said, pointing to Kate's pajamas. "I'm glad none of the deputies had a speed trap going at this hour. I know I broke the sound barrier."

"She would have gotten a ticket for reckless driving," Kate muttered.

"Was the barn locked when you got here?" Cassidy asked.

"Nope. The big doors were shut, but not locked. I wondered why it was open, but I'm glad it was. In my mad dash out, I forgot my keys," Aileen said.

Well, that explains how Anastasia and Kelly got in. "I'm going over to the office to see if the contract had any more names on it," Cassidy said. "I have no idea if we're hosting today's event or if anyone will even show up. And Anastasia broke a window by the kitchen when we were looking for Kelly. I have to let Levi know."

"We'll swing by when they're done in the barn," Kate said. "To see if you need anything else."

24

LATER SUNDAY MORNING

After a long walk with Elvis, who was overly interested in what was going on at the barn, Cassidy settled in at her desk. The endorphins pumped through her, and she felt herself getting a second wind after the all-nighter. Not finding any other people to call on Britt's contract, she made an executive decision to move the final event outdoors if Annie agreed. Who knows, maybe some curious folks would show up for today's brunch. Glancing at the clock on her laptop, she punched in Annie's number. *I hope she's up at eight o'clock.*

After a couple of rings, Annie chirped, "Good morning, Cassidy. What's up on this beautiful autumn morning?"

"Hey, there. It's been a little crazy here. You sound so full of energy."

"Always. I'm an early bird. What's up?" Annie stirred something in the background, obviously something cooking on her stove.

"The police are here. They arrested Anastasia for injuring Kelly and for the two murders. She put up a big fight and denied everything."

"I guess when I think about it, she always seemed so unhappy and upset about everything. I can't believe it. Why in the world? I thought they were all friends." Her voice trailed off.

"I think it had been building up for a while. From what I could piece together, Britt wanted Vince back, and she and Anastasia conjured up a way to get Darcy out of the picture. After Anastasia did the deed and hid the body, Britt got cold feet and tried to deny her involvement, and Anastasia snapped. She said she was tired of cleaning up Britt's messes."

"Wow. I got the impression all of them were used to getting their way and being the popular girls. I never dreamed it would lead to a double murder and the other attacks. The other night, Austin said he remembered more stuff like talking to Kelly and Anastasia right before he got clobbered. He said both were drunk and flirty. He said he offered to call an Uber for Anastasia, and she got mad when he wouldn't drive her home. She could have hit him in the back of the head when he wasn't looking, but how did she get his body to the garden? He's a pretty big guy."

Before Cassidy could comment, Annie continued, "This is going to sound crass, but what do we do about today's event? I've got a ton of food ready to go. There probably aren't that many people who are in a celebratory mood. What should we do?"

"I checked the contract, and there are no more committee members left to call. We can't get into the barn, but if they'll let us drag the chairs and tables out, we can set up in the garden if that works for you."

"I can make it work with a nice buffet. We'll be over in about an hour."

"Sounds good. I'll text you if anything changes. Thanks." Cassidy disconnected.

Before taking Elvis upstairs to her apartment, she filled a to-go mug with the strongest dark roast she could find. *Zombie Apocalypse should do the trick. Where does Ruthanne get this coffee from?* A slight headache was building behind her eyes. *Hang in there, girl. Just a couple more hours until you can crash. It'll all be over soon.*

Before she could close up the office, the back door swung open, and the Pearly Girls tromped in like a hurricane blowing up the coast and over the mountains.

"I can't believe it, Cassidy. We helped the police solve some more murders. What a rush!" Ruthanne waved her hand in front of her face like a fan and plopped into her desk chair. She dropped her satchel on the floor, and it made a loud thud.

"That is a dangerous weapon," Kate said.

"Books are powerful," Aileen added.

"Use what you have," Ruthanne said. "I've always loved my books. This is the first time I've ever used them to stop a crime."

"We're going to get a reputation," Roxie said.

"Speak for yourself," Kate said with a half-grin. "Coffee, anyone? We're in for a long day."

"I haven't pulled an all-nighter in a while," Aileen said. "I'm going to pay for this later."

"Since our knit-a-thon," Ruthanne giggled. "But this was way more exciting. We stopped a cold-blooded killer. And we got to meet Kyle and Jake."

"Who?" Cassidy asked.

"Those two hunky state troopers. Hurry up with the coffee. I want to go back over there and see what else is going on," Aileen said.

"Annie and Austin will be in the garden. I need to call Levi to see if he can help me move the chairs and tables."

"Do you think anyone will show up?" Kate asked, putting another mug under the coffeemaker's spigot. "If I were part of that class, I'd be afraid of what's going to happen next."

"This is the class reunion that just wouldn't end," Roxie muttered. "I would run if I were them."

"Maybe the past is better left in the past," Kate added.

Cassidy pulled out her phone and tapped in Levi's number.

"Hey, boss," he answered. "Congrats on helping apprehend

another killer. I heard from some of the cops that you had a hand in solving another one. What's up?"

"Thanks. The Pearly Girls were responsible for the take-down, especially Ruthanne and her huge bag full of books. I'm glad we're almost done with this event. Speaking of that, can you help me move some tables and chairs to the garden?"

"No problem. Be there in about fifteen minutes. Meet you at the barn." He hung up before she could comment.

"Elvis, you look all comfortable in your bed. I'll leave you here to guard the place."

"We'll be over to help you in a minute," Aileen said.

A white forensic van sat in the grass in front of her barn, and several police officers milled around near the entrance. The grassy area where the tactical team and the state police had been parked stood empty.

Cassidy poked her head inside the barn, and Zac stopped his conversation with someone in a Tyvek suit. "Hey, Cassidy. We've got another hour or so here."

"Is it okay if we pull out some of the tables and chairs?" she asked, blinking to get her eyes to stop burning.

"That's fine. It's probably better to start at that end." He pointed to the far side of the room as Levi rolled a flat cart in from the back.

"Hey," Levi said with a wave. "The strangest thing happened. I found this cart out back near the woods. I know I left it in the storage room when I set up last week. I have no idea who moved it outside. Glad it didn't get rained on."

A light bulb flicked on in Cassidy's head. "That might explain how Anastasia was able to move the bodies by herself. With the cart, she could move Britt, Darcy, and Austin almost anywhere."

Levi started to break down tables and stack them on the cart. "How many should we take outside?" he asked.

"Maybe enough for twenty or twenty-five. I can't imagine we'll have a crowd. The reunion numbers have been dwindling steadily."

"We can knock that out with like five tables. Shoot, we can probably get all that in one trip, including the chairs."

Cassidy folded up chairs and stacked them near the cart. "Annie and Austin will need some of the six-foot tables for their buffet."

"No problem," Levi said, hoisting the last round table onto the cart. "Let's get those chairs on here, and I'll come back for the long tables."

"Oh," she said: "I forgot to tell you. When I was here earlier with Anastasia, she broke the barn's kitchen window. Do you think you can look at that later?"

"Sure thing. I can get it fixed as soon as the hardware store opens. See you in a bit," he said.

By the time Levi pushed the loaded cart into the serenity garden, the Pearly Girls were fluttering around and chatting. The caffeine must have kicked in—not one of them looked like they had been up all night. Suddenly aware of how she must look, Cassidy rubbed her eyes and ran her fingers through her hair.

"Here, let us help," Ruthanne said.

Her team had the five tables and the surrounding chairs set up in a matter of minutes.

"Let's put the buffet table over there," Aileen said. "That way it won't block the view of the mountains."

"I'll be back in two shakes of a lamb's tail with the big tables," Levi said, heading for the barn.

"Fall is here," Aileen said. "The leaves are beginning to turn."

"Yay, the roads will be clogged with all those visitors," Kate said.

"Who spend money in town," Cassidy added.

"Yep, that too," Kate said.

The gals busied themselves with their phones until Levi returned with the buffet tables.

"Over here, Levi," Aileen said. "Let's go with one long one. Annie can readjust them if she wants something different."

About fifteen minutes later, Levi hustled back to the barn with the cart.

"Whew," Kate said, sinking down in one of the chairs. "I'm definitely going to need a nap today, or maybe I'll make it an early night."

"We're just gettin' started," Roxie said with a wink. "You can rest when you're dead."

Kate waved her hand like she was flicking away gnats.

Whistling filtered into the garden, and all heads turned toward Austin, who guided a pushcart over the grassy area. "Morning, ladies. How are you on this sunny Sunday? Heard you all had some excitement around here."

Before anyone could comment, Annie hauled a wagon full of gear to the row of tables. She started unpacking tablecloths.

"Here, let us help," Aileen said.

"Austin, are you okay? Shouldn't you be resting?" Roxie asked, clutching his bicep.

"Thanks. I'm fine," he grinned. "I'll have this unloaded in a minute. No big deal."

"Those smaller white ones go on the round tables." Annie did a quick count and pointed toward her wagon. "I have enough in that box. I brought enough food for an army. I hope y'all are hungry."

"I am," Austin chimed in.

His sister punched him lightly in the shoulder. "You're always hungry. It's a good thing I can get food wholesale with your appetite. Get busy and earn your keep."

"Gotta keep these athletic types fed and healthy," Roxie said with a wink.

Right before eleven, smells from the warming trays wafted through the garden. The Pearly Girls had taken up residence at one of the back tables. Only the birds were chattering in the nearby trees. Cassidy felt like she would fall asleep if she sat still too long.

Annie paused next to Cassidy. "Doesn't look like there are too many from the class of 2009. Why don't you go let the police know they should come and eat before they take off? Austin filled all the coffee carafes. So everything is hot and ready. We need some hungry folks. Tell them we've got plenty."

Cassidy pulled out her phone and fired off texts to Levi and Zac.

"Ladies, help yourselves to a plate or two," Annie said, pointing to the buffet. "You too, Austin. I know you're always up for a snack. And it'll hold you over until lunch." She winked at her brother, who held a chair for Ruthanne and then for Aileen.

After filling her plate with bites of everything on the brunch buffet, Cassidy made her way to an empty table. Several of the police and technicians filled a table near the front. The police spoke in low tones when they weren't chowing down on Annie's gourmet brunch.

Nodding to his colleagues as he passed with a plate laden with food, Zac paused at Cassidy's table and rested his hand on the back of her chair.

Cassidy steeled herself for more of his questions. *This guy is always in detective mode.*

After a long pause, he leaned forward and said, "Thanks for the hospitality. It was a long night. And all of us missed breakfast and coffee."

"Here, pull up a chair," she said. "We've got lots of space. I'm glad all this is over. Not sure if we'll do any more reunions any time soon," she said, letting out a little puff of air.

He nodded and settled in next to her. It didn't take him long to shovel in a forkful of egg casserole. When he was done chewing, he continued, "But it feels good to wrap up two murders and two assaults. Thanks for your help. I don't like it when you put yourself in dangerous situations, but your information turned out to be valuable. And you all had the suspect restrained when we arrived."

She shrugged one shoulder. "We did what we had to do." She looked up at his intense stare and stifled a nervous giggle. "Plus, I have a knack for solving puzzles. And people tell me things."

"You and your gang over there are always ground zero for whatever is going on in town." He nodded his head toward the Pearly Girls, who were whooping and laughing with Austin at a nearby table.

"They're the best support team. Even if they do stir things up," she said with a wink.

"Hey, boss," Levi said, slightly breathless. "Sorry to interrupt, but Vern is going to drop off the estimates, drawings, and contract for the cave work first thing tomorrow. Will you have time to look them over while he's here?"

Cassidy nodded. "That sounds awesome. I'll be in the office early. Any time in the morning works. Make sure you get yourself a plate or two. There's lots of food."

"Thanks. I've already had breakfast, but I might make a to-go plate." Levi wandered toward the buffet table.

Zac paused. "The cave?"

"I think I've figured out what to do with it. We're going to have an underground venue. Wanna have a party in a cave?"

He raised one eyebrow. "Maybe."

A little jolt rocketed through her. *Was he hinting at something?*

"We're thinking we could do parties, small concerts, comedy clubs, and other events."

After a long pause that seemed like an eternity, he said, "Hey, I was thinking." He stopped and gazed out toward the mountain skyline. "I'm going to be tied up for a couple of days with all the paperwork from this investigation, but the sheriff owes me a couple of days off. After I catch up on my sleep, you want to get dinner one night?"

Proud of herself for not blurting out "like a date," Cassidy smiled. "I'd like that." *Maybe he's not all business* all *the time.*

Cassidy's phone rang as the bells on the front door jangled, announcing the entrance of the Pearly Girls. Elvis chose to be the greeter while Cassidy answered her phone. "Hi, Detective," she said, feeling the heat rise in her face.

"Oh, it's Zaaaaaaac," Roxie said louder than she needed to. She set her black Michael Kors bag on the table and stepped closer to Cassidy's desk.

Aileen's eyes widened as the rest of the Pearly Girls encircled Cassidy's desk to hear her half of the conversation better. Cassidy tried to shoo them away, but, like with a flock of seagulls eyeing a french fry, it didn't work.

"Hey," he said. "I'm buried in paperwork, but I'm determined to get out of here tomorrow before the sun goes down. You free for dinner then?"

"Dinner sounds like fun." Suddenly tongue-tied, Cassidy hoped she didn't sound like an airhead. Ruthanne clapped as Kate and Aileen patted her on the back.

"I told you," Roxie whispered. "We all knew it was inevitable."

"Good. I'll pick you up at six," Zac said, drawing her back to the conversation. "I know a nice Italian place in Staunton; and if we're up that way, we'll have to swing by Mrs. Rowe's for a slice of her famous pie."

"The best pie in the Blue Ridge Mountains. Sounds like fun. See you then."

"Bye, Zac," all the Pearly Girls yelled like a chorus.

Cassidy made a face and disconnected.

"It's a date," Aileen squealed. "I'm so excited for you. He is so handsome and smart."

"We all knew there was some magic between you two." Ruthanne hugged Cassidy.

"It's just dinner," Cassidy said.

"And dessert," Roxie cooed.

She can even make pie sound spicy. Cassidy shook off the desire to defend herself. *Let's see where this goes.*

"Well, I'm excited for you. You make a great team. Your investigative skills always help him nab the bad guy—or gal, in this case," Ruthanne said.

"I'm relieved you all apprehended Anastasia and now she can't hurt anyone else." Cassidy rubbed her elbow and her knees. She'd ended up with some bumps and bruises after yesterday's altercation. *I'm glad that's over. Maybe we can all move on.*

"We're a great team, but we already knew that. Cassidy, we've always got your back," Roxie said with a sly grin.

"I'm wondering if Anastasia will ever stand trial. Her lawyer may try to get her declared incompetent," Kate said.

"I heard her mother has already hired a cadre of lawyers. Right now, they're all claiming that Britt bullied her and subjected her to years of mental abuse." Ruthanne's voice drifted off.

"Ha. A sorry attempt at blame-shifting and trying to frame herself as being the victim," Roxie scoffed.

"She may be nuts, but she packed a mean punch. It took a bunch of us and a couple of officers to finally subdue her," Kate said.

"Good riddance. Now we can get back to important things like the renovations to the cave and Cassidy's love life."

Blood surged to Cassidy's cheeks. "Let's see what kind of design ideas you have for the space."

"Sure, try to change the subject," Roxie said. "We'll get back to Detective Zac in a bit."

The gals rummaged through their bags and the desks for design samples and drawing tablets. Lively conversation about names and themes filled the conference room.

The office line sounded above the chatter, and Cassidy rose to answer it. "Celebrations at Ivy Springs, this is Cassidy. How can we help you with your next event?"

"Hi, Cassidy. This is Niles Johnson. I'm with the Blue Ridge Brewers Vintners and Distillers Association. It's a professional organization for those in the craft beer and Virginia wine and spirits industries. We're looking to do an event for our members, and I'd like to set up some time with you to talk about the use of your venue."

A tingle zinged right to Cassidy's stomach. "That sounds wonderful. We'd love to meet with you and discuss what we can offer your members. When do you have some availability?"

"I will be in your area on Thursday and Friday of this week. Will either of those days work for you?" he asked.

"How about Thursday afternoon?"

"Great. Shall we say two o'clock?"

"Perfect. Our conference room is in the restored farmhouse next to our property's parking lot at the main entrance. And when were you planning to hold your event?"

"We'd like to do something in the spring. We love your outside venues and your barn. We want to have tastings, lectures, workshops. Kinda like a fair. We want to do some members-only events and others that will be open to the public."

"That's not a problem," she said. "My team can work with you to provide venues for all your events. And we're looking forward to seeing you Thursday at two o'clock."

"See you then." He disconnected, and she finished jotting notes on her calendar.

"This could be good," she announced to the Pearly Girls. "The Blue Ridge Brewers Vintners and Distillers Association wants to talk to us about having an event next spring. Mr. Johnson will be here on Thursday afternoon."

"That sounds right up our alley. I hope he brings samples," Roxie said.

"It'd be cool to use the cave," Cassidy said. "I wonder if we can have it ready by spring."

Acknowledgments

I am eternally grateful for all the support of so many family and friends who stick with me during this crazy writing journey. Thank you, Stan Weidner, for all your love and support and for always being there (and for making me look good in the photos); my parents, who instilled in me a lifelong love of reading; Cortney Cain for all the five a.m. sanity checks; Meagan Van Laeken and Jocelyn Cain, my pop-culture gurus; and Bill Cain for always keeping everyone entertained.

I am so grateful for my talented Sisters in Crime, Guppy, James River Writers, and Writers Who Kill friends. Your support is invaluable! Many thanks to Jackie Layton, Sue Minix, and Paula Charles for all the great advice.

Many, many thanks to my fabulous agent, Cindy Bullard, for all her guidance and hard work. And I am eternally grateful to Amanda Chiu Krohn, Ashlyn Inman, and the entire team at Turner Publishing. You all are amazing and make the publishing process seamless!

And most of all, thank you to all the mystery lovers who follow Cassidy, Elvis, and the Pearly Girls on their adventures.

ABOUT THE AUTHOR

Through the years, **HEATHER WEIDNER** has been a cop's kid, technical writer, editor, college professor, software tester, and IT manager. She writes the Pearly Girls Mysteries, the Delanie Fitzgerald Mysteries, The Jules Keene Glamping Mysteries, and The Mermaid Bay Christmas Shoppe Mysteries.

Her short stories appear in the *Virginia is for Mysteries* series; *50 Shades of Cabernet*; *Deadly Southern Charm*; *Murder by the Glass*; *First Comes Love, Then Comes Murder*; and *Crimes in the Old Dominion*. She has non-fiction pieces in *Promophobia* and *The Secret Ingredient: A Mystery Writers' Cookbook*.

She is a member of Sisters in Crime: National, Central Virginia, Chessie, Guppies, and Grand Canyon Writers; International Thriller Writers; and James River Writers. Heather blogs regularly with the Writers Who Kill.

Originally from Virginia Beach, Heather has been a mystery fan since Scooby-Doo and Nancy Drew. She lives in Central Virginia with her husband and a crazy Jack Russell terrier.

www.ingramcontent.com/pod-product-compliance
Lightning Source LLC
Chambersburg PA
CBHW031218020726
47499CB00002B/639